BRIGHT HOPES

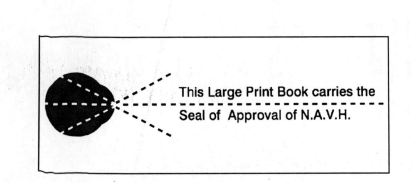

This Large Print Book carries the
Seal of Approval of N.A.V.H.

A ST. ROSE QUILTING BEE MYSTERY

BRIGHT HOPES

ANNETTE MAHON

WHEELER PUBLISHING
A part of Gale, Cengage Learning

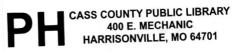
GALE
CENGAGE Learning

Farmington Hills, Mich • San Francisco • New York • Waterville, Maine
Meriden, Conn • Mason, Ohio • Chicago

GALE
CENGAGE Learning®

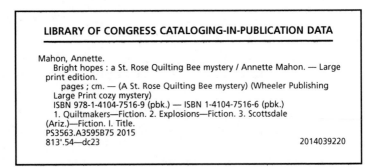

LIBRARY OF CONGRESS CATALOGING-IN-PUBLICATION DATA

Mahon, Annette.
    Bright hopes : a St. Rose Quilting Bee mystery / Annette Mahon. — Large print edition.
        pages ; cm. — (A St. Rose Quilting Bee mystery) (Wheeler Publishing Large Print cozy mystery)
    ISBN 978-1-4104-7516-9 (pbk.) — ISBN 1-4104-7516-6 (pbk.)
        1. Quiltmakers—Fiction. 2. Explosions—Fiction. 3. Scottsdale (Ariz.)—Fiction. I. Title.
    PS3563.A3595B75 2015
    813'.54—dc23   2014039220

Published in 2015 by arrangement with Annette Mahon

Printed in the United States of America
2 3 4 5 6   19 18 17 16 15

Bright Hopes

CHAPTER 1

It was her worst nightmare come to life.

On a beautiful summer morning, Maggie Browne stood at her open door staring at a uniform-clad Scottsdale police officer. While one part of her mind closed with trepidation, another segment recognized Nick Hunter, a longtime friend of her son Michael. Maggie feared this was the moment she'd dreaded ever since Michael had announced his intention to enter the police academy.

"Dear Lord . . ." Maggie's lips mumbled a prayer as her hand clutched at the solidity of the wooden door frame. Nick's image turned blurry, and Maggie realized her eyes had filled with tears.

"It's all right, Mrs. Browne. Michael is all right. Injured, but all right."

Nick's words penetrated her fear-fogged mind and Maggie was able to breathe again. Funny how you don't realize you are holding your breath until you suddenly draw in that first refreshing lungful of air, she thought.

Stepping forward, Nick took her arm and led her into the house. His warm hand on her suddenly cold arm sent a physical reassurance through her tired body. Odd, but she'd felt well rested and invigorated, ready for the day before she'd opened the door.

"You like tea, don't you, Mrs. Browne? Would you like me to make you a cup?"

Maggie had an unfortunate urge to giggle at this question. She felt as though she'd been transported into the pages of an Agatha Christie mystery story, with an inspector offering her tea. She did manage to quell the urge to laugh, realizing that it would bring on full-blown hysteria. This was just not like her. She'd always prided herself on being a practical, commonsense type of person.

"Thank you, but no. What happened? Where is he?" She allowed Nick to lead her to a chair, but she perched at the very end of the cushion. "Can I go to him?"

"Yes, of course. Michael really is all right." He smiled his reassurance. "You might know that he's currently on night shift."

Maggie nodded.

"He was patrolling in the area where those

explosions have been going off late at night."

Maggie swallowed. For the past week nightly explosions had awakened people in one of the older Scottsdale neighborhoods. The Quilting Bee at St. Rose had been talking about it every day, since most of their members lived in the area. They had all heard the explosions, which they described as loud bangs. The first of the explosions occurred around midnight, but then moved to much later — or earlier — in the morning.

The whole thing was a great nuisance and was scaring people in an area where many of the residents were elderly couples or young families. But, as far as Maggie knew, no one had been hurt by them. Maggie's heart squeezed tight in her chest. Until now.

Nick tried to relieve the tension with a light-hearted remark. "Don't worry, he still has all his fingers and toes."

Maggie realized he was trying to get her to relax, but she just wanted him to get it over with.

Perhaps Nick picked up on that vibe because he quickly turned serious.

"A homeowner reported hearing activity behind his rear fence. Michael was investigating what he thought was a suspicious object in the alley behind the house. Unfortunately, the object exploded as he was approaching and threw him back against a block wall. He thought he blacked out for a moment, so he had to be checked out at the hospital. The doctor thinks it's a concussion and he wants to keep him today, and probably overnight for observation. His hearing was impacted too, but they say that will pass. If you'll get your things, I'll take you to the hospital now."

Maggie was up out of her chair in less than a second, rushing to grab her purse and a sweater. It might be a hundred degrees outside, but it was likely to be chilly in the hospital. She would call Victoria on the way over, to let her know that she would not be meeting with the Quilting Bee this morning.

CHAPTER 2

Everyone stared when Victoria Farrington entered the Quilting Bee workroom alone. Victoria and Maggie usually carpooled and everyone expected to see the two women together. Maggie had started the St. Rose Quilting Bee and was still the unofficial leader of the group. It was almost unheard of for her to miss their morning quilting sessions.

Victoria was Maggie's best friend and lived in the same condo complex. She was actually a member of the nearby Lutheran church, but she loved working with the quilting group at St. Rose Catholic Community. The other quilters had all become her close friends, and they felt the same about her.

"Oh, my, has something happened to Maggie?" Clare asked. One of the more emotionally charged members of the group, Clare Patterson was also the quintessential people person. She seemed to know everyone at St. Rose parish, and was always quick to offer sympathy and a helping hand and/or a sympathetic ear when someone suffered an injury or a personal loss. "She hasn't missed Quilting Bee since that terrible flu two years ago."

"Maggie is fine." Victoria reassured everyone as she put her purse on a shelf in the closet. "Apparently Michael was hurt in the line of duty early this morning and she's at the hospital with him."

All the women around the quilting frame had questions, and the onslaught of voices was loud. It was impossible to determine what any one person said as one voice slid over another. Everyone there knew Michael and all were concerned for his welfare as well as for Maggie's. For a time, stitching on the Delectable Mountains quilt top was totally abandoned. ·

"Give the poor woman a chance to sit down and tell us herself," Louise suggested. Louise Lombard was a nurse with a practical turn of mind similar to Maggie's. Her calm but firm tone acted as a soothing balm.

Needles once again pushed through fabric as everyone calmed down. Everyone except Edie Dulinski, that is. Edie was the feisty one, the one most likely to speak her mind.

Which she did now.

"It's those explosions, isn't it? I heard another one last night, around four o'clock. Woke me right up. All the dogs in the neighborhood started barking too. And this morning's news said a police officer was injured."

Anna pulled in a noisy breath, her hand hesitating over the leafy pattern she was stitching.

Edie was constantly complaining about the rise of crime and the proliferation of gangs in their part of town. They usually dismissed her rants as her personal form of paranoia, but in this instance she was proving only too correct. While the possibility of pranks did exist, if these *were* pranks, they were taking a nasty turn. Most recently, there was property damage, and now a police officer in the hospital.

Victoria took a seat at the quilt frame and picked up a threaded needle. She was eager to share the little information she had, but all of the women felt more relaxed with needles in hand. "Michael has been on night shift, and, yes, it has to do with the explosions. Maggie called on the way to the hospital — an officer had come to tell her about it and was driving her over there. I said I would pick her up after lunch and

13

take her home. She just said Michael was injured while checking on a suspicious device and was thrown back by the blast. They think he has a concussion, but other than that he is all right."

Edie clicked her tongue. "It's these teenage boys. They have nothing to do so they join gangs and then they cause trouble."

"Now, Edie," Louise began.

But Edie was having none of it. "Don't you 'now Edie' me. You live farther north so maybe you haven't been awakened every night this week. Clare knows, don't you, Clare?"

Clare nodded. "It is very frightening having these explosions going off every night. Waking us up, scaring the poor dogs. I'm afraid to take Samson out for his walks at night. I used to like to walk in the evening, when it was a little cooler right after the sun went down. But I'm afraid to go now. I take our last walk between six and seven when there's plenty of light. Who knows what those things are and when they might go off. They sound like bombs." Clare ended her tirade with a shudder.

"And you know what bombs sound like, do you?" Louise asked. The corner of her mouth twitched, but she did not allow a smile to appear.

Clare tightened her lips but didn't answer. Of course she didn't, she'd never heard a real bomb go off, but she imagined it would sound like the nightly noises that woke her, her husband and their miniature Schnauzer. "No," she admitted. "But the latest ones have an extremely loud pop that makes the windows shake and scares the life out of poor Samson."

Edie made a gruff sound in her throat. "It sounds like the bombs that go off in television shows and movies, and that's enough for me. I don't know why the police can't seem to find anyone involved when it's been going on for over a week now."

"Don't you think it might just be kids who purchased fireworks on sale before the Fourth of July?" Theresa asked. One of the newer bee members, Theresa Squires had joined the bee when she retired after a long career in the offices of a local auto dealership. She'd found her passion on their trip to Hawai`i for a quilt seminar earlier in the year, deciding that Hawaiian quilts were the most beautiful things she'd ever seen and devoting herself to creating them — that is, when she wasn't quilting with the bee for their yearly auction to benefit the church. "I think it's ridiculous that they allow those sales when none of the cities around here allow fireworks to be set off."

"Well, of course I agree with you," Edie said. "About the sales. Ridiculous. But you must be able to hear them from your house. Does it sound like fireworks to you?"

Theresa had been with the group long enough not to be intimidated by Edie. "Well, yes and no," she responded. "Because it usually wakes us up, I don't really hear it as well as I might. But it could be fireworks, I think. It certainly gets all the dogs barking and howling. And that's the same way they reacted to the legal fireworks on the Fourth. The official displays aren't really close by, but we can hear the noise and see some of the sky rockets. The dogs hate it."

"Hmpf," was Edie's reaction. "I think someone is playing around with explosives, maybe practicing for some local terrorist activities."

Edie nodded her head with a sharp jerk as though agreeing with her own conclusion. Not that anyone else would. Sewing stopped as everyone stared at Edie in surprise.

"Terrorist activities?" Anna repeated. Anna Howard was the oldest and frailest member of the group. She lived with her daughter and son-in-law and watched her grandchildren after school. She had some health issues that often worried the others, but she loved to quilt and came regularly to the bee meetings. "Do you really think we might have terrorists operating in Scottsdale? Right here in our own neighborhood?"

Concerned at the fear in Anna's voice, Victoria was quick to reassure her. "Don't be silly. Edie was just speculating, weren't you, Edie?"

Knowing she was outnumbered in regard to her theories, and not wanting to further upset Anna, Edie backed down. "I'm just offering up possibilities, Anna," she said. "It could also be amateurs trying to manufacture methamphetamine, for example. I understand that's an extremely volatile process."

"Every night?" Louise asked, her eyebrows raised.

"As I said," Edie replied with calm dignity as she pressed her needle back into the quilt, taking the first stitch in another leaf. "Amateurs."

"You know," Clare began, speaking slowly as though considering something. "There's a neighbor of mine I often see when I walk Samson. He goes out with his dog at about the same time, and we stop to let the dogs greet each other. And we visit a little."

"And what does that have to do with this?" Edie asked. She was still annoyed at

17

having to tone down her ideas about terrorism in the community.

"I just remembered something Paul said." Clare stopped to look around at the others. "That's his name, Paul. He's kind of a gruff old guy, but I can tell he loves his dog, and he has the sweetest little grandson who usually walks with them."

Edie rolled her eyes. Clare didn't see her, as she was sitting along the same side of the quilt frame.

"What did he say?" Edie inquired, hoping Clare would get to the point.

"It was right after the explosions started and everyone in the neighborhood was talking about them. So it was natural to ask if he'd heard the explosions." Clare's eyes sparkled and her hands stilled momentarily on the quilt top. "He told me he heard the noise all right, that the first explosion was right behind his fence. He was out in his yard, even though it was midnight — he has insomnia, you know. And he went right out there. He claims he caught some kids in the alley, setting off fireworks and laughing about it. He told me he 'scolded them good.' " She raised her eyebrows.

"It is terribly dangerous to set off fireworks here in the summer," Victoria said. "That's why none of the cities allow it. Everything is so dry, the fire danger alone is enough to urge prevention. And with teenagers, I worry about them getting too close and losing fingers — or worse."

"So it *is* just a matter of teenagers causing trouble." Louise nodded her head in satisfaction at this conclusion. "Looks like our original idea was correct, Edie."

"Did he say whether he recognized the kids?" Theresa asked.

"I don't think so. But you know, that was early on. Those first couple of explosions were earlier, around midnight, no later. And they weren't as loud as these most recent ones."

"You're right," Theresa said. "Carl and I didn't even hear the first ones. But these latest have awakened us every time."

"It's most likely another group," Edie said. The eagerness in her voice could not be missed.

"Terrorists?" Louise asked, looking pointedly toward Anna.

Edie got the hint. "Copycats," she said. The firm tone of her voice left little room for the others to comment. "Some teens set off some illegal firecrackers and gave some other, more dangerous, people ideas."

"There were people in tents everywhere selling fireworks for weeks before the

Fourth," Theresa said. "Who knows how much of the stuff might still be around in garages or sheds."

There was a moment of silence as the others contemplated this.

"It sounds dangerous," Anna said, "to keep that kind of thing in a garage or a shed. I can't help worrying that the heat buildup would set them off. I've often wondered if that's why they sell fireworks from tents in parking lots rather than in real stores."

"Interesting idea," Theresa commented. "I agree about the danger of storing that stuff."

"If you see Paul again," Victoria said, returning to their earlier topic, "ask him if he recognized the teens he saw that first night."

"There are a lot of parish members living in that area," Louise said. "Perhaps we'll know the families."

"Why didn't he go to the police and report seeing them?" Anna asked.

"Well, he said he scolded them, and he probably thought that was enough," Clare replied. "He's an odd one, but I enjoy talking to him. He loves his dog and his grandson means the world to him."

There was no answer to that, so the women sewed in silence for a while. The Delectable Mountains quilt top had been

20

pieced by both Anna and Louise and was a lovely top sure to bring a high price in their annual auction. They had used a multitude of green fabrics for the mountain blocks, with a creamy ivory tone on tone for contrast. Anna had stitched a swag border to contrast with and complement the jagged look of the pieced blocks. They were stitching a soft leaf pattern into the ivory fabric, and a chevron in the green. They had already done the borders with parallel lines.

Their moment of quiet was interrupted by the ring tone from Victoria's phone. She took a short call from Maggie, informing everyone that Maggie was happy with Michael's appearance and that he seemed to be fine.

"Should we take some meals over for her?" Clare asked. "Will Michael be in the hospital for a while? Will he have to stay with Maggie to recuperate?"

Victoria shrugged. "I'm afraid I can't answer any of those questions. I don't know any more than I've told you."

"Concussions can be serious," Louise said. "I'm sure they'll want to keep him in the hospital for at least twenty-four hours."

"I'll call everyone after I pick Maggie up," Victoria said. "She'll have more information then, and I can let you know if there's anything new. I have a feeling what she just told me is going to be it though."

Aware that they should not all bother Maggie by calling her individually at a time like this, that would have to do for now.

CHAPTER 3

Maggie arrived at the Quilting Bee room the next morning looking exhausted, which did not go unnoticed.

"You look tired, Maggie," Louise mentioned as soon as she saw her.

"But your cheeks are nice and rosy," Anna commented.

Victoria frowned. "I hadn't noticed, sitting beside you in the car, but they're right."

"You aren't feverish, are you?" Louise asked, putting the back of her fingers against Maggie's forehead, then her cheek.

"No." Maggie brushed her hand away, though she was grateful for her friends' concern. "I woke up at three and couldn't get back to sleep. So I drove out to the ranch and took Chestnut out for a ride. We watched the sun come up and communed with nature." As she finished speaking, her mouth relaxed into something very near a smile.

"That sounds lovely," Anna said. "I loved spending early mornings in the garden back in Ohio. It's just not the same here in the desert. The plants are different, and the scents. I often miss my flower garden." She finished with a heavy sigh. "I had beautiful hydrangeas and daisies, but they don't do well here in the heat."

"The oleanders in town are beautiful at this time of year," Maggie suggested as she stored her bag in the closet and pulled out a chair at the quilt frame. Not everyone had started stitching when the questions began. Her friends were all anxious for information about Michael.

"I saw the news report about Michael last night," Clare said.

All of the local television stations had been following the story of the late-night explosions, and all four had carried the story of Officer Browne's injury. In fact, the quirky story of Scottsdale's explosions in the night had moved from the middle of the newscast to the very beginning after Michael's injury.

"Is he still in the hospital?" Anna asked.

Maggie sat at the quilt frame, settling herself before answering. "Michael is still in the hospital; the doctor wanted him to stay overnight for observation. He said concussions can be tricky. I spent most of yesterday with Michael and he wasn't happy. I talked to him this morning and he claims to feel just fine. The headache he had yesterday is gone and his hearing is back to normal. He's never liked being cooped up indoors so this is driving him crazy. He'll be leaving today, but not until the doctor sees him. Victoria and I drove separately so that I can leave as soon as he calls. They thought it would be around eleven or twelve, so I should be here for most of our session."

Louise nodded her agreement. "It's best to be careful. You just never know about concussions."

"Will he be all right on his own?" Clare asked. They all knew that Michael lived alone in a Scottsdale town home.

"He'll be staying with me through the weekend," Maggie said. "The doctor insisted he not be alone for a day or two."

"And he's listening?" Theresa inquired. "Good for him."

Louise grinned. "You'd better think up something to keep him in bed. Or resting, anyway. He'll be going nuts within a few hours."

"Are you kidding? He's already stir crazy," Maggie said, but she said it with a smile. "He does not like being kept indoors, much less having to rest. But I'm already working on it," Maggie assured her. "I have a nice lounge chair set up on the patio so that he can spend time outdoors. It's been awfully hot, but the heat has never bothered him."

"A real desert rat," Louise said with a smile.

Maggie nodded absently. "I've enlisted the boys to play video games with their uncle on Saturday." Maggie's oldest son, Michael's older brother Hal, had two young sons who would be happy to distract their uncle. "I've promised them an indoor picnic for lunch. We used to do that when they were little, but we haven't done it for years. They're looking forward to it."

"Now don't you worry about anything today," Louise said. "We've already talked about it and we're bringing over dinner for the two of you tonight."

"I'm making my meatloaf," Edie announced. "Michael's had it before and claims to like it."

Maggie was touched by their kind offer. She thanked Edie, assuring her that Michael did indeed like her meatloaf.

The others went on to detail what they would contribute, outlining an entire meal specially intended to appeal to a man's tastes.

"You're all terrific for doing this," Maggie

said, her eyes suspiciously watery. "I could have managed fine, you know."

"Of course we know," Louise said. "But why should you have to when we can help out?"

"That's what friends are for," Clare added. The others nodded.

"Did Michael have anything to say about the explosions?" Clare asked.

"We didn't hear anything last night," Theresa said. "Unless it was another of those quieter blasts, like the early ones."

But Clare shook her head. "It's the first night since this started that nothing's happened. I heard it on the morning show on TV. But there was a copycat explosion in northwest Phoenix."

"Scared them, having a police officer injured," commented Edie with a smug smile.

"Perhaps, if it is only a teenage prank," Victoria said. "I don't think terrorists would be scared off so easily," she continued, giving Edie a pointed look.

"A terrorist would be sorry Michael wasn't killed," Louise stated, her face grim.

Startled, Maggie glanced between the speakers. "Terrorists?"

Victoria sighed. "It's one of Edie's theories."

Maggie gave one short nod of acknowledgment. Victoria didn't have to say more for her to understand. Outlandish theories were nothing new for Edie.

"I merely suggested various reasons for these late-night explosions," Edie said. "One was the possibility that a terrorist might be practicing making explosives. They don't all operate in groups, you know. There have been some American men who have tried to do something on their own to support Al Qaeda. And then there are those lone American nut jobs like Timothy McVeigh."

Even knowing Edie's propensity for paranoia, Maggie stared at her. "I can't believe a terrorist — homegrown or not — is operating in our parish."

"I don't see why not," Edie said. "Isn't that just the kind of thing that would terrify people? And isn't that what they try to do?"

No one answered. After all, what could be said? She was exactly right.

They all worked somberly for a moment, stitching the softly twining leaf pattern. The pretty stitches were a pleasant contrast to recent events — and Edie's theories — and offered a moment of escapism. Until Theresa looked over at Clare.

"Have you seen your friend Paul again? Were you able to question him about the kids he saw setting off firecrackers in his alley?"

"What?" Once again Maggie's surprise was apparent from the stunned look on her face. "I seem to have missed a lot, not being here yesterday. Do you mean to say you know a person who actually saw someone setting off explosives? Why hasn't he spoken to the police?"

The others quickly brought Maggie up to date on the conversation she'd missed the day before.

"Goodness, Clare," Maggie said. "This could be very important. If you have any information, I'll pass it along to Michael and he can have someone contact your friend."

"Well," Clare began, squirming a little in her chair. "He's not really a *close* friend. He's just someone from the neighborhood who walks his dog about the same time I do." She tugged at a knot that had snarled her thread. "He belongs to St. Rose, so I felt we had a few things in common. I ask him in for a glass of iced tea now and then."

"He sounds like a friend to me," Anna said quietly.

"An acquaintance perhaps," Victoria offered.

Clare appeared grateful for this distinction. "Yes, more an acquaintance. He's quite gruff, and curmudgeonly. But he's good with his dog, a little dachshund named Max. He told me once that he always has dachshunds and he always calls them Max. Isn't that odd?"

"It is a bit eccentric," Louise conceded.

"Wait." Theresa looked toward Clare. "What's this Paul's last name?"

"I don't know. Why?"

"There was a mechanic at Gilligan's named Paul. Paul Tipton. Brilliant mechanic, but noticeably lacking in people skills. That was okay, though, because he didn't work directly with customers and he got along with the other employees." Theresa's brows furrowed in thought. "I'm sure I recall his saying that he had a dachshund named Max, though that was years ago. But his mannerisms were also gruff and I could imagine him being an old curmudgeon. He retired about five years ago."

"Paul Tipton." Maggie repeated the name slowly. "I think I knew his wife. We were in the altar society together, years ago. She moved out — just up and went to LA after they lost their son in a tragic accident."

"Goodness," Clare said, her eyes wide with all this new input about her longtime acquaintance. "I know his daughter lives there with him, but he doesn't talk much about himself. I assumed he was a widower."

"Do you know his address?" Edie asked Clare. "We could look it up online and see who lives in that house."

"You can do that?" Anna looked amazed. She did email and used Google now and then, but did not do a lot online.

"Not much is private these days," Louise said, regret in her voice.

"But what about his seeing who set off the fireworks?" Maggie demanded. "Did he inform the police?"

Clare seemed to recall that she was supposed to address the issue of who was in the alley that night and quickly apologized. "Sorry. I get sidetracked so easily. I did see Paul early this morning. We both try to avoid the worst of the heat," she added.

"Did you ask him who he saw?" Edie was impatient with Clare's meandering conversational style and wanted her to get to the important stuff.

Maggie frowned, and Clare hurried to continue.

"I asked him about that. He said he didn't know the names of all the kids he saw. He said that there was a group, mostly guys but a couple of girls too. Teenagers, maybe as many as a dozen. He said he knew two of them lived next door, two teenage brothers, he said. He didn't know their names but the family name is Rivera. Those were the two boys he scolded since he felt he knew them. He said most of the others took off when they saw him come out of his yard."

"He didn't know the names of his neighbors?" Anna asked. "That's a shame. It isn't like the Midwest here, is it? We knew everyone in the neighborhood there."

"He does know the family name," Theresa said. "That's something."

"Wait a minute." Clare looked excited. "I just remembered. There's a woman in the Senior Guild whose daughter married a Rivera. Raquel Moreno."

"I know her," Edie said. "She embroiders."

"Yes. And she and her husband live on that block where I usually see Paul. They have the corner lot. I wouldn't be surprised if it is her daughter who lives next door to Paul. She might easily have bought there to be close to her parents." Clare smiled happily at her conclusion.

Just then Maggie's phone rang. While the others listened in to see what they could learn, Edie pulled out her smartphone and started tapping on its little keypad.

After a brief conversation with Michael,

Maggie stood and gathered her things.

"Michael is ready to leave the hospital," she said. "I'll see you when I can. Victoria, I'll call and bring you up to date." She turned to Clare. "Keep me informed about anything more you learn from Paul."

As Maggie hurried from the room, Edie brandished her phone. The small screen was brightly lit. "I've called up this real estate app, Clare. I have it on Appletree Lane. The arrow is there on the Morenos' house." She moved her finger around on the screen, then held it up again. "And here's the Riveras. Which house is Paul's?"

Clare stood and moved to stand beside Edie. "Imagine that. And it tells you how much the house is worth too?"

"I think it's what it sold for the last time it was on the market. Or it could be the estimates from the tax office."

"It's this one," Clare said, putting her finger on the house to the east of the Riveras. To her surprise, the phone's picture zoomed in on the house, and she quickly pulled her finger back.

"Theresa was correct." Edie spoke in her most didactic tone. If they weren't all so interested, there might have been some sniping. "The name on that lot is Tipton."

Clare headed straight for the door. "I

think I'll go see if Raquel is here today."

To everyone's surprise, Edie stood and followed. "I'll go with you."

CHAPTER 4

Clare and Edie made their way to the embroiderers' room, where they had to take time to visit with acquaintances and admire the works in progress before making their way to Raquel's side. They invited her to join them for tea in the break room, claiming to have a question about her neighborhood. In the break room, Edie poured glasses of iced tea and Clare passed lemon slices.

Once they had settled down with their iced drinks, Clare asked Raquel about her family. Edie sipped her tea and drummed her fingers on the table, shooting meaningful looks toward Clare every minute or so. Clare, however, ignored her. After all, hearing about Raquel's family was the reason they sought her out. Even Edie had to realize that just coming out and accusing Raquel's grandchildren of being involved in the explosions that were rocking the neighborhood would be all wrong. She might just get mad and leave, and then where would they be?

"So that is your daughter living next door to Paul Tipton." Clare gave Edie a triumphant smile. "Paul and I walk our dogs at about the same time every day and we've taken to visiting for a bit. Like everyone else, we've been talking about those explosions that disrupt our sleep every night."

Edie had had enough. "Paul claims he saw your grandsons with a group of teenagers, lighting firecrackers in the alley behind their house the night of the first explosion."

"Paul is an insomniac, and he sometimes sits outside by the pool," Clare rushed to say. "He told me he heard that first explosion in the alley and went right out there. Your grandsons were the only ones he recognized. He gave them a talking to, he said, while most of the other kids took off."

Raquel looked from Clare to Edie then back to Clare. "So that's why you asked me to have tea with you? So you could accuse my family of this terrible thing? I've heard how the Quilting Bee has solved murders, but accusing my grandsons of this — this is too much."

She half rose from her chair and Clare thought she might just walk off without saying anything more. So she rushed to re-assure her. "Oh, no," she said. "We're not accusing anyone, Raquel. Are we, Edie?" The look she cast toward Edie dared her to disagree. "It's just that we're all so concerned about these noises that have been disturbing our sleep. Surely you've heard the explosions? I've been afraid to take Samson out after dark."

Raquel nodded but remained silent. As she sat back down, her mouth was pulled so tight, her lips almost disappeared.

"When Clare told us that Paul claimed to see several teenagers in the alley that first night, we asked her to see if he recognized anyone." Edie's voice was uncharacteristically contrite. "We were all concerned about the disturbances before, but now that Maggie's son was hurt . . ." She allowed her voice to trail off.

"I heard about that." Raquel finally relaxed a little, leaning against the back of her chair. "Poor Maggie. You know, my youngest son is a police officer in Phoenix. You always worry that something dreadful might happen."

"I didn't know that," Edie said. "That your son was a police officer, I mean. So you know how Maggie must feel."

Raquel nodded.

"I heard on the morning news today that there was an explosion in Phoenix last night," Clare said.

"An obvious copycat," Edie claimed.

Raquel fidgeted with her tea glass, turning it around and around on the tabletop. "I did hear that, and it made me worry about my Antonio." She stopped playing with the glass and looked at Clare. "How is Michael?"

"Michael is fine," Clare told her. "Maggie was really scared when they came to get her to go to the hospital yesterday morning. As I'm sure you can understand," she added. "He has a concussion but Maggie says he feels okay."

"Poor Maggie," Raquel said again, running her fingers down the moisture forming on the side of her glass.

"He'll be fine," Edie concurred. "Maggie just left, in fact, to pick him up from the hospital. He's going to spend the weekend at her place."

Raquel nodded once more. "That's good." She took a sip of her tea, swallowed hard, then looked Edie straight in the eye. "But as far as my grandsons go, I cannot see either one of them causing that kind of trouble." She frowned as though considering, trying to be unbiased. "Maybe just to set off some firecrackers, like Paul said. Boyish mischief, you know. A prank with their friends. But not something big enough to injure a large man like Maggie's son."

Clare nodded and was surprised to see Edie nod her agreement. "It's like I said," Edie told Clare. "The first few explosions might have been teen pranks. They weren't nearly as loud as these later ones. The explosions the last few nights have been different. Bigger. Louder." She nodded again as though satisfied with her own opinion.

"These last ones have been louder. Bigger too," Raquel agreed. "There wasn't any damage reported at first. But I know the last couple caused some serious property damage."

"That's right," Clare said. "I can't believe I didn't think of that. These last few, besides harming Michael, there's been destruction of property. The Krakowskis had to have their mailbox replaced, and the Stanleys had a large shrub at the side of their lawn burnt."

"And the Thorntons had some damage to their wooden fence," Raquel reported. "They live two doors down from us. They said the device exploded near their back fence gate and they will have to have the gate replaced. It knocked down a palo verde tree in the alley, too, one that came up on its own, right beside the fence. They said they've been thinking of removing that tree for the past few years, and they're glad it's gone. But they thought it would be expensive to replace the gate," she added.

"If the teenagers started all this by setting off some firecrackers late at night . . ." Edie paused while she considered. "Just as some mischief, as you said. They may have given someone else ideas." She ended with a firm nod, quite happy with her conclusion.

"Not that theory about terrorists again," Clare said.

"Terrorists?" Raquel looked puzzled. "You think there are terrorists? Here in our neighborhood?"

Edie didn't look fazed at the disbelief apparent in others whenever she mentioned her ideas. "It's a theory. There could be someone practicing to make explosive devices for a larger purpose. You said yourself that the explosions are getting bigger, and causing more damage."

"You mean you think someone is trying to make bombs." A frown marred her attractive face, and Raquel's voice oozed disbelief.

"It could happen," Edie insisted.

The other two women exchanged a look. Both remained skeptical.

"The thing is, Raquel," Clare began, "do

you think you could ask your grandsons about it? Find out what happened that first night and if that was the only time they set off firecrackers?"

Edie picked it up. "Maybe they know if any of their friends decided to try it as well. If we knew which of the explosions were teenage pranks, maybe we could figure out what else is happening."

Raquel nodded, though reluctantly. "I'll do it, but only because I would like to help Maggie. My grandsons aren't bad kids. But like I said, mischief, yes; that they might do. Especially if their friends were also involved." She sighed, her large chest rising and falling with the effort. "I know my son-in-law bought a few *legal* fireworks for them to set off for the Fourth of July. We all had BBQ, and enjoyed the sparklers. Then the kids and some of the *male* adults" — she put a slight emphasis on the gender of the miscreants — "played with the firecrackers afterward."

"It would be great if they know anything about these most recent explosions," Clare told her.

"Maybe their friends decided to try something bigger?" Edie suggested. Her voice moved upward at the end of the sentence, turning it into a question.

41

Raquel unbent enough to nod, and to thank them for coming to her instead of going to the police. "I appreciate you asking me first," she added.

"And thank you so much for offering to help," Clare said.

"By the way," Edie asked as the three rose to rinse out the glasses and put them in the dishwasher, "did you know Paul's wife? Maggie thinks she remembers her from the altar society years ago."

Raquel smiled and nodded. "Fay Tipton. I do remember her. Nice woman. She just went to pieces after their son was killed in a freak helicopter accident. He'd only been in the army for a few months if I recall correctly. Just shattered the family. Though we women thought they were having some trouble already — thought that might be why Fay had gotten pregnant again when their only child was fifteen."

"So the second child is the daughter who came back to live with Paul a couple of years ago?" Clare asked.

Once again, Raquel nodded. "She was only five when her mother left, and Paul had to raise her alone. She was a mess as a teenager. Wild. I haven't seen her much since she got back, but I see Paul with his grandson sometimes. Cute kid."

The three women left the break room together, Clare telling Raquel all about Paul's sweet little grandson. They separated in the courtyard to return to their respective craft rooms.

Clare spoke as they walked back toward the Quilting Bee's room. "That's interesting about Paul's wife. I guess that's why he never talks about her, if she just up and left him with a five-year-old daughter."

"There's no way for us to know what was going on," Edie told her. "But she must have been very depressed about losing her only son."

"Wouldn't you think they both would be?" Clare asked. "If that had happened to Gerald and me, I would have needed him to comfort me."

"Well, we're all different," Edie said. "But I know where I'm going from here."

"You mean where you want to have lunch when we leave today?" Clare asked.

"Of course not." Edie sounded exasperated, but she did explain. "I mean, where I want to go in our investigation into the explosions. As soon as I get home today, I'm going to do some online surfing."

"Really?" Clare was impressed. "That sounds very professional."

"Well, I don't know about that," Edie

replied, though she did appear gratified by the adjective. "But I'm going to check out those social network sites I keep hearing about and see if anyone is talking about these incidents. If teens are involved, they might say something on their pages. From what I hear, young people put their whole lives up for anyone to see. I don't know if there will be any information, but it will be interesting if there is. Especially with this new incident in Phoenix."

CHAPTER 5

Maggie and Victoria arrived at the church parking lot at their usual time on Friday morning. But there was nothing usual about the two young men who suddenly appeared before them, seemingly out of nowhere. In reality, they had been concealed behind a tall SUV with dark tinted windows that kept them from being seen by the women. Victoria gasped and Maggie took a step back even as she clutched her purse tightly, ready to fling it at one of them if necessary.

"Mrs. Browne, ma'am?"

The young man's voice was hesitant but polite. It was the tentative nature of his inquiry rather than the fact that he knew her name that allowed Maggie to relax. As she did so, she realized that they were not men at all, but teenage boys.

"Yes," she replied, but she frowned at him. "You startled us." She took in his appearance: slim and wiry with thick, dark wavy hair — a good-looking young Hispanic man. The second teen looked much like the first, but younger — probably his brother. "Do I know you?"

"Sorry, ma'am. I didn't mean to do that. Scare you, I mean. But we wanted to talk to you private like, you know? I'm Ramon Rivera and this is my brother Angel. Raquel Moreno is our grandmother."

Maggie was finally able to smile and she offered her hand, shaking his and his brother's both, to their obvious surprise. "And what do you think I can do for you?"

Maggie thought she saw Ramon's mouth twitch, as though he was amused by her supposition that they wanted something from her. Angel looked uneasy. Maggie hid a smile of her own. She could like this young man, she thought. He was polite, dressed fairly well for a teenager. He wore jeans that were clean, unripped, and did not sag below his underwear.

"Our grandma, she came over yesterday and talked to us. She said some lady came to her and said someone saw us and some other kids around that first explosion."

"And did they?"

Ramon and Angel both hung their heads. While Angel had been doing this for most of their conversation, Ramon had up to then

46

looked into Maggie's face. "Yeah. Our neighbor, that Mr. Tipton, he came out and saw us standing around where the firecrackers went off. Laughing and having fun, you know. You could still smell it, the sulfur smell, you know, and there was some of the paper and stuff on the ground."

Maggie cleared her throat, uncertain of what to say next. She didn't want to accuse them, but she did want to know if they had continued to play with explosive materials.

Victoria stepped in. "Why did you come to us? Shouldn't you be telling this to the police?"

Angel kicked at a loose piece of gravel on the lot surface, but Ramon stood still, hands shoved into the pockets of his jeans. Once again his eyes dipped toward the ground.

"We heard around church how you helped that other dude, you know? The one whose house exploded."

"I thought maybe we could call Silent Witness. Tell them about that first explosion, you know." Angel finally joined the conversation. "But Ramon says we should talk to you, that you help people."

His eyes darted back and forth, from Maggie to Victoria to his brother, and his feet moved back and forth so that he almost appeared to be dancing in front of her. Not ballroom dancing or even street dancing, but the kind of back-and-forth "dance" that prize fighters did in the ring.

"We do try to help when we can," Maggie said. "People who need our help." And it was obvious to her that these boys needed their help.

Ramon, looking slightly embarrassed now, took back the conversation. "My grandma says that was your son, the cop who got hurt the other night."

Angel quickly intervened, his voice high and nervous. "We want you to know, we was nowhere near that. We were home all night that night. Our parents can tell you."

Ramon nodded vigorously. "Yeah, we were embarrassed after Mr. Tipton yelled at us. We stayed away, but one of our friends had some firecrackers and he set them off the next night around the same time. Early, you know. He did it in his front yard, and a bush caught on fire. It scared him bad, and the others too, but it didn't catch on anything else and the fire just went out. But after that, we were all scared, especially after there were a couple really loud bangs the next nights. And real late. We only did it once, and then our friend another time. And early, not two or three in the morning, because we all had to be home by midnight." The older boy hung his head — what Maggie thought was a gesture more of regret than shame. "They should never have done nothing after that first time. Mr. Tipton, he was mad. He yelled at us, said he would tell our parents if it happened again." He hung his head. "I'm sixteen. I should have known better."

Maggie did not disagree, though she did feel sorry for the boy.

Victoria, though, had a kinder disposition. Having worked in high schools for her entire teaching career, she understood teenagers. "Sixteen *is* old enough to know better, but you aren't an adult yet. You've learned an important lesson and you're much wiser now." She smiled kindly at them. "Coming to speak to us was a very mature decision."

"Our grandma was pretty mad," Angel mumbled.

His brother nodded agreement. "After things started getting damaged, we were afraid to say anything in case everybody thought we were still involved."

Maggie could understand that and how it would frighten them into keeping silent. And especially after Michael was injured.

"Let's go inside," Victoria suggested. Before anyone could say more, she began walking toward the church building. "It's very hot out here on the pavement. I'm sure we can find a private corner of the court-yard."

The two boys exchanged a look, and Ramon gave a quick nod. Then they followed the women into the courtyard. It was still very warm there, but not nearly as hot as out on the parking lot where the sun beat down on one's head and shoulders and the intense heat from the pavement surged up through the soles of one's shoes.

Maggie's initial surprise had morphed into — pity? Excitement? Yes, excitement that the authorities might actually learn something from these boys that would help find whoever was responsible for hurting her son and disturbing the sleep patterns of so many people. And perhaps pity, too, for these teens who seemed like decent young men, but who may have started something that turned sinister. Even though she didn't believe Edie's ideas about terrorists, she thought with an inward smile.

Maggie had to admit to a frisson of fear at first seeing the two boys appear from behind that large SUV. It was well known that one should never leave a purse or any other valuables in a car parked in the church lot as things had been stolen in the past. A possible purse-snatching was her initial fear.

She wouldn't be human if that didn't scare her. Older women were so often the target of young people — often drug addicts — looking for some quick cash. And they were a smart target, too, as they could rarely defend themselves against younger, stronger, quicker opponents.

Chiding herself now for such unfounded fears, Maggie eyed the two boys. As she'd noted initially, they were well groomed, though their clothes were worn. Their hair was cut in a neat style and recently combed, and they did appear sincere in what they were telling her. Fear radiated off them, from the foot-shuffling of the younger boy to the nervous hand movements of the older. Maggie found that she believed everything they said.

Victoria, she noted, was busy with her own keen observation. They exchanged a quick look, a short nod. Maggie knew that meant that her friend also believed the boys. She had to repress a chuckle when she realized they were imitating the boys in their nonverbal communication.

They stopped in a shady corner of the courtyard, closer to the church office and away from the Senior Guild break room.

"Wait here for a minute," Maggie told them. "We have a retired attorney in the

Senior Guild. He helped with Kenny Upland too, and you can trust him to keep things confidential. I'm going to get him, have him come and talk to you. You can see if he thinks he should go with you to talk to the police. Have you told your parents?"

The boys hung their heads as they mumbled an affirmative answer. Maggie hid a smile. It must have been difficult facing their parents, but she had to give them credit for doing it.

Maggie looked them over again. Ramon said he was sixteen. His brother looked younger, perhaps fourteen. But she asked anyway. It was important. "Are you both under eighteen?"

They nodded.

"What about the others who were involved?"

They exchanged a frightened look. It looked like telling on their friends would be harder than admitting guilt to their parents.

"Don't start lying to me now," Maggie scolded. "Are the others all under eighteen too?"

They exchanged another look but remained silent.

"You can't do this halfway," Maggie warned. "If you lie to the police, they are sure to know it. You have to go in and tell them what you were doing and why, show them any fireworks you might still have."

"We don't," Ramon quickly interrupted.

"Well, just let them know that what you did was different from the more violent explosions that came later and that you say you are not involved in."

"We aren't," Angel pleaded. Maggie thought he looked close to tears.

She gave them a stern look before asking again about accomplices.

"There were a lot of others," Ramon finally admitted. "All about our age." He paused. "Maybe Angela's brother, he might be eighteen. But everybody else is still in high school. I think they're all younger like us."

"Okay. Stay here for a moment. I'll be right back." Maggie turned to go after the person she'd mentioned, but then reconsidered and turned back to the boys. "The retired lawyer is Walter Jackson. He handled Kenny Upland's affairs *pro bono* — that's for free. I'm sure he'll do the same for you."

Both boys nodded. Maggie realized she should have considered that they watched television and knew all about such legal terms. "Okay then. Be right back."

CHAPTER 6

Maggie and Victoria were seriously late entering the Quilting Bee room after their encounter with the Rivera brothers. Which understandably produced a spate of questions once they did arrive.

"Maggie! We didn't think you'd be able to make it," Clare said. "And, Victoria, we were getting concerned about you."

The questions came too quickly for the two newcomers to reply.

"How's Michael?" Louise asked.

"What's wrong?" Edie asked. "You look flustered."

"Is Michael worse?" Theresa asked.

Maggie dropped her purse on the shelf in the closet, grabbed a bottle of water and sat down. "I am flustered." She turned toward Louise. "But Michael is well. Chafing at the bit to get back on the job. Which means he's feeling just fine. And he asked me to thank you all for the excellent dinner last night."

She took a long drink from the water bottle. "And I thank you for that too. I enjoyed having a nice dinner I didn't have to cook. As much as I enjoy cooking, it makes for a nice change."

While everyone smiled and commented on how it was no problem, Victoria sat down across the frame from Maggie with her own bottle of water. "We've been outside for the past twenty minutes," she said, patting her forehead with a lace-edged hanky. "We had an encounter in the parking lot."

"The parking lot?" Anna looked confused.

"An encounter?" Louise raised her eyebrows at the word choice.

"Are you all right?" Edie asked. "It wasn't a mugging, was it?" She looked them up and down. "You don't appear to be hurt. Of course you know not to leave any valuables in your car, or even here in the church buildings."

The diocese often ran notices in the church bulletins warning of robberies in the various church parking lots and buildings, and asking parishioners not to leave valuable items in their cars. They especially warned the women to keep their handbags with them, even when walking to the altar to receive communion during mass. Thieves had no respect for religious observations.

Maggie shook her head. "No, nothing like that. As we got out of the car, two young men appeared from behind a large SUV. It was rather startling."

Anna gasped. Edie raised a brow.

"Don't worry." Maggie addressed herself to Anna. "It turned out they were Raquel's two grandsons and they wanted to talk. They were very polite. Well-spoken. They don't dress like thugs either. It was just such a surprise the way they popped out from behind that truck."

"Oh!" Clare's eyes lit up. "Raquel said she would talk to them and ask if they really were involved in that first explosion like Paul said."

"Well, they claim that they were with the group that set off the first explosion with some firecrackers they had." Maggie reached for a threaded needle, slipping her thimble onto her finger. "But they said they stopped after that scolding from Paul. They say their friends still had some fireworks and they set them off the following night, burning a bush in their yard and scaring them in the process. So they stopped then too. They don't know anything about these larger, louder explosions."

"And they were adamant about not causing Michael's injuries," Victoria added.

"Aha." Edie almost chortled. "So the others are copycats. Didn't I tell you?"

"Yes, but you also implied terrorists were involved," Louise reminded her.

"It's still a possibility," Edie insisted.

"Only in your mind," Louise muttered.

Edie ignored this, if she heard it at all. "You say they only admitted to causing the first two explosions, and there have been seven, counting the one that injured Michael. A full week. Plus a new one last night — or rather, very early this morning."

"I didn't hear anything last night," Louise said. "I'd hoped that injuring a police officer scared off whoever is doing it and that they'd backed off."

"There was nothing overnight on Wednesday, but there was an explosion last night," Edie said. "Woke me around three. About the same as the last few. A loud bang, the dogs barking."

"Yes, we heard it too," Clare said. "We thought it was the same as these latest, too. We thought it seemed more like a loud muffled bang. Like those ground-level fireworks they let off during the big shows on the Fourth. I wonder why you didn't hear it," she said, turning toward Louise.

Like Louise, Maggie had not heard anything, but then she hadn't heard all of the

57

explosions. Her condo was well insulated, and the air conditioner fan added to the muting effect whenever it turned on. And with the recent high temperatures, it was running a lot.

They all stitched quietly for a few minutes. The soothing strains of a Mozart concerto filtered into the room from the sound system in the courtyard. Father Bob enjoyed Mozart and Beethoven and usually shared his enthusiasm with the Senior Guild. Now and again he shook things up with a little Vivaldi or Bach.

"Clare and I talked to Raquel yesterday," Edie said. She finished off a line of stitches, smoothed them over with her index finger and looked up. "We told her we had information linking her grandsons to the first explosion. She said she would look into it."

"That explains a lot," Maggie remarked.

"The older boy said they heard how we've helped others in the past," Victoria said. "Perhaps from their grandmother?"

"Oh, everyone in the parish knows about our amateur sleuthing," Clare declared, sitting up proudly. She loved being able to help solve mysteries, fancied herself as a modern-day Miss Marple or Amelia Peabody. Her idol was Jessica Fletcher.

"They agreed to tell the police what they

know," Maggie said, going back to the topic of their recent visitors. "I introduced them to Walter, and they were talking to him when we came inside. I told them they might want to have him go with them to the police when they tell their story."

Edie nodded in satisfaction. "That's good. I think they may know a lot, maybe more than they realize."

Maggie drew her brows together as she looked at Edie. "What makes you say that?"

"They were in with the group that started it all. It could be one of those other boys continued without telling his friends. A potential terrorist, for all we know." Edie pursed her lips in satisfaction at her pronouncement. As was often the case with her more bizarre ideas, the others ignored it.

"Raquel thanked us for going to her first rather than involving the police with what we'd heard," Clare said. She snipped off her thread and reached for the spool lying on the quilt top. She went on to tell Maggie about the conversation she and Edie had with Raquel, and her comments on the Tipton family. "You'd already left to pick up Michael, so you didn't hear about it," Clare explained.

"After we talked to her, I decided to do some checking online," Edie said. "I spent most of the afternoon and evening looking at social media sites, trying to find any mention of the recent explosions by teens in this area."

"And did you find anything?" Louise asked.

Edie's smug expression told Maggie that she had indeed found something. "What did you find?" she asked. Better to just ask outright. Otherwise Edie might take her time leading up to the good stuff.

"I discovered that teenagers must waste hours and hours each day on those sites," Edie said, clicking her tongue. "I must admit, I don't see the appeal."

No one disagreed. While the others weren't as proficient as Edie on the computer, they all had some amount of competency. They emailed with family members in other states, shared photos, even Skyped with them. But they were all of a generation that had grown up without computers. Their children and grandchildren were much more comfortable with the new technologies and that was how most of them were drawn — or dragged — in. Modern families lived in scattered locations and if the older generation wanted to keep in touch it was necessary to learn about sites where their children shared photographs and videos or did video conferencing.

Edie continued. "I managed to find numerous references to the recent explosions. These kids don't seem to realize that all this information about their lives is available to anyone — unless they make it private."

"Oh, I think they know," Louise said. "But they don't care. They like communicating with the world. Look at all the awful stuff they post on those video sites."

"It's a side effect of all this reality TV," Victoria suggested.

Louise nodded. "I think you're right. They want their fifteen minutes of fame, but they want it now and they want it often. Even when I was young, I can't imagine my friends and I doing the things today's young people freely post on the Internet. Imagine letting the whole world see what a fool you can make of yourself!"

"And it's on there forever!" Theresa added.

"Hmm. You may be right," Edie conceded. "Anyway, I found lots of references about the incidents, asking who was doing it — that kind of thing. Some people offering to participate. *Anxious* to participate." She frowned. "I found two young men who bragged of their involvement. But of course it's difficult to know if they were telling the truth." She reached into her pocket and brought out a piece of paper. "One of the problems with these places is that the participants often use code names. There were some Tristans and Erins posting, but the two boasters called themselves 8player and — if you can believe it — loverboy18. Must be something about the number eight." She muttered the final sentence while shaking her head at the incomprehensibleness of teenagers. "There were also a large number of videos posted that show various things being blown apart, but I couldn't tell if any of them were of our recent incidents."

"Did they say anything that might help us identify them?" Victoria asked.

"We have the two Rivera boys admitting to it," Maggie reminded them. "When they go to the police, they'll have to identify the others."

"Will they do that?" Theresa asked. "Go to the police?"

"Oh, yes," Maggie replied. "They said they would even before I suggested having Walter go with them. You could see that they were nervous about it, but determined to do the right thing. Don't you think so, Victoria?"

Victoria nodded. "They seem like well-brought-up young men. They were neat and polite. Respectful. They must have a good family relationship to do something difficult like meeting with us because their grandmother said they should."

"They do seem reluctant to identify the others, but I think between Walter and their parents, they will say something." Maggie tugged gently at her thread to pull a knot through the top layer of fabric and into the quilt batt. "I did tell them they needed legal representation. Besides injuring Michael, a couple of these latest explosions have caused considerable property damage. They claim no responsibility for those, but there's bound to be some initial skepticism."

"I wonder why the police haven't looked online like you did?" Clare asked, looking over at Edie.

Edie shrugged, but Maggie replied, her voice strong with her confidence in their local police force.

"What makes you think they haven't? The police don't announce all their methods. And they watch those social media sites for sexual predators, so why not for something like this? As you said, kids put everything online these days. You can probably sketch out a teenager's whole day by what he or she posts online."

"That's true," Edie said. "They tell their friends where they are, what they're doing, where they're going next, what they're eating. It's amazing. There were lots of posts that were simply things like 'at Jake's house,' and 'Starbucks for a latte.' " She shook her head. "Unbelievable."

"I guess that's why they're always fooling around with their cell phones," Maggie said. "My grandchildren are a little young for that yet, but I know they are already asking for phones of their own. Sometimes I wonder what today's teenagers would do if they couldn't have a phone in their hands at all times."

"They'd find some other mischief to get into," Edie said.

"Maybe all that texting and calling is helping to keep them *out* of mischief," Louise suggested, a twinkle in her eyes.

But Edie wasn't to be drawn in. "I think we did the right thing, speaking to Raquel yesterday."

No one disagreed. In the brief silence, the faint strains of the "Promenade" from Mussorgsky's "Pictures at an Exhibition" filtered into the room.

As Anna finished off a line of stitching, she looked toward Maggie. "We weren't sure you'd be able to come this morning,

Maggie. We didn't know if you'd want to leave Michael on his own. Is he still staying at your place?"

"Yes," Maggie replied. "Reluctantly. His girlfriend has the day off and is visiting him this morning. That's why I decided to come."

"Well, you look happy about that," Louise said.

"I am," Maggie admitted. "The quilting is relaxing, which I need, and besides, I like her."

"Is he still dating that other police officer?" Anna asked.

"Oh, no," Clare said. "Don't you remember, she moved out of state, back to her hometown."

Maggie hid a smile at Clare's reply. Leave it to Clare to recall all the personal details of everyone's life.

"Lauren was a wonderful girl," Maggie said. "But, as Clare said, she returned to her hometown in Colorado back in March. Her mother's been diagnosed with cancer and she wanted to be closer to her so she can help her fight it. Michael and I were both sorry to see her go, but he wasn't devastated, so I guess she wasn't his special someone. For the past two months he's been dating Kimi Tanaka, and she's a very nice person. I like her a lot." Maggie pulled her thread through, then concentrated on making and hiding a knot. "I don't know that I should be calling her his girlfriend. That makes it sound more serious than I've been led to believe."

"What does this Kimi do?" Theresa asked.

"She's a crime scene photographer. She's from LA, but she said that getting a job there was very difficult and terribly competitive, so she thought she'd try here. She has some cousins in Tempe, and they put her up while she interviewed and got established."

"It sounds like a good match," Edie decided, much to everyone's surprise. "A cop and a crime scene photographer should have a lot in common."

"As I said, I don't know how serious they are at this point." Maggie finished rethreading her needle and looked down at the quilt top to find a spot to insert it once more. "But, yes, I do think it could be a good match."

"Did they meet at work?" Anna inquired.

"Actually they did and they didn't." Maggie smiled at her contradictory reply. "Michael says he'd seen her at crime scenes a few times and thought she was 'a cute little thing.' His exact words, by the way."

There were a few laughs and a "hmpf" from Edie.

"I'm sure Kimi would have said the same thing if she'd heard him say that." Maggie tugged the thread to bury the new knot in the batting and pushed her needle in to begin a new line of stitches. "But it was at an art festival on the Scottsdale mall where they really got together. Michael was working security there, and Kimi was taking pictures. In her spare time she likes to take art photographs, and some of them are very good. She posts them on a website," she added, in case anyone wondered how she'd happened to see them.

"You'll have to share the link with me," Victoria said.

"Didn't I?" Maggie was surprised she hadn't already done so, as Kimi's art photos were just the type of thing Victoria enjoyed.

"So go on with how they met," Clare urged. "Was it love at first sight?"

Maggie laughed. "I don't think so. Remember, they'd seen each other before. But Michael told me when they met on the mall that day, they did the don't-I-know-you-from-somewhere thing and started talking. They've been seeing each other ever since." Maggie smiled as she ran her finger over her last line of stitches, and it was easy for the others to see how fond she was of Kimi. "It was nice of her to offer to spend time with Michael this morning. She knows I come here to quilt, so she arranged her schedule to have the morning free."

"She sounds like someone who would make a good daughter-in-law," Louise said. "Think that might happen?"

Maggie sighed. "I don't know. I think it might be too soon. But then the kids surprise me all the time. Do you know that Joshua showed me how to clean out the email on my phone? I couldn't figure it out myself, and he's only eight. Did it just like that!" she added, bringing her left hand up from beneath the quilt and snapping her fingers.

The others began talking of wonderful things their own grandchildren did, especially having to do with electronic devices, and the time passed swiftly and pleasantly. Maggie almost forgot about the ongoing explosions. Almost.

But as she and Victoria returned to the parking lot to leave, she remembered again how the two teens had appeared seemingly out of nowhere. They had given her a right good start, and she wasn't proud of that. She turned to Victoria as they got into the car and pulled on their seatbelts.

"I can't believe I was so startled when those boys confronted us this morning. They gave me quite a scare."

"They startled me too," Victoria admitted. "I was reaching into my bag for my phone when I realized they were friendly."

Maggie sighed. "Most of the time I don't feel old. But every now and then, something like that happens and I realize I can no longer do a lot of things I used to do."

Victoria nodded. There was no need to say more. They both understood how things were. And while they both expected to be around for a good number of years yet, they both knew they were no longer young.

CHAPTER 7

By the time Maggie got home from her quilting session, Michael knew all about the Rivera brothers. He grinned at her from the kitchen, where he had sandwiches made and a plate of fruit. He gestured for her to sit down while he poured the iced tea.

"That was smart of you, having Walter take them to the station."

Maggie's eyebrows shot upward. It wasn't only the information that the Rivera brothers had already spoken to the police but the idea that her "sick" child had done such a nice job with lunch. "They already went in? And you know all about it? How did it happen so quickly?"

"Walter wanted them to go in as soon as possible." Michael pulled out a chair for Maggie. "He may have already heard the news, but I don't think you have."

Maggie suddenly realized Michael was alone in her condo. "Where's Kimi?"

"She got called in to work. It's bad news, for the neighborhood and for those boys."

Maggie sank down into the chair. "Sit," she directed her son. She picked up a napkin and shook it out before laying it over her lap. "Tell me."

"There was another of those large explosions last night, around three o'clock."

"Edie mentioned it," Maggie said, spooning some fruit onto her plate. "I didn't hear a thing, but Clare said she did."

"Lots of people called it in. Patrol cars checked around the area but no one saw anything suspicious. It just seemed to be another damaged tree and fence. This morning, a woman calls nine-one-one. She's hysterical. Her five-year-old just found her father in their backyard, dead in a lounge chair. A large palo verde tree fell on top of their ramada and the ramada roof fell onto her father who was troubled by insomnia and often fell asleep outdoors."

"Oh, no," Maggie said. "And did the explosion topple the tree?"

Palo verde trees were popular throughout the valley, pretty trees with dark green trunks, leafy branches and yellow blossoms. The trees appeared everywhere, the wind-scattered seeds sprouting after rainfalls. But they had a shallow root system, often attacked by boring beetles that compounded the problem. Therefore they were common victims of high winds and a familiar sight lying across roads or lawns after storms. Could one of the explosive charges have toppled a tree large enough to cause so much serious damage?

"Yes," Michael replied, his face somber. "It sure looks that way. The house is old, and the ramada was the same age. I guess it was weak after so many years of hot sun."

"Do you know who it was?"

"I don't know him personally. The name hasn't been released yet, but it was a Paul Tipton."

Maggie had just speared a chunk of melon when she heard the name. The fork went back to her plate, and her audible groan made Michael sit up. "You know him? Is he in the Senior Guild?"

"No." Maggie felt tears dampen her eyes. Those poor boys. They were bound to be in big trouble now, and it was her fault for urging them to report what they had done. On the other hand, she *had* provided them with counsel.

Maggie extracted a tissue from her pocket before commenting further. "Oh, Michael, he's the man who told Clare he'd seen the Rivera boys and a few of their friends set off the first explosion. He lives — ah, lived — next door to the Riveras." She swallowed. "His wife and I were good friends once, long ago. We were in the altar society together."

Michael shook his head. When it came to parish members, it was a very small world.

"There wasn't mention of a wife," he told her. "Or maybe I just didn't get all the information. I just heard of a daughter and grandson."

Maggie nodded. "She left him. It was years ago, right after their son died in a tragic accident. It was a nervous breakdown, I guess, but she never did come back. She sends me Christmas cards from LA."

Michael took a bite of his sandwich, not sure what to say.

"I feel so guilty," Maggie continued, dabbing at her eyes with the tissue. "I was the one who told the Rivera boys they had to go in. What have I done?" Maggie's hands twisted the soft tissue and bits of white flaked off, drifting toward her lap. She suddenly felt very old.

Michael put down his sandwich and walked around the table to his mother. He put his arm around her shoulders and leaned over to kiss her forehead. "You acted as a responsible citizen, Ma. You gave them

73

the best advice you could. And you provided Walter to help them find their way through the legal system. I'm sure having him there was a big help."

"They'll think the boys did this for revenge." Maggie's voice was soft, her tone fearful. "Do you think they'll charge them with murder?"

"They may question them about it, but I doubt there will be any charges, especially murder. If it was an *accident,* the charge would probably be manslaughter."

Suddenly, Maggie sat upright; she straightened her shoulders and squared her jaw. "When did the news come out about this latest . . . event?"

"I heard about it when Kimi was called in, of course. Then someone I know at the station called to tell me about the boys coming in. But I turned on the television for the midday news and it was the leading story. No names were mentioned," he added.

"Did they show the house?" Maggie asked. She knew how the local stations covered these stories. They parked their satellite trucks right across from homes where disaster struck, so even though no names were given, it was simple enough for those familiar with the area to know who was involved.

"The cameras showed the police cars in front of the house, yeah." Michael knew exactly where she was going. "Does Clare watch the midday news?"

Maggie nodded. "She would get home the same time I do, which is past the time for the lead stories. But Gerald watches it every day, and he'll tell her. I'm sure he'd recognize the house too. It's not very far from theirs." She rose abruptly and stepped purposefully toward the phone.

"The others will want to know," she told Michael, and he understood her to mean the other bee members. "Poor Clare. She knew him, you know. They walked their dogs at about the same time and would stop and talk. I'm sure she'll be upset."

"A lot of people are going to be upset," Michael said. "There was already an outcry about the late-night noise and the property damage. A ruined fence might not seem like a big deal to a newspaper reporter, but in that neighborhood, it could mean a week's pay to repair it for the homeowner."

"And don't forget the damage to your head," his mother said, a grin playing at her lips. She couldn't resist reaching out to ruffle his hair. "It's a good thing you always had such a . . ."

". . . hard head," he finished along with

her. He didn't return the grin, but she could see the amusement in his eyes.

Maggie picked up the phone handset but did not punch in any numbers. "I hope they listened to those boys, Michael. They might know something about all this, maybe something they don't even realize they know. Or their friends might. I believe them when they say they only did it once. But it's going to sound very bad."

Michael did not disagree. "The media are all over this. They had already been reporting on the nighttime explosions, and the story became slightly bigger when I was injured. But now someone is dead, so all the stations are jumping on it. Kimi said there are television vans and trucks all over the area."

Maggie shook her head. She'd like to blame a prurient public, but she had to admit to just as much curiosity about the case as any of the media people. She stared down at the phone in her hand, turning it so that the number pad faced upward. "I'd better call Clare. I'm sure she'll want to talk. She thought of Paul as a friend."

However, before Maggie could punch in a single number, the phone rang. As she suspected, the caller ID showed Clare's home number.

"Clare," Maggie began, then stopped when she heard a stifled sob. Maggie sighed. "I guess you heard about Paul."

"Gerald saw it on the midday news. He recognized the house right away. And he said a police officer stopped by this morning to ask if we'd seen or heard anything last night. It was after I left for the church."

Maggie could hear the tears in Clare's shaky voice.

"We should get together to discuss this," Clare suggested.

"That's a good idea. We could meet at the church tomorrow and get this quilt finished. It should only take another hour to finish the last bits and we can set up the new top." Maggie knew that there was a lovely Dresden Plate quilt top in the closet, one that Louise had made out of the pastel thirties' reproduction fabrics, which always did well in the auction. And they were relatively easy to quilt, as most just involved a wide cross-hatch pattern.

"Thank you, Maggie. I really need to talk about this." Clare paused and her voice dropped to a near whisper. "Gerald's a good husband, but he doesn't understand why I want to talk. He says I'm dwelling on it and should move on. But it just happened, and it's so senseless. I need to talk."

"He's just being a man," Maggie said, eyeing her son, who was back seated at the table and starting his second sandwich. He looked up and raised one eyebrow as he listened to her describe the male species. "Men deal with these things in a different way. They hate to talk about emotional things. Feelings. Hank was the same."

Clare sighed. With relief? "You're right," she said. "I didn't see Paul this morning, you know. But we don't always meet up, so I didn't think anything of it. And all the time he was lying there . . ."

"Better not to think about it, Clare," Maggie replied. She certainly didn't plan to tell her that the boy she called "his sweet little grandson" had found the body. "We'll get together tomorrow morning and you can talk all you want. It will be a celebration of Paul's life."

Maggie could hear the smile in Clare's voice when she responded. "What a lovely idea. Thank you, Maggie. I'll call the others and tell them about meeting tomorrow morning. I feel better already."

CHAPTER 8

Later that afternoon, Maggie sat stitching, engrossed in an audio book mystery. She not only enjoyed the stories, but they took her mind off recent events. Michael had gone out to the patio after lunch and had dozed off on the lounge chair. She grabbed quickly at the phone when it rang, not sure if the sound would travel outside and waken him. The caller ID told her it was Victoria.

"Are you watching the news?" she asked.

"No," Maggie replied, reaching across her sewing supplies for the television remote. "I was sewing and listening to an audio book and got involved in the story. I didn't realize it was already five. What station?" she asked as the picture came up on the screen.

"It probably doesn't matter," Victoria informed her, though she provided the channel number that she herself had on. "It's about the boys. They didn't give out their names, as they're underage, but they know that two boys confessed to starting the explosions. The reporters are speculating on whether or not they believe their story of not causing the damage at the Tiptons'."

"Oh, dear," Maggie said. "It's a good thing they're juveniles, though that won't keep the names from coming out."

They hung up when the Scottsdale Police Department spokesperson came on. He reiterated that they had spoken to two minors who came in voluntarily and admitted to playing with illegal fireworks late at night, causing the first of the explosions that had rocked the neighborhood.

"What about the later explosions?" a reporter asked.

"What about the injured officer and the death of Mr. Tipton?"

The questions came fast and furious from the several reporters surrounding the police representative.

But he maintained a calm dignity. "The investigation into all the recent incidents is ongoing. We have no reason not to believe the boys' confession," he said. "At this time, we believe they and their friends set off some fireworks, creating the first two explosions that were heard in the south Scottsdale area."

Maggie's lips thinned as she listened to this last statement. The reporters were bombarding the poor man with questions about the further explosions, but he wasn't giving out any new information. They were switching back to the news anchor at the station when she realized Michael was standing behind her. She hadn't even noticed the patio door sliding open.

"I was just watching the news," she told him. "Victoria called to tell me the boys' story was the 'breaking news.' "

"Not surprising," he said. "I'm guessing there was a lot of coverage of the incident at Paul Tipton's."

Maggie nodded. "Oh, Michael, the media will crucify those poor boys."

"They'll just have to live with what they did," he said. "I bet they'll think twice about causing any more mischief."

"You're probably right. At least some good will come of all this." Maggie sighed.

"Listen, Ma. This is for your ears only." Michael walked around her chair to seat himself on the sofa.

"I can keep a secret," Maggie said, indignant that her son might think she'd blab important information to her friends. She might like to reassure them when it came to something important to the neighborhood, but she could be silent if she had to be.

Michael sighed.

"What is it?" Maggie urged.

"I heard from Kimi. The forensics supports their story. The earliest explosions — the ones you mentioned that were not as loud and that happened around midnight — those are the ones the brothers and their friends confessed to setting off. They claim to have only done it once, and their friends said they did one other. Those were the blasts that did not cause any major damage, just woke people up and upset the area dogs. Those *were* simple fireworks. They put a bunch of small fireworks under a can, lit the fuse and ran off. Dangerous in itself, and illegal, but not something to cause major damage."

"So we were correct in the beginning, thinking it was just a teen prank."

"Yes. In the beginning, that's all it was. Unfortunately, the prank gave someone ideas. Some nutcase must have liked the idea of disrupting everyone's sleep and got busy on the Internet. The latest explosions, the ones causing property damage, are more sophisticated, made with stronger mixes of chemicals. The one that injured me was basically a pipe bomb. I'm just lucky I didn't get peppered with shrapnel. It's odd, but the construction and the placement seemed to ensure a big boom and that was about it. I was close enough for the flash and the noise to throw me back against the block fence and that's how I was hurt."

Maggie caught her breath. "Oh, Michael, do you think someone really meant to hurt you? That they set off that . . . thing . . . when you were near it?"

"I don't know, Ma. Maybe, maybe not. As I said, it wasn't made for major destruction."

"If someone set it off, he could have been the nine-one-one caller, trying to get an officer to the scene so that he could press his detonate button."

"No," Michael said. "That was checked. The call did come from the homeowner. He was up late, heard something in the alley, and because of the recent activity, he called nine-one-one right away. It was probably just bad luck on my part that I was nearby and got there so quickly. If I had been one minute later, I wouldn't have been hurt. I might have seen the flash from the end of the alley, but that would have been it."

"Where would the person get the chemicals and things to make these bombs?" Maggie asked, though she had a suspicion she knew the answer.

"You can get some of them in Mexico," he replied, "but it's getting harder to get that kind of stuff back over the border. However, there's a lot you can get off the Internet without even leaving the comfort of home."

"So we can't rule anyone out." Maggie heaved a heavy sigh. Clare would not be happy.

CHAPTER 9

It was a difficult night. Maggie had trouble
falling asleep, concerned about both Clare
and the Rivera brothers. She felt she'd
barely gotten to sleep when something
awakened her. Lying in her dark bedroom,
staring at the ceiling while she decided if
she was truly awake, she thought there
might have been a loud noise.

She sat up quickly, earning herself a short
dizzy spell. Forced to sit on the side of the
bed for a moment while her head grew ac-
customed to being upright, Maggie's mind
raced. Could something have happened to
Michael? He'd been so good all evening.
But they'd warned her that concussions
were tricky. Had Michael gotten dizzy, fallen
out of bed?

She heard the sirens just as she realized
that the room seemed darker than usual. A
quick glance at the nightstand showed that
the digital display on her clock was out. Nor

was there a soft glow coming through the bathroom door from the nightlight she kept in the windowless room. No electricity!

Pushing herself into a standing position, rewarded for those few seconds of quiet with good equilibrium, Maggie fumbled in the nightstand drawer for her flashlight. The temperature in the room was still comfortable, so the power had not been off for long. She'd check on Michael and then call it in, though if the sirens were anything to go by, the electric company must already be aware of the problem.

She wanted to check the window, to be sure the power outage was more widespread than her condo, but it was more important to be sure Michael was all right. That impression of a loud noise still bothered her. Could he have fallen out of bed? Or bumped into something when he got out of bed — the result of being in the dark in a strange room? Or was it another of those explosions? Did someone else get injured or, heaven forbid, killed?

Hurrying now, she left her bedroom, crossing the hall to the guest room. A quick pass with her flashlight showed that the bed clothes were twisted and rumpled, but the bed was empty. Heart pounding now, Maggie swung her flashlight beam across the floor then breathed a sigh of relief. Michael stood in front of the window, drapes pushed to one side. He was doing what she had put off, checking to see if the power was out to the entire neighborhood.

Maggie approached Michael, who glanced down, not surprised to see his mother. That was when she realized he had his cell phone to one ear, but he disconnected just as she stepped up to the window. He draped an arm around his mother's shoulders, pulling her against his side. Everything beyond the glass was black. So the whole neighborhood *had* been affected. Luckily, there was a bright half moon, so they could see the outlines of buildings and trees, even a cat creeping along the top of Maggie's back fence.

"Michael, I'm so glad to see that you're all right. I was afraid something had happened to you." She looked him over as carefully as possible in the dim glow of the moonlight. "I thought I heard a loud noise."

Michael grinned. "You didn't think I'd fallen out of bed, did you? Haven't done that since I was seven."

But his teasing tone quickly disappeared and his mouth tightened into a grim line. "You did hear a loud noise. There was an explosion at the power substation two blocks over. That's why the power is out."

Maggie frowned. "You don't think . . ." She was almost afraid to voice her suspicions about teenage boys and nasty pranks. But not the Rivera brothers; she believed they were truly sorry for their actions and had told the truth about their early, and brief, involvement.

Michael tried to be reassuring. "It could just be that a transformer blew. That can happen, especially when it's as hot as it has been and there's a big demand for electricity."

Maggie could see enough of his face to know that he didn't believe that. Neither did she.

"This is getting out of hand," she mumbled.

"It was already out of hand, Ma. And if this explosion *was* set, it will be considered an act of domestic terrorism. The FBI and Homeland Security will be all over it. And the media will be too." He let his breath out in a hard swoosh, a sign of his frustration.

"Oh, dear." It was all Maggie could think of to say. There had already been a lot of local coverage about the "noises in the night," but this would be sure to bring in reporters from outside the area.

Michael's cell phone rang, a snippet of

the *Star Wars* theme music sounding loud in the quiet house. It wasn't until there was no electricity available that one noticed the white noise created by refrigerators and air conditioning, Maggie thought.

Maggie tried to eavesdrop, but she couldn't hear the caller and Michael said little. When he disconnected, she looked eagerly into his face. "Well?"

"Definitely sabotage. SPD sent someone over to the Rivera house right away, but they found the family all together, in their night clothes. Just like everyone else in the neighborhood, they were looking outside and trying to figure out what happened. They took the two boys in for questioning, but they aren't under arrest."

Maggie's chest tightened as though a hand had closed around her heart. Those poor boys. When they lit those firecrackers with their friends, they had no idea what they were setting off. "Do you think I should call Walter?"

Michael shook his head. "They have his number. I'm sure they'll call him if necessary."

Maggie frowned, thinking about an explosion at the power substation. "You know Edie has been suggesting there are terrorists here in Scottsdale, that these previous explosions were their practice bombs."

There was enough moonlight for her to see Michael raise his eyebrows. "Looks like she could be right for a change."

"Do you really think so?"

"There's more going on here than teenage pranks, that's for sure. I don't know what it is, but right now terrorists are as good a suggestion as any other."

It wasn't what Maggie wanted to hear.

CHAPTER 10

As arranged, all the Quilting Bee women arrived at the quilt room at their usual time on Saturday morning. Despite dark circles beneath red eyes, they could hardly wait to get started. Everyone commented on the power outage and their great good luck that power had been restored by breakfast — in time to make coffee! And although they planned to meet to discuss the tragedy of Paul Tipton's death, their conversation began with talk of the explosion at the power substation.

"It was such a loud noise," Anna declared.

Edie gave a curt nod. "Just the kind of thing terrorists get up to."

"It scared poor Samson something awful," Clare told them.

Maggie thought it probably scared Samson's mistress even more, but she refrained from saying so.

"I did wonder if they would get the power

up and running in time to make the coffee," Louise said. "I wouldn't want to start the day without a cup of coffee."

"It was getting pretty warm inside," Theresa agreed. Her voice lowered, she dipped her head and her cheeks turned pink. "We never did get back to sleep, so Carl and I went skinny-dipping just before dawn — to cool off."

There were grins and some laughter. "Good for you," Edie declared. "That's what keeps you, and your marriage, young."

Louise agreed. "I'm past skinny-dipping, even with Vinnie," she laughed. "But I'm sure it felt good. Even at dawn it's warm out. We're lucky to have backyard pools."

They were seated around the quilt frame in their usual community bee style, stitching busily while they talked. Maggie was glad Theresa had started them out with something happy. But Clare quickly turned their attention to the reason for this special meeting.

"We were going to meet this morning to finish this quilt and talk about Paul Tipton's death. But now we have this awful sabotage to talk about too."

Edie almost smirked. "Terrorists. I told you."

"Are they sure the transformer didn't

blow on its own?" Louise asked. "They do that sometimes when demand is high."

"I don't think so," Maggie said. "When we drove by there, there were masses of media trucks, but we could still see people wearing shirts that said FBI, ATF and even DHS."

"DHS?" Anna asked, a puzzled frown marring her forehead.

"Department of Homeland Security," Edie replied. "The group that looks out for our safety. They would definitely look into terrorist attacks. There were already reporters here from LA and CNN; I wouldn't be surprised if we get some media folks from overseas after this."

"But don't you think it might be connected to all this other business?" Theresa asked. "And the boys already confessed to the earliest incidents."

"I told you," Edie said. "The earlier explosive devices were practice for the big ones." She pulled her thread through the cloth and tugged lightly to set the correct tension to her stitches. "Not those little firecracker explosions the Rivera boys and their friends caused. That was just mischief. I mean the bigger explosions, the loud ones that followed. The ones that damaged mail boxes and fences. The teenage pranks gave someone evil ideas and they took it and ran."

Terrorists? Evil ideas? Maggie wanted to dismiss it all — to go back home and hide under one of her quilts. But this latest trouble precluded that. Something more than teen pranks *was* going on here.

"But what about Paul?" Clare asked. "Why would terrorists tamper with his tree?"

"It was an accident, wasn't it?" Theresa asked. "It had to be. It was late and no one would expect that he would be out in his yard at that hour. Why was he sleeping outside, anyway?"

"Goodness, how could Clare know that?" Louise asked.

But Clare did know. "He told me he had terrible insomnia and he often found that he slept better outdoors. He didn't like air conditioning. Before his daughter came to live with him, he used his evap cooler all summer."

There was some murmuring about this. The old-style evaporative coolers were cheaper to run and worked well at cooling the house until the air became humid, which it usually did in July and August, the valley's "monsoon" season. At that time, people who still used the old-fashioned coolers switched over to air conditioning to keep their homes comfortable. Maggie and Hank had used evap coolers at the ranch in their early years together and she'd liked them then. But she had to admit that air conditioning was infinitely better. She'd never want to go back to coolers.

"In those earlier explosions the terrorists were perfecting their technique," Edie proclaimed. "Practicing their bomb-making. The explosions, and therefore the bombs, are getting progressively larger and more destructive." Edie glanced around the frame. "The first damage was a burnt bush."

"We learned that was the Rivera brothers' friends," Clare said. "Remember, they told Maggie and Victoria that their friends set off fireworks one more time, but it set a bush on fire and scared them."

Edie barely nodded, intent on her listing of the damages. "A mail box was destroyed, and part of a wooden fence. Then a backyard shed and another fence. And then Paul's tree and fence. Don't you see? They were building up to last night's destruction of the power station."

"It wasn't a major power station," Maggie corrected. "And it wasn't destroyed. It was just a transformer that made a neighborhood lose power for a few hours."

Edie didn't reply, just continued to stitch with a smug expression on her face. She was sure she was correct in all her assumptions, especially since they fit so nicely with her earlier theories about terrorists.

"Why wouldn't terrorists attempt to find larger targets?" Louise asked. "As Maggie said, all that happened last night was a small-scale power outage. It seems to me that terrorists would want to target something bigger, like the state capital or the Palo Verde Nuclear Plant."

But Edie had an answer for everything. "Obviously, a nuclear power plant would be too well protected. Same with the capitol building. It's apparently a small terror cell and they are starting out on a minor scale. Besides, the purpose of terrorism is to create terror among average citizens, and don't you think that's what all these explosions are doing?"

Both Clare and Anna nodded.

Maggie sighed. There would be no changing Edie's mind about this. For years she'd predicted lawlessness and danger and Maggie suspected she was enjoying this moment, now that some of her predictions were coming to pass.

"You know that a few of the nine-eleven hijackers trained here in the valley. So there's a history of terrorism here," Edie said.

"Oh, Edie," Victoria countered. "You can't *really* say that. Some of the hijackers took flying lessons here. I don't think having them here as student pilots can be called a history of terrorism."

"They should never have been allowed into the country," Edie declared. "And they certainly should *not* have been allowed to take flying lessons. They weren't interested in learning how to land the planes, you know, just how to fly them."

"Hindsight is twenty-twenty," Louise mumbled.

"I thought we came to talk about Paul," Clare said, hurt that the discussion had veered so far from her intent. "You can't really think terrorists killed an old man like him."

"She's right," Maggie agreed. "We set up today's meeting so that we could talk about Clare's friend and what happened to him. A celebration of his life. Let's try not to dwell on how he died."

"Why don't you tell us about Paul, Clare." Victoria looked to her friend. "The best tribute to someone who has passed on is to remember the happy times we had with them."

"What a lovely sentiment," Anna said.

"I didn't know him *really* well," Clare began. "We kept passing each other walking our dogs and we started stopping and visiting a bit. But we've been doing it for years and years. I should have known something was wrong when I didn't see him yesterday morning," she added, leaving her stitching to swipe a tissue over her eyes.

"Did you see him every day then?" Theresa asked.

"No, not every single day," Clare admitted. "But just about. Sometimes I'd ask him in to have a glass of iced tea after our walk. Gerald enjoyed talking to him too. Paul has — had — this darling little dachshund named Max. Max and Samson got to be friends."

"There's nothing like a pet, is there?" Edie asked, surprising them all with her warmhearted statement. But everyone nodded in agreement.

"Didn't you say something about a daughter and grandson?" Victoria asked. "Did they live with Paul?"

"Yes." Clare smiled now, thinking of her neighbor and his grandchild. "Paul's daughter's marriage didn't work out, I guess. Paul didn't say much about it except to call his son-in-law a no-good bum. But his daughter moved back home with little Brad two years ago." Clare took a few stitches, knotted her thread, then clipped it. While finishing up, she remained silent. "I think Paul was conflicted about having her there. From things he said, I got the impression that he and his daughter didn't always get along. But he doted on his grandson, and he loved having him so close. In fact, Brad often walked with Paul and Max and he's just a sweet, polite little boy. Samson loves him." Clare sighed heavily. "Losing his grandfather is going to be very hard for young Brad."

"It's always hard for a child to lose a beloved grandparent," Louise said. "They don't really understand the concept of death. But young children are also very resilient. He'll be fine."

As Louise finished her sentence, Edie took the final few stitches in the quilt. The women looked around their circle, smiles on all faces despite the dour topics of their morning's discussion. There was something special about completing a quilt, no matter how many times they experienced it. Their autumn quilt auction was a major moneymaker for the parish and they were all proud to contribute their talent toward the support of St. Rose.

With quick work born of experience, they unrolled the frame and removed the quilt.

"I'll do the binding," Anna offered. "I kept some matching fabric to use."

As she took the bundled quilt to put aside with her things, Maggie turned toward the supply closet. "We have that Dresden Plate top that Louise did. I thought we could start that next."

"Wait." Victoria touched Maggie's arm, stopping her. With quick movements, Victoria retrieved her tote bag and pulled out a folded, pieced top.

"After all that's been going on, I decided to start something with a happier motif," Victoria announced. "Not that the Dresden Plate isn't a pretty pattern," she quickly added. "Cheerful too, with the thirties' pastels."

Maggie stared at her friend in surprise. She found it hard to believe Victoria hadn't shared this news with her before now. They usually discussed everything together, especially news about new quilts started, or even contemplated. Maggie realized that she hadn't even noticed that Victoria had brought the tote bag with her. She shook her head slightly, bemused with herself for being so distracted. Not that there wasn't more than enough to distract her . . .

Victoria began to unfold a colorful top made from batik fabric. "It will need ironing again," she said with a frown.

Maggie took one side and together they opened the pieced top. Victoria had used expensive batik fabrics, beautiful Asian-inspired cloth splashed with vivid dyes. All the primary colors were represented, the colorful rectangles pieced around a creamy tone-on-tone square.

"What pretty fabrics," Anna commented.

"The pattern is called Bright Hopes," Victoria told them. "I thought bright hopes were something we could all use right about now. I hope you'll all agree that this can be our next quilting project."

"Of course," Maggie said. "It's lovely, Victoria."

"I like it," Edie said with a quick nod. "Very modern, even though it is an old pattern."

"It's a great idea, Victoria," Louise complemented her.

"I brought multicolored thread for the quilting," Victoria said. "And I thought we could quilt fun things in the cream squares — hearts, stars, flowers, that kind of thing."

There were more accepting comments and compliments.

"Well, what are we waiting for?" Maggie

asked, her voice sounding happier than it had for some days. She gathered the new top into her arms. "Get out the ironing board."

"It will be nice working on that quilt," Anna declared. "The colors are so happy."

"Let's hope that all this business will be resolved well before we finish it," Louise commented.

Bright hopes indeed, Maggie thought.

CHAPTER 11

A half hour later, as they pinned the new top into the frame, Clare suddenly stopped and stared into space. "You know," she began, her voice stuttering a bit as she organized her thoughts. "I just thought of something. There was a book I read . . ."

Maggie smiled, but Edie heaved a loud sigh. "Really, Clare."

Clare often mentioned books with plots that reminded her of whatever events were brought up for discussion. Some tied in nicely but others were extremely far-fetched. However, they all loved mysteries, so Maggie for one did not mind listening to Clare's theories.

Neither did Anna. "Hush," she urged. "What is it, Clare?"

"I just remembered. There was a story about a son who didn't want to wait for his inheritance. And he planned what he thought was the perfect crime."

"What did he do?" Louise asked.

Clare had their attention now — even most of Edie's reluctant interest — as they all loved a good mystery novel.

"Well, he did all kinds of calculations and planning and stuff. Then he waited for a big storm, and when there was one, he snuck outside and knocked this tree over. He made it look like the storm had done it, but it fell precisely on the part of the roof above his father's bed, crashing down and killing him while he slept."

"That seems a little chancy to me," Edie decided. "How could he be sure the tree would damage the roof enough to fall on the bed, and how could he be sure his father would be in just the right place on the bed?"

"Oh, Edie, it was just a story," Louise said. "And it sounds like a pretty good one too. I don't think I've read it."

"The son didn't rely completely on chance," Clare said. "He caused some damage to the roof supports beforehand."

"But the police would be able to detect that," Edie said.

"Yes!" Clare happily agreed. "That was how they came to suspect him."

"So he wasn't so smart after all," Theresa said.

"Well, they had a hard time pinning the

damage on him, so it wasn't real cut and dried," Clare said. "But don't you see?" Clare paused in her pinning to glance around at the other bee members. "Doesn't Paul's death seem a little like that? Maybe someone wanted to kill him and planned it like in that book."

Clare seemed so proud of herself Maggie hated to say anything. She should have realized she didn't need to. Edie spoke right up.

"Don't be silly," Edie said. "The bomber would have had to do it. We've already discussed Paul's family. His son died years ago and his only other child is a daughter with a small child. Maggie said his wife, or ex-wife, is in California and has been for years. His daughter is the only heir in the area. Is she smart enough to plan something that involves so much math and physics? Even then, getting that tree to fall in exactly the right place to topple the ramada roof would be extremely chancy." Edie paused long enough to replenish her supply of pins. "Anyway, do you think he had enough of an estate to tempt someone to kill him in such an elaborate way? While it's a nice neighborhood, the houses are old and not nearly as high-priced as in other parts of Scottsdale."

Everyone paused for a moment, thinking

this through. Edie had a point, Maggie thought. From what they'd heard, Paul's daughter had been a wild teenager and rebellious teens didn't always do well academically. And even if she did want to kill her father, there were easier, less unreliable ways to do it. A little oleander in his food, for example; in an elderly man oleander poisoning could easily be mistaken for a natural death.

Still, Maggie was glad for the moment of levity when Theresa broke the silence by asking, "Do you think his daughter knows anything about explosives?"

Once the chuckles had cleared, and Theresa's cheeks had gone from red to pink to normal, Louise commented. "Somehow it doesn't seem like a woman's kind of crime, does it? All these explosions, I mean."

"It doesn't," Maggie agreed.

Clare still looked miffed by Edie's devastating comments. "It was just an idea." Clare's voice seemed smaller than when she'd first mentioned the book plot, showcasing her hurt feelings.

Maggie shot Edie a quelling look. "It was a good idea, Clare. It's just human nature to try to find explanations for such senseless deaths. And gender doesn't *really* matter on something like this," she added, with a sympathetic look toward Theresa. "It doesn't take strength to make a bomb. From what I hear, anyone can make one from instructions on the Internet, and you can get the supplies you need that way too."

"*Did* Paul have much of an estate?" Anna asked. It was one of Edie's questions, but one they had passed over as irrelevant.

"I would doubt it," Theresa said. "He worked all those years at Gilligan's. It was a good job with nice benefits and an adequate retirement package. But I don't see how he could have saved all that much. And, like Edie said, the neighborhood is old, so the houses aren't worth much, especially in the current market."

"I don't think he had a lot of expenses," Clare said, frowning. "We talked mostly about the dogs, but I do remember him mentioning that his refrigerator had broken down and he asked about the best place to get a new one. He was more interested in price than in quality I think." She cocked her head to one side as she considered. "Yes, I'm sure he just wanted the cheapest model he could find. And I'm sure he owned his house, as he did tell me he'd lived there since before his daughter was born. So, really, he didn't spend much money."

"So he might be termed a cheapskate,"

Edie declared. She ignored Clare's frown at the disparaging term. "There have been many instances of people who lived with almost nothing amassing thousands if not millions of dollars and no one even realizing it until they died."

"Interesting," Theresa commented.

"Yes, I remember reading about a woman in Chicago who cleaned at a school," Louise said. "From the description, she was almost a bag lady. Then when she died, they discovered she left over a million dollars to the school. She didn't have children and she felt the schoolchildren were her family."

Clare's eyes brightened. "Maybe Paul was a secret millionaire. Wouldn't that be exciting!"

"Why?" Edie asked. "Do you think he left the money to Max, and named you as executor?"

Louise and Theresa laughed, and Victoria smiled. But Clare just looked stunned at such a thought.

"There's no real way for us to find out about something like that," Maggie reminded them.

"I think it's public record once the will goes through probate," Edie said. "But I'm sure that takes a while. You know how slowly bureaucracy works."

Maggie nodded, missing the calculating gleam in Clare's eyes. "Didn't you say you knew his wife?" she asked Maggie.

"Or is it his ex-wife?" Edie asked. "If she ran out on him so long ago, wouldn't she have gotten a divorce?"

"No, I doubt it," Theresa said. "Paul was a devout Catholic. I'm sure he would never have agreed to a divorce."

Maggie frowned. "I knew Fay through the altar society, but then she left town and no one heard from her for years. It was ten years or so ago that I got a Christmas card from her. She said she was too embarrassed to write for a long time, but she regretted not saying goodbye. I've gotten a card every Christmas since then." She pulled her thread through the fabric and then looked around at the others' faces. "I can't say that I know her very well. It's been too many years. Who knows how she's changed. After all, she left here because of a serious tragedy — the kind of thing that could change a person's whole outlook on life."

"And you say she's been in Los Angeles all this time?" Edie asked.

Maggie nodded.

"Surely that's too far away for her to be involved in a plot to murder her husband," Anna declared.

"Well," Clare began, drawing out the word. "That might depend on how she gets along with Shannon. There's the possibility they got together and planned something . . ."

"I doubt it," Maggie said. "Fay usually writes a newsy letter at Christmas time, and one thing she often talked about was how she regretted leaving her young daughter. She said that Paul wouldn't allow her to contact her at first, then by the time Shannon was a teenager, there was too much resentment there for her to set up a relationship."

"Another good idea busted," Edie announced.

"Paul wouldn't let his daughter see her mother?" Victoria frowned. "That's very sad. He must have been deeply hurt when she left him that way."

"Do you think Fay will come back to Scottsdale for the funeral?" Victoria asked Maggie.

"I would think so. She was involved with church activities, so it may have been a mutual decision not to pursue a divorce. I don't recall her ever saying anything in the Christmas notes about that. She mostly talks about work and any trips she might have taken."

"We'll have to talk to her," Clare announced. "I wonder if she'll stay with Shannon."

"I doubt it," Louise replied. "Not if what Maggie said is true, and she was never able to reconcile with Shannon. And especially if there's any truth at all to Clare's theory about the estate being a motive if Paul's death was planned."

"What do you mean?" Anna asked.

"If they're still legally married," Maggie said, "and Paul didn't have a will, she'll get everything as his wife. It will be different if he had an updated will. Then it's anyone's guess."

CHAPTER 12

Sunday did not improve the climate in the neighborhood. A new window-rattling explosion detonated early Sunday morning, this one outside the high school offices. Although the sky was overcast, it remained blisteringly hot. Air quality was bad, and while there were monsoon storms in the forecast, the chances were a mere ten percent. Everyone was agitated about the ongoing explosions, and the electric company was still tinkering with the new transformer, which resulted in rolling blackouts. Word got out about the Rivera boys and their friends, but as often happens, the truth of the matter was lost and many thought them responsible for everything that had happened for the past two weeks. Rocks had been thrown at windows and nasty comments spray-painted on fences and garage doors.

In addition, copycats were causing explosions all over the valley, using anything from fireworks to gunpowder to household chemicals. An explosion in south Phoenix caused a fire in a dumpster, and there was an arrest in Glendale following a loud explosion in a previously quiet neighborhood. Unfortunately for the Glendale teenager showing off for his friends, his device went off earlier than planned. Luckily, his friends called nine-one-one and he was rushed to a west-side hospital. He suffered serious burns on his arms and chest in addition to losing most of his fingers. Police and fire officials were using him as an example when urging other young people not to try explosives themselves. News stations were resurrecting public service footage of exploding melons from the days before the Fourth of July and showing them on all broadcasts.

Bleary-eyed parishioners stood in the St. Rose courtyard before the seven o'clock mass to talk about the current situation, and continued their discussions outside after mass. The explosion at the high school had awakened many of them around four that morning, and most had not gotten much rest after that. Everyone was too upset about the entire matter, and finding it difficult to sleep at all. The explosion at the high school brought things much too close to home. At four o'clock on a July morning, only one security guard was at the school and he was not injured. But all the parents, whether they had children at the high school or not, were horrified by the what-might-have-beens. The parishioners were worried; the school was located on the block just behind the church, and there was a great deal of concern that the church itself might be the next target.

To make matters worse, the media had descended onto the neighborhood from all over the country and even the world. Maggie passed a crew of Asian reporters on her way to mass, taping a report on the street a block from the high school. Curious, she lowered the driver's-side window and was almost certain they were speaking in Japanese. She could also see a large remote transmission truck with the logo of a Los Angeles television station, a pretty blond reporter standing in front of it holding a microphone. Maggie was too far away to hear what she might be saying.

From what Maggie and Michael could glean from the morning news programs, there was little more official information about the explosion of the transformer and none at all about the newest explosion at the high school. Maggie knew that now more than ever Edie would be shouting "terrorists."

Colleen Kirkpatrick, who lived across the street from the high school, held court outside the church doors, telling eager listeners about the damage she was able to see from the front of her house. "Lots of broken glass — just everywhere. There were some scorch marks on the stone, but I didn't see any flames. The fire department carried out all this office equipment, so there must have been a lot of damage inside."

And, as Maggie had suspected, Edie found a wide audience as she broadcast her theories about terrorism. With the damage to the power station, and now to a school, many were ready to believe her. They were certainly listening, and with no snide remarks about imaginary conspiracy theories.

Maggie ran into Raquel, who told her that Bianca's family was huddled down in their house, afraid to leave even for Sunday mass.

"There are reporters all over the street in front of their house. And if anyone comes out, they're bombarded with questions about whether the boys set the explosives to damage the power station. It will probably be even worse now that the high school has been hit. It's the same with all the families of the boys who came forward."

Maggie tried to offer words of comfort, but it wasn't easy. With this latest damage to the school, she'd wondered too — if only for a moment — whether the teenagers had been busy once again. Not the Rivera boys, whom she liked and who seemed properly cowed by their notoriety. But the high school could be an attractive target for another teenager. Or maybe she just didn't want to consider urban terrorism, no matter how sensible Edie made it sound.

Maggie and Michael drove to church separately, as Michael planned to return to his apartment after brunch. Maggie knew she would miss his reassuring presence in her condo. For now, she enjoyed having his steady presence beside her for the weekly service. With his varying work schedule, he didn't always attend with the rest of the family. Afterward, they continued on to brunch at the family ranch, a Browne family tradition. The family brunch was a weekly event where the extended Browne family caught up on what was happening with the rest of the clan. Maggie had four grown sons and all but Michael were married with families of their own. Hal was the oldest and he and his wife Sara had two sons, Jason and Joshua — the two boys who entertained their Uncle Michael on Saturday, keeping him safely on the sofa playing video games for most of the day. Hal's family lived on the ranch where the brothers had grown up, though the property was much smaller now and no longer a working ranch. Still, family was always welcome. Maggie kept her aging riding horse there and enjoyed going out into the desert for relaxing rides.

Maggie's second son, Frank, was a veterinarian and he and his wife April had a seven-year-old daughter named Megan. Being the only granddaughter (so far), she was the apple of Maggie's eye and they often did things together, baking and shopping being big favorites. Visiting the mall with Megan was the only time Maggie didn't abhor shopping.

Bobby and Merrie were both teachers, and the relatively new parents of a baby boy. They had decided to name him Harry after his grandfather, Maggie's late husband. He had just started walking and loved playing with his cousins on Sunday mornings. All together, it was a large and rambunctious group, sometimes supplemented with friends. The Quilting Bee women were frequent additions to the family group.

On this Sunday morning, however, Kimi was the sole non–family member present. She had attended mass with Michael and Maggie, although Maggie had questioned whether her presence wasn't needed at the crime scene across the street.

"No, the feds have their own people," she replied.

Maggie had noted the proliferation of jackets sporting an alphabet soup of abbreviations: ATF, FBI, DHS.

The atmosphere at the Browne ranch matched that at the church earlier. There was a somber undertone to the meal, as the adults were all aware of the danger Michael had encountered and of how much worse his injuries could have been. Even the children seemed to sense there was some sinister current running through their town.

"Is it really firecrackers, Uncle Michael?" Joshua asked him.

"They were," Michael replied. "In the beginning. But the one that got me — that was more like a small bomb." He shook his head. "It was too powerful to be firecrackers," he added, more for the adults than for his nephews. "Not that firecrackers can't be very dangerous," he added quickly, glancing at his nephews.

"From what people have said, these latest explosions seem like they're providing a pretty big boom, too much so for firecrackers," Hal said.

His wife agreed. "We got a few of the legal ones for the Fourth," Sara said, "and they don't have nearly the power that the papers are reporting in these explosions. The firecrackers we set off might have burnt a dried-out bush or singed a wooden fence, but they could never had taken out a transformer."

Michael shrugged. Maggie knew he was of two minds about the situation. On the one hand, he wanted to talk about it, but on the other it was an ongoing investigation. And he was still mad about being sidelined after his concussion. He was itching to get back to being legitimately involved in solving this problem, out in the field, not at a desk.

"The latest explosions — the transformer and the high school." Michael shook his head. "There's no way that was caused by firecrackers. I doubt it was even a gunpowder bomb, the kind of things kids make and blow up in the desert. Those explosions were big and caused a lot of damage."

Jason and Joshua listened wide-eyed. They had loved their first experience of setting off firecrackers and were brimming with excitement when they told their uncle all about it on Saturday. They couldn't comprehend the difference between their loud, fun explosions and the enormity of the recent attacks in the city.

"We had firecrackers for the Fourth of July, Uncle Michael," Joshua said. "We were really careful with them, weren't we, Dad?"

"They were," Hal agreed. He rolled his eyes toward his mother. She knew what he meant to tell her. Given recent events, he was sorry he'd bought any fireworks for the boys.

"The sparklers were cool," Joshua added, his big grin infectious.

His older brother, Jason, not taken in by his brother's grin, contradicted him. "They were lame."

"Now, boys," their father warned. Joshua's grin had faded to a sad look closer to tears.

"I liked them," Sara said, causing her older son to roll his eyes. But Joshua gave her a weak smile.

"I think sparklers are pretty cool," Michael said, winking at Joshua who grinned in pleasure while his brother frowned.

"I wish we lived where we could hear the explosions," Jason announced. "Tyler at school hears them from his house and he says it's real exciting."

Michael glanced at him, his face set in his stern cop look. Maggie was surprised Jason didn't cringe in fear. "It's not exciting," Michael told his nephew. "It's dangerous. Look what happened to me." He pointed to a patch of shaved skin near the back of his head where a couple of dark stitches highlighted the spot where he'd hit his head when he'd fallen back, away from the bomb.

Maggie was satisfied to see Jason look abashed. He even straightened his back, seeming to pull away a little, as though trying to put some distance between himself and his uncle.

"You should be glad you *don't* live near them," Maggie said. "As your uncle says, it is not exciting. It's dangerous." Maggie's voice, firm until now, softened as she continued explaining to her grandsons. "Some of my friends live where they can hear them every night, and I've heard the latest from my house. And we're all *frightened,* not excited. It's not fun to wake up to loud, unexplained noises in the middle of the night. My friend Clare is afraid to take her dog out for a walk after dark because she doesn't know if one might go off that early."

Maggie's gaze moved from her young grandsons to her youngest son. She stopped short of saying how scary it was to have an officer come to your door early in the morning to report your son was in the hospital. But all the adults realized it was left unsaid. Michael's three brothers had worried about him, too, and all three had been to visit him during his short hospital stay.

Maggie returned her gaze to the children, all sitting together at a smaller table. "Your Uncle Michael was injured by one of those explosions — and harmed seriously enough to put him in the hospital. He could have been hurt very badly. It's possible to lose fingers or even a hand when setting off fireworks."

"Which a young man in Glendale learned last night," Hal added. "He'll never be the same."

Maggie nodded. "Please remember that."

Both Jason and Joshua looked down at their hands before nodding solemnly. Maggie saw Joshua blinking rapidly and felt sorry for being so tough on them. His brother would ride him hard if he started to cry. But this was such a serious matter, she thought they needed to be tough.

"I guess it's not exciting," Jason mumbled.

Joshua, young as he was, was a little braver. He looked up at his grandmother. "Dad told us all about losing fingers. We were really careful, weren't we, Jason?"

His brother nodded, head still down. While Maggie felt unhappy at causing such deflation in her grandson's attitude, she knew it was necessary. He was at a tough age, neither teen nor child. His twelfth birthday was coming up, and soon enough he would be thirteen — a teenager. She was glad she didn't have to deal with teenagers in these troubled times. She'd had her turn with four sons who had all become upstanding citizens. Now it was up to them to raise stalwart young men — and women, she added to herself, not wanting to forget Megan.

Maggie was getting ready to ask Bobby about teenagers and social media braggadocio when they were distracted by Kimi's cell phone. Her facial expression remained stoic as she listened, but her gaze traveled quickly around the table. Maggie wondered what had happened now, and if it would have repercussions for the family. Why else would Kimi look at them all that way?

"I have to go," Kimi said as she finished her call. She tucked her phone into her purse and stacked her dishes. "Another explosion," she mumbled.

Maggie touched her arm. "Leave those.

I'll take care of them. You go on to work."

Kimi nodded, her lips tight. Maggie wondered where this latest incident had occurred. Kimi's reaction seemed more emotional than she would expect from a seasoned professional.

Michael got up to walk Kimi to her car, but Maggie clearly heard his "damn" as he rose from the table. Maggie shot one of her "mother" looks toward her youngest son. He didn't usually swear in front of the children, but she did know how frustrated he was about being sidelined in the midst of all this action. He would return to work tomorrow, but was sure he'd be relegated to a desk.

Michael apologized, then rushed after Kimi, who had not waited for him.

Maggie watched them for a moment, before turning back to the other adults at her table. "Well, this is a chance for me to ask Bobby a few questions."

Bobby, startled, looked up quickly. "What did I do?"

Everyone laughed.

"Nothing," Maggie said. "I just wanted to ask you about teaching summer school."

Bobby taught at the local middle school, and this summer he was doing a special science program for the honors kids, as well as the usual review for those who needed it.

"I just wondered," Maggie said. "The kids must be talking about all these explosions and about the Rivera brothers. Have you heard anything interesting?"

Bobby nodded slowly. "There's a lot of talk all right. But most of it isn't supposed to be overheard by the teachers."

"No kidding," Michael muttered. Maggie had barely registered his return. But she could see that his interest level had shot upward at this new topic.

"After the first explosions," Bobby continued, "the students were all grouping together, talking. I couldn't overhear much, but my impression was that they were wondering what was going on and who might be involved."

"Did they seem to know who might have done it?" Maggie asked, just as Michael asked, "Do you think any of the younger kids are involved? The Rivera brothers are in high school and I assumed their friends were too."

"I don't think any of them are really *involved,* but it's hard to tell," Bobby said. "I think some of them are *pretending* they are. For the prestige."

"You're kidding," Sara said.

"Oh, no." Bobby shook his head. "It's true."

Michael agreed. "The school is on the fringe of neighborhoods heavily involved in gang activities. Some of the kids are sure to think gangs are cool, and want to be involved for that reason."

This time it was Bobby agreeing.

"Do they seem to know what's going on?" Maggie asked.

"Not that I could notice. It was more a lot of speculation, I think. Lots of texting. Lots. I've confiscated more cell phones in the past two weeks than in the entire last semester."

"What about after Michael got hurt? Or after Paul's death?"

"They got a lot more secretive after that. I think they were thinking the same as you in the beginning, that it seemed like a teen prank and who was doing it. More of a fun thing, even if it was mischievous, bordering on illegal. But now, they don't know. And a lot of them don't *want* to know."

"So no names were mentioned?" Michael asked.

"I've heard a few names bandied about, and some are kids I'm sure would never get involved. Others, not so sure. That's why I said some of them are pretending involvement, trying to be big man on campus. But they are all pretty young. The oldest kids in the school are maybe fourteen or fifteen, if they were kept back for some reason. Most are closer to Jason's age."

"And you think they're too young to make bombs?" Michael asked. His voice was rising, and the children looked over, becoming interested again. Maggie shot a stern look his way and his voice dropped down so that only the adults at the large table could hear him. "I've got news for you. Kids as young as ten have committed murders." He took a swig of his coffee before realizing it had grown cold; he grimaced. "You better give me the names you're heard," Michael said. "The ones claiming to be involved."

Maggie cringed. The words were practically barked out as an order, and Maggie knew his older brother wouldn't like it. And he didn't.

"I'm not going to set up some innocent young kids who don't know any better than to brag about things they didn't do," Bobby declared. "You'll have to find them by checking the social networks. I'm sure there will be some boasting and some applause, so to speak."

Michael frowned, but also nodded. "We have people who check on the social networks, though I don't know if they've been monitoring these latest activities. They mostly check for sexual predators. A lot of them are online, searching for new interests." He glanced at the kids' table, then refrained from saying more. "I hope you monitor the sites the boys go on," he told Hal, who nodded briefly.

"Edie is convinced there are terrorists at work in the neighborhood." Maggie kept her voice low, not wanting the children to hear and perhaps become frightened.

Michael shook his head. "Leave it to Edie. I suppose she's spreading her opinion all over St. Rose."

"Of course," Maggie agreed. "At first we all thought it must just be teenagers — pranks, you know. Summer fun. But even early on, Edie was talking about terrorists and bomb-making. Or meth-brewing. The supplies explode, you know." She shook her head. "After the two new episodes this weekend, she's just gotten worse. People are starting to listen to her now."

Michael's phone rang before the conversation could go any further. As he reached into his pocket for it, Maggie's phone rang. The other family members exchanged puzzled looks. Something was going on. But what?

Michael was already speaking when Maggie fumbled the phone from her purse and finally pressed the talk button.

"Maggie, it's Louise. There's been an explosion at the church."

Maggie was shocked to hear the tremor in Louise's voice. Maggie didn't remember ever hearing her sound so upset, even when she was a murder suspect in the death of a sometime member of the Quilting Bee.

"Louise! What's happened? What's wrong?" Maggie arose from her place at the table and moved off to the side of the patio. Pressing the phone closer to her ear, she heard Louise suck in a large breath of air before she replied.

"Oh, Maggie. There was something in the donations they collected at mass this morning. Vinnie was helping, you know, with the sorting."

Maggie's heart almost stopped. Her breath did. "You mean an explosive device? Is he all right?"

Maggie was almost afraid to hear the answer, but it was not what she expected. From the state Louise was in, Maggie had suspected the worst.

"He's okay. But he was right there, Maggie. He was so close."

Despite the sound of her breath as she finally released it, Maggie could hear Louise swallow hard. "Was anyone hurt? What was it?"

"It's Deacon Adam. He was emptying a box of clothing, Vinnie said, when he held up a flashlight — one of those large yellow plastic ones with the handle on top. He said, 'Hey, look at this. We could use one of these around here.' And he said something about it being heavy, so there must be a battery in it. Then Vinnie thinks he must have turned it on and it exploded in his hands." Louise choked, her voice coming out hoarse as she finished speaking. "Oh, Maggie, it could so easily have been Vinnie. He said Deacon Adam's hands were all bloody and he's sure to lose some fingers."

"Were you there when it happened?" Maggie asked.

"No. Vinnie called me. He said he had to hear my voice." At this sweet sentiment, Louise finally broke down. Maggie heard her trying to stop a loud sob, but it was hopeless.

"Where are you now?" Maggie raised her voice to be sure Louise would hear her over her sobbing.

"Vinnie didn't want to go to the hospital,

but I insisted. I'm at the hospital, in the ER waiting room. They just took Vinnie back. He has some shrapnel wounds. Everyone who was in that room has some kind of small injury. But Deacon Adam was the only one seriously hurt."

"Oh, Louise." Maggie was sure her sigh carried clearly across the open line. "Shall I come wait with you?"

"No, no. It's too much trouble. But I needed to tell someone."

"It's no trouble. Just tell me what hospital." Maggie listened as she looked back to the table at the rest of the family. "I'm at the ranch, so it will take a while for me to drive down there. But I'll call Victoria. I'm sure she'd like to be there too."

Maggie placed the call to Victoria, telling her as quickly as possible what had happened and where to find Louise and Vinnie. "It will take me twenty or thirty minutes, depending on traffic," she told her. "Do you know if Gerald was helping with the donations?"

"I don't think so," Victoria replied. "I'm sure Clare would have mentioned it yesterday, but I'll check with her."

"Thank you," Maggie murmured as she ended the call.

The rest of the family waited anxiously to

hear what news Maggie might have. They had begun to clear the table and Maggie headed for the kitchen, glad to see they had moved well away from the children. And she had to fill them in before she left. This was terrible news, and just what so many people at mass that morning had feared — an attack against St. Rose. How convenient it had been for the perpetrator that the back-to-school drive scheduled so long ago happened to take place this morning! It would have been so easy to slip the bomb into a bag or box of donated clothing or school supplies.

Sara and Hal looked up, uneasy about what she might say. Sara nodded toward Michael who had also left the table. He stood in the farthest part of the kitchen, outside the door leading into what might have been the maid's room but had always been used as an office.

"He's talking to Kimi," Sara told her mother-in-law. "It sounds serious."

Maggie nodded. "That was Louise. There was an explosive device hidden in a flashlight among the donations at the church this morning. Vinnie was right there when it exploded, and he thinks Deacon Adam will lose some fingers. Deacon Adam was holding it when it exploded. Louise is pretty shaken about the close call."

"Were others hurt?"

"Louise said everyone who was in the room had some kind of injury, but Deacon Adam is the only one with serious injuries." Maggie looked toward Michael. "Is that what they're talking about?"

"Probably," Hal said as Michael pocketed his phone and headed straight toward them.

"Was that one of the bee ladies filling you in?" Michael asked, raising one brow as he looked at his mother.

"Louise," she replied.

"Come on, then, let's go."

Maggie was relieved. Usually, he told her not to get involved.

As they rushed toward the front of the house and their parked cars, the rest of the family watched. Apprehensive looks were quickly neutralized so as not to worry the children. But more than one Browne sent a silent prayer heavenward to "Please protect my mother and my brother."

CHAPTER 13

It was a subdued group that sat around the quilt frame on Monday morning. They had to run a gauntlet of media types just to get into the church building that morning. Father Bob had had to ask the police for help after remote satellite trucks representing media from across the country clogged the parking lot after the previous day's bombing. The trucks now lined the once quiet street instead, but the reporters — television, print and digital — continued to accost anyone entering or leaving the church buildings. Maggie cringed as she saw one bright-eyed blond TV anchor interviewing Edie. It looked like the rest of the valley was about to hear of the local terrorist cell.

Even the cheerful colors of the Bright Hopes quilt top could not make recent events better. Louise had dark, almost purple, circles under her eyes. Everyone else had lighter shadows beneath their eyes, and all eyes were pink where they should be white, underscoring an inability to get enough sleep.

Maggie had tossed and turned for much of Sunday night, unable to cut off her whirling thought processes. Recent events cycled through her mind, and she could not stop worrying about what might happen next. She'd spent most of Sunday afternoon with Victoria and Louise at the hospital emergency room waiting area. There were many others from the church there, waiting for relatives who had been injured in the blast. Most had only experienced cuts and bruises, but there were many like Vinnie who required stitches.

Maggie also continued to worry about Clare. Usually, Clare was energized by being near a crime scene. She loved to see herself as an amateur sleuth, loved comparing herself to her favorite fictional characters. Nothing pleased her more than comparing herself to Miss Marple or Jessica Fletcher. But here they were, sitting some hundred feet from an important crime scene, media all around them, and she looked drawn and listless.

"How is Vinnie?" Maggie asked, once everyone was seated at the quilt frame. She knew Vinnie's presence at the bombing the day before was the reason for Louise's present state. She still wasn't sure why Clare remained so downhearted. Surely she wasn't still fretting about Paul Tipton. Though Maggie remembered that she had been upset about the explosions even before anyone was injured, and concerned over neighborhood safety. Perhaps she was worried that there might be more bombs around the church itself.

Before Louise could reply to Maggie's question, Raquel burst into the room, bulging tote bag swinging from one arm. She must have just arrived at the church, Maggie thought, wondering what could cause her to come into the quilting room first thing.

"You all just won't believe this," Raquel began.

"Your grandsons were arrested?" Edie asked, surprising the others.

Raquel turned to face her. "No, of course not." She seemed startled by Edie's suggestion and not a little hurt.

"I'm glad to hear that," Maggie said.

"They're good boys," Raquel said, dropping down into an empty chair with a loud sigh, as though she was happy to be off her feet.

Maggie noted that Raquel had gained

quite a bit of weight since joining the Senior Guild — probably retirement weight. People talked about the "freshman fifteen," but no one seemed to notice that men and women who worked all their lives seemed to gain weight once they retired. Perhaps it was being home and able to snack at will. Or perhaps it was too much time in front of the television. Probably it was just age and a slowing metabolism — but Maggie didn't want to go there.

"My grandsons are helping the police," Raquel stated, her forehead wrinkled in a troubled frown. "Though the police did ask them to come in after the new bombings — at the power station and at the high school. Bianca said they were knocking on their door before dawn both days, demanding to see the boys."

"Weren't they here yesterday, helping with the donations?" Louise asked. "Are they all right?"

"Yes. They *were* here helping. They came over as soon as the police let them go. The police asked them if they knew anything about the new bombings. Just because they were good citizens and admitted they set off a few firecrackers two weeks ago." Raquel glanced around. She was indignant at the local police and at Edie for suggesting her grandsons might have been arrested. She wanted to be sure they all knew her grandsons were responsible young men. "They had promised to help sort the back-to-school stuff and they came straight here from the police station. They were injured in the explosion, just like everyone else. I hope the police leave them alone now," she added.

Maggie didn't want to point out that being so close to one of the explosions could be good cover for the real bomber.

"They were injured?" Anna repeated. "Are they all right?"

"Yes. Nothing serious. They had lots of cuts from flying debris, and Ramon hit his head trying to duck. Angel is probably hurt the worst. He sprained his ankle when someone pushed him down as the blast went off. The man was trying to help, but Angel twisted his ankle pretty bad. It's all taped up now, but he's still limping bad." She shook her head. "They were proud of their injuries, showing off to a steady stream of their friends visiting yesterday evening."

"So what is it we just won't believe?" Maggie asked, returning to Raquel's provocative statement when she first entered the room.

"Oh, yes." Raquel seemed to take a moment to collect herself. "I knew you'd want to hear this."

The women paused in their stitching, waiting to hear what she had to say. Whatever it was, they were definitely interested after waiting for her to explain.

"My daughter Bianca called last night. She lives next door to the Tipton house, you know."

There were a few nods.

"She called to tell me about a big fight over at the Tipton house last night just before sunset. Bianca said there's been a man over there the last couple of days, and then, last night, an older woman arrived." She looked around as though this was quite a significant event.

"Who is she?" Edie asked.

"Well, Bianca says some of the neighbors got together to talk about it afterward — after that big scene, you know," she clarified. "They all agree that it's Paul's widow, but otherwise no one can seem to agree on what they heard. One person says Shannon yelled at her that she had a lot of nerve coming back now, after all this time."

Raquel paused, creating a moment of drama, and Maggie remembered that she liked to appear in amateur theatricals. Maggie didn't mind giving her her moment, but she could see Edie fidgeting.

"She's come to collect her inheritance," Raquel finished with a flourish. "That's what everyone decided. They never got a divorce, you know."

"Oh, my."

Anna's comment pretty much said it all as far as Maggie was concerned. And this interesting news acted to perk up Clare. She seemed more her old self, as she paid close attention to hear what else Raquel might have to say.

"So, it is Shannon's mother?" Clare asked.

"We were talking about this the other day," Edie said. "About what might happen if the widow came back. If Paul didn't leave a will, she could get the house."

"We heard that she and Shannon don't get along," Clare offered.

"And for good reason," Raquel said. "I remember when she left. Poor Paul was just lost. Still grieving for his son and all alone with a five-year-old girl. Some of us in the neighborhood took meals over for a while, until he could get his feet back on the ground. Did you know her, Maggie?"

Maggie nodded. "We both belonged to the altar society. I liked her. She wasn't involved in much else though. I think she was shy."

Raquel merely shrugged. "Well, if she was, I think she may have outgrown it. Another neighbor called the cops last night because they were making so much noise over there. Bianca said it was the woman across the street who called nine-one-one. She talked to her afterward, and she told Bianca she was afraid someone else would end up dead." Raquel lowered her voice to a near whisper. "She thought she saw the man over there waving a gun around."

"Who is it, this man?" Edie's voice wasn't as quiet as Raquel's and sounded extremely loud after the other woman's delicate whisper. "I thought it was just the daughter and her son."

"It seems to be Paul's daughter's boyfriend. Or husband. We know Paul insisted she get married when she got pregnant in high school, but no one knows if she ever got a divorce. And no one knows if this is the guy she married or a new boyfriend. She just appeared on Paul's doorstep one day, with that little boy in tow, and there's been no sign of any man until now. Paul didn't talk much about her either. No one saw much of her, just of her little boy." She sighed deeply. "Paul doted on the little guy. He really is a nice, well-mannered child. It's hard to believe with that mother of his."

"Oh?" Maggie hadn't heard much about

Paul's daughter. "What is the daughter like?"

"Her name is Shannon," Clare informed them, although they had been using her name in the conversation all along.

"That's right," Raquel said. "She was a wild one growing up."

Theresa nodded. "She worked at the dealership one summer and she wasn't well liked. She wasn't at all like her father. He was gruff and preferred to be left alone, but most people liked him. Shannon was immature and lazy and always looking for a way to have someone else do her work." She shook her head. "Maybe Paul spoiled her, since she didn't have her mother around. And she was still very young when he lost his son."

Anna looked up, sadness in her eyes. "You said his son died suddenly?"

Theresa nodded again. "He was a lot older than Shannon. We talked about it at work — you know the kind of gossip you have during breaks. He was a teenager when Shannon was born. We all figured the marriage wasn't going well and they tried to save it by having another child. But the wife left as soon as Shannon started school." Her brow furrowed in thought. "I can't remember the wife's name. I believe the son was named Robert; Paul always called him Robbie."

"His wife's name is Fay," Maggie provided.

"I remember Robbie," Raquel said. "We've lived in our house as long as Paul has been in his — over forty years. I remember Robbie riding around on his bike. That was when the young neighborhood boys used to deliver newspapers on their bikes, and he was our paperboy for years. We never had any trouble when he was delivering, either."

"I miss those days," Anna remarked. "The service just isn't the same with these adults who toss the paper out the car window."

"We probably won't even have newspapers much longer," Edie said, "let alone home delivery. The Scottsdale paper has been gone for years, and the Phoenix paper is getting thinner and thinner. And now they want us all to subscribe to their online edition too."

No one replied to Edie's observation. They all knew that she was correct as far as the Phoenix paper was concerned. And Maggie was sure everyone was curious about what had happened to Robbie.

"So, what happened to him?" Louise asked, looking toward Raquel. "The son."

"Oh, it was awful," Raquel said, and

Theresa nodded. "He was attending community college but we thought he might have started clashing with his father. That's the age, isn't it?"

Louise nodded agreement.

"Anyway," Raquel continued, "one day he up and joined the Marines. Paul wanted him to go to college, but you could see how proud he was when he took his son in his uniform to mass with him. Then Robbie was killed in a training accident down in Tucson. Two helicopters crashed. You must remember it," she added, looking around at the others. Maggie and several others nodded. "If you lived here then, I mean. It was just awful. Eight young men died. The news stations showed pieces of the helicopters spread all over the desert. It must have been terrible for Paul."

"It was," Theresa said. "We all felt so bad. Gilligan's closed for the day so that everyone could attend the funeral, and Mr. Gilligan gave Paul time off with pay so he could deal with his grief. It must have been awful for him."

"It was shortly after that that Fay disappeared," Maggie remembered. "No one saw her for a while after the funeral, but we all figured that was to be expected. But when the head of the altar society called the house, Paul just snapped at her that Fay was gone and wasn't coming back."

"We didn't realize she had gone either — those of us in the neighborhood, I mean," Raquel said. "It was some time before it got around, and that's when we started dropping by in the evening with casseroles and baked goods. I made lots of cookies for that little girl back then. Wouldn't make her any now," she added with a frown. "Paul may have been too strict with her, but she turned into a wild teenager, rebelling against everything he believed in."

"It would be easy for him to act that way," Victoria said, "a single father left with a little girl. He probably didn't realize she was growing up."

Raquel nodded before continuing. "She got pregnant while she was in high school, then she ran off with that bad-boy boyfriend of hers. Paul chased after them and saw they got married. Paul told me once that the husband left soon after the baby came. Didn't like the noise or the responsibility. One thing, though, Shannon did stick it out on her own for a few years before she came back to live with her father. As far as I know, she hasn't gotten a job since she's been there. At least, I never noticed her coming and going like someone with a job."

"How did she earn a living to support her son before she came here?" Louise wondered, pulling her thread through and snipping it.

"Oh, I don't think she did," Raquel said. Maggie could see that she was enjoying the gossip session. Maggie might not have approved of such gossip except that she and all the others were curious about Paul and his family after what had happened to him.

"What do you mean, she didn't work?" Anna asked. "How could she have managed? Did Paul send her money?"

"I don't think so," Clare said, her brow furrowed. "I hate to say something derogatory about the dead, but Paul just wasn't the type who would hand out money that way."

"Even to his daughter?" Anna asked.

Clare shook her head sadly.

"I think Shannon just got welfare and food stamps and that kind of thing," Raquel said. "Once Brad was older, they probably got after her to get a job, and that's when she came back home."

Edie nodded. This kind of thing didn't surprise her. "There's a lot of welfare fraud out there, and I'm sure a healthy young woman should be working rather than collecting government handouts. Good for them if they pushed her out of the system." Welfare fraud was one of Edie's pet peeves, and she often regaled the others with stories that she heard on the news or read about online.

"It wasn't fraud if she had a baby and couldn't get out to work," Victoria said quietly, looking straight at Edie.

Edie shrugged. Maggie was sure she wanted to say more, but Clare interrupted.

"I know Paul often said how hard it was having her back home and with a young child. But Brad really captured his heart."

Maggie smiled at Clare's romantic phrasing. She noticed Victoria's lips also twitched.

"He used to walk Max with his grandfather quite often. Cute little guy. He's going to start kindergarten next month. He called Paul 'Papa'," Clare finished with a sigh.

"Three-year-olds can have a lot of personality," Maggie said.

Before things got any more sentimental, Raquel asked Louise about Vinnie.

"How is Vinnie, Louise? You know, Rodrigo was there too, but he wasn't in the room at the time of the explosion. He ran in real quick though once he heard that explosion because he knew Ramon and Angel were in there."

Maggie and the others were also anxious to hear how he was doing. Raquel had burst into the room before Louise could bring them up to date.

"Vinnie's all right," Louise said. "He does have some scratches from shrapnel, but there was nothing serious. He just scared me half to death when he called to tell me about it. He didn't want to go to the hospital either, but I insisted. Good thing too; he did need a couple of stitches to close a gash on the side of his head."

"You can't be too careful," Raquel agreed. She reached over to pick up her bags.

"What are you working on?" Theresa asked, looking at the lumpy tote bag with interest.

Raquel pulled out some tea towels she'd been working on at home, spreading them out on top of the quilt. The quilters exclaimed over the beautiful embroidery work. The towels had sprays of lovely flowers in delicate thread colors. Anna exclaimed over one with a bunch of yellow daisies and a beautiful blue butterfly.

As Raquel refolded her towels, the Quilting Bee women returned to their seats around the quilt frame.

"Do you think Paul could have lived alone all those years and never divorced his wife?"

Anna asked. "When she was the one who left him?"

Both Raquel and Maggie nodded.

"Paul and I have been nodding acquaintances for years," Clare said. "Max and Samson are the same age, you know."

Edie rolled her eyes.

"And I don't ever recall him mentioning a wife. I thought he was a widower. But then he didn't talk much about his family. I'd never heard he had a son, and I didn't know about Shannon for a long time either. It was here at church that I first heard Shannon got pregnant in high school and ran off with someone. That was after she returned," Clare added.

Raquel nodded as she put the tea towels back into the tote. "Paul was the quiet kind, pretty much a loner. He didn't make friends easily and he didn't share a lot. But he was a good neighbor. His house and yard always looked nice."

"Sounds like the Paul I knew," Theresa agreed. "He was always a little gruff because he just liked to be left alone to do his work."

"A loner," Louise said, and Maggie agreed.

"I doubt he did get a divorce," Theresa said. "He was quite devout."

"I agree," Maggie said. "Fay still uses the

name Tipton, though I know a lot of women do even after a divorce. But when she first got back in touch, she wrote a kind of summary of what she'd been doing over the past years, and there was no mention of divorce. Also, she's never mentioned a man in her life."

Theresa nodded. "I don't think it would be in character for him. He came to mass every Saturday evening without fail and he always went to communion."

There were several knowing nods then from the other quilters. That was why they didn't know him. All of the Quilting Bee members attended mass on Sunday morning, most of them the popular nine o'clock service. It was impossible to know everyone in the large parish, so most members knew others who attended the same mass or belonged to the same organizations associated with the parish.

"Yes," Raquel agreed, pushing the tote bag up onto her shoulder. "He always dressed nicely too, not like people nowadays who wear their shorts or ragged jeans. He always wore pressed khakis and a nice shirt. Even a suit in the cooler weather. Rodrigo and I often saw him leaving. We eat out most Saturday evenings," she said with a shy grin. "It's like our date night. That's what the kids call it, anyway." Her cheeks turned a bright pink.

"Wonderful," Theresa said with a bright and mischievous smile. "Do you ever go skinny-dipping together?"

Raquel's eyes went wide, but the other women all laughed.

CHAPTER 14

That evening, about an hour before sunset, Clare rang the bell at the Tipton house. Samson sat quietly beside her, satisfied with the quality of their walk so far. However, he did keep an intense watch to see what might come next, since this was a departure from the norm.

A young woman who Clare took to be Shannon answered the door, opening it just enough to look out. Her eyes suspicious, she looked Clare up and down. "Yes?"

Clare proffered the covered dish she carried — her popular chicken and rice casserole. "I thought I'd bring this over for you and Brad," Clare said. "Paul and I were dog-walking friends," she added.

Shannon was forced to open the door further to accept the dish. Before she could say thank you — Clare assumed she planned to say thank you — Brad came barreling toward the door. "Miz Clare! And Samson!"

He threw himself down beside the miniature Schnauzer and ruffled the fur on top of Samson's head.

His stump of a tail wagging like a metronome, Samson reared up on his hind legs, put his front paws on Brad's shoulders and licked his face. Brad laughed in delight.

Shannon turned, looking at her son in surprise. "You know this woman?"

"Yes. It's Miz Clare." He continued to ruffle Samson's fur, running his hands down his sides. "Papa and I always see her and Samson when we walk Max."

"Oh." Shannon seemed at a loss as to how to proceed.

"Perhaps you'd like to put that dish in the oven," Clare suggested. Might as well be helpful, she thought. And perhaps get into the house at the same time. She didn't know what she hoped to see but she figured a look around wouldn't hurt. She might see something interesting. "If you haven't eaten yet. Otherwise, you can put it in the refrigerator or freezer, then heat it up later."

Shannon looked doubtful, but proceeded to move further into the house. Clare wondered if she cooked at all. Or was she nervous for another reason?

Clare glanced around, wondering if she might get a glimpse of the man the neighbor thought had brandished a gun at Fay Tipton. But she didn't see or hear anything other than the two people in front of her.

"If you want to eat it tonight, just keep it in the oven at two twenty-five for now; that should keep it perfect for your dinner. It's fully cooked," Clare explained. "If you refrigerate or freeze it, you can warm it up at three twenty-five until it's nice and hot."

Clare turned to Brad then. "How is Max? Are you still giving him his walks?"

Brad's face fell and his hands moved off Samson's sides. Samson once again sat properly beside his mistress, but he kept his eyes on the young boy hoping for more attention. "No. Seth doesn't like dogs, so Max is mostly outside. Mommy says he has lots of room to run around out there."

"Oh, it's not the same," Clare told him, immediately wondering if Seth was the wayward husband/boyfriend. "Dogs really enjoy their walks and it's the perfect exercise. Then they don't chew on things or bark too much."

Shannon returned, looking anxious. What was the deal with the woman? Clare wondered. She should be grieving or upset, but she seemed more nervous than anything. Perhaps a little angry. At fate?

"Come inside, Brad." Shannon stood with

one hand on the door, ready to push it closed. "Thank Miz Clare for the dinner she brought."

"Oh," Clare interrupted, speaking quickly in case Shannon tried to push her out more forcefully. "But the dinner isn't the only reason I came. I wanted to offer to take Brad and Max with me when I walk Samson. I thought you might be too busy to take them, what with everything," she said vaguely, waving one hand in the air. She had no idea what the young woman did with her time, but she hoped Shannon would fill in the blanks. "I have to take Samson anyway, so it's no bother. And I always ran into Paul and Max, and sometimes Brad here." She smiled sweetly at the little boy. "So I know he usually took Max out at the same time. What do you say?"

Brad popped up from the floor and stood beside his mother, bouncing on the tips of his toes. "Oh, please, Mom. Max and I would like it so much." He had bright blue eyes, filled with pleading. How could his mother possibly resist? Clare thought.

Shannon looked between the two of them. Clare knew she was torn. But why would she object? Because she didn't know Clare personally?

"I can give you references," Clare offered,

before Shannon had the opportunity to say no. "You can call Father Bob at St. Rose and he'll tell you that I'm a nice and responsible person. A grandmother. You can trust your son with me for an hour."

"Oh, it's not . . . I mean . . ." Shannon stumbled over her words for a while, looking between the placid Clare and her anxious and excited child. "Okay. I guess it will be okay." She turned to Clare, looking dubiously down at Samson, as Brad whooped with delight. "Did you mean to begin tonight?"

"Yes, if you wouldn't mind. I'm sure Max and Samson would enjoy it."

If Shannon thought it odd that she would mention the dogs' wishes, she didn't say so. But she did get a strange look in her eyes — a "save me from this crazy lady" look. But Clare had survived worse, and she merely waited patiently in the foyer.

Shannon turned to Brad, who was once again bouncing on his toes, and told him to get the dog. "And get your shoes on," she called after him, before turning back to Clare.

"It's nice of you to offer. Brad seems excited."

No kidding, Clare thought. As thank yous went, it wasn't a lot, but still better than

156

nothing.

But to Shannon she said, "When will Paul's funeral be? You'll have it at St. Rose of course."

"Yes, of course. Daddy went to mass there every week. But we have to wait for the police to release the body."

"They haven't done that yet?" Clare was shocked, and realized that Shannon must see it.

"No." Shannon frowned. "I don't know why it's taking so long. Something about a backup at the medical examiner's, I think they said." She frowned. "It's a nuisance too, as we can't clean up the mess in the yard until they give us the go-ahead. Seeing that pile of lumber just reminds me of how he died. I'd like to throw it all out, and the next big trash collection day is coming up."

Clare tried not to frown, and even managed a sympathetic look as she patted Shannon's wrist. "That must be very difficult for you." Shannon seemed taken aback by this caring gesture, taking a step to the side to put a bit of distance between them.

"Oh, here's Brad. And little Max!" Clare bent to pat the little dachshund who leaped into the air in glee. His tongue flew out and he managed to swipe Clare's chin before she was able to straighten back up. She laughed. "Fastest tongue in the west," she said. "Isn't that right, Brad?"

"Yes." The little boy laughed too. Shannon looked at him in surprise. Then she put her hand on Clare's arm as they started up the walk. She lowered her voice, so Brad wouldn't hear. "Thank you. He hasn't laughed much since his Papa died. And now that's twice since you've been here." Clare thought she saw tears in her eyes, and suddenly she felt sorry for her. So the woman had feelings after all. Maybe the cold-hearted woman was a facade she put up in order to cope. Clare smiled at Shannon before hurrying up the sidewalk to meet boy and dog.

Clare and Brad started out on what Clare assumed was Paul's usual route, since Brad turned confidently at the end of the street.

"Brad, how are you feeling?" Clare asked him. "It must be very sad for you losing your grandfather."

He replied in a grave voice that should have belonged to a much older child. "Yes. I miss him." He paused for a moment to pat Max on the head. "Max misses him too." He straightened back up and looked at Clare. "He's with the angels now."

Clare almost cried at the sweet seriousness of his voice.

"The roof fell on him," he continued. "I went to call him for breakfast and the roof was covering part of him. But I could see his face and he wouldn't get up. I had to call Mommy and she called the police and the am-boo-lance."

Clare tried hard to block the horror she felt, learning that little Brad was the one who discovered his grandfather's body. The poor child! It took all her self-control not to scoop him up into a bear hug. And to contain the tears that threatened.

"He told me he liked to sleep outside," she said in what she hoped was a normal voice.

Brad smiled, even as he paused to let Max sniff at an interesting bush. "Yes. He had a special chair outside that he liked for sleeping. He called it his outside bed. He showed me how he made it comfy by putting the top part up."

Clare could hardly stand it. Such a sweet child, and he and his grandfather had been so close. It was terrible that some teenage pranks might have ended his life. Surely there must be more to it than that.

They walked on in silence for a while, just enjoying the sight of the two dogs sniffing and exploring.

But Clare was curious about several things, and she thought she might get at least one answer from the boy. "You said Max had to stay outside because Seth didn't like him."

She saw Brad nod.

"Who is Seth?" she asked.

"Mommy says he's my daddy. But I've never had a daddy. He said I can call him Seth, since I told Mommy I didn't want to call him Daddy."

Clare heard the serious tone and knew Brad was struggling with this.

"Do you like Seth?" she asked, hoping she wasn't butting in where she shouldn't. But it sounded to her like the child wanted to talk about this and she didn't think he'd be able discuss it with his mother. And his "Papa" was gone.

Clare could see Brad thinking it over.

"I don't know yet," he finally said.

"That's a very grown-up way of looking at it," Clare told him.

"It is?" Brad puzzled over that for a while then decided it was good. "Not all the kids at my school have dads. But I hear my friends talk about doing things with their dads, and it sounds like it would be really nice to have one. Dads play ball and take you to ball games or learn you how to ride a bike."

"Teach you how to ride a bike," Clare corrected automatically.

"Yes," Brad said. He kicked at a pebble on the sidewalk and watched it roll forward a yard and a half. "I asked Mommy once why we didn't have a dad at our house, and she told me my daddy wasn't very nice. But now she told me he's back and he wants to be with us. And that I should try to like him."

Clare could sympathize. "Things get very confusing sometimes," she told him.

He nodded solemnly.

"Max doesn't like Seth," he suddenly said.

"He doesn't!" Clare found this extremely interesting, but declined to discuss it with Brad. Clare herself felt that animals were excellent judges of character. Children, too. So Seth already had two strikes against him to add to his youthful reputation as a "bad boy."

"Why do you suppose Max doesn't like him?"

Brad considered. "I think it's because Seth doesn't like Max. He yells at him all the time, and pushes him away when he tries to make friends. He doesn't like him to lick, either, and Max loves to lick people. It's

161

how he kisses," he added.

"Yes, I know," Clare said. "I like dog kisses myself."

"Me too." She was happy to see the bright smile that bloomed on Brad's face. But it quickly disappeared. "Seth yells at me too."

"Does he?"

The little boy nodded.

"Why does he yell at you?" Clare asked.

Brad didn't look at Clare, just kept his eyes on Max. "He doesn't like me either," he said, his head bowed and his voice so low Clare had trouble hearing him.

"Oh, I'm sure that's not true," Clare responded quickly. "He's your daddy; I'm sure he loves you."

But Brad shook his head. "He says I make too much noise, and that I'm always leaving my toys where they get in his way."

"I think he's just not used to being around a little boy," Clare offered. "He'll get used to having a family." Clare sincerely hoped this was true. She also wished she'd been able to meet Seth while she was at the house. She was very curious about the man no one seemed to hold in high esteem. And why on earth was he here now?

"Your mother must like him," she suggested. "Their love made you, you know."

"It did?" Clare could see his busy mind

trying to process this new information. "Papa said that God made me."

Clare laughed. "Well, yes, God did make you. But your mom and dad helped."

As they turned the corner, Brad's feet began to drag. Clare realized they had circled the block and were approaching the Tipton house. The time had breezed by.

"This has been very nice, Brad," she said. "I really enjoyed it."

"Me too," he said quickly.

They strode up the front walk, Brad's feet slowing even more with each step.

"Don't forget, I'll pick you up in the morning, early. Will you be up?"

Brad's smile returned. "Oh, yes. Papa and I always got up early. But Mommy and Seth like to sleep late."

"Well, remind her that I'll be here for you early, before it gets too hot. Around six, okay?"

"Okay. I have an alarm clock. I can get up by myself."

"That's wonderful," Clare told him, though privately she thought it very sad that his mother would allow this. And what about his breakfast?

They had reached the door and it opened almost immediately. Shannon looked Brad over as though she expected there to be something amiss. "Are you okay?" she asked.

"Oh yeah," he replied, a big smile on his face. "Max and me had a great time. Miz Clare is coming for me at six tomorrow morning so we can go on our walk before it gets too hot. I'm gonna set my alarm."

Clare saw Shannon's eyebrows shoot upward at the early hour, but she didn't object. Even she had to see how much her son enjoyed walking Max, Clare thought.

Happy with her evening's work, she turned toward home. "I can't wait to tell the others," she muttered, pulling her cell phone out of her pocket.

CHAPTER 15

Michael hadn't wanted to come to dinner that Monday evening, despite their usual arrangement. He claimed he'd already imposed upon his mother too much in recent days.

"You can't impose upon me," Maggie retorted. "I'm your mother." With that she hung up the phone, not giving him time to think up another excuse. She wanted to see him, to reassure herself that he was indeed all right. And, of course, to see if he would let slip any new information about the recent explosions.

To her surprise, when he arrived — very late — Kimi was standing beside him.

Maggie smiled, reaching out to give the young woman a hug.

"Kimi, how nice to see you again." She threw a reproving glance toward Michael. "Michael called to say he'd be late, but he didn't say you were coming. I'm so glad you did; it's nice to see you again. Just give me a moment to put out another place setting."

"Let me help," Kimi said, following Maggie into the kitchen.

It was one of the things Maggie liked about Kimi. She was always ready to lend a hand. Look at how nice she'd been to sit with Michael so that Maggie wouldn't have to miss a session of the Quilting Bee. So this made three days in a row that Kimi and Michael had been together. The realization made Maggie smile.

When they reached the kitchen, Maggie opened the cupboard with the plates, and gestured Kimi toward the drawer holding the flatware.

Kimi cast a quick look at the door, then spoke in a low voice. "Michael's been put on desk duty for now, and he's not happy."

"I bet." Maggie could imagine how irritated he would be after a few days chained to a desk. "But he must have known that would happen, at least until the doctor gives the all clear on his concussion."

Kimi shrugged.

"So why is he so late?" Maggie asked. "He usually gets delayed when he has to finish up paperwork."

Kimi blushed. "I'm afraid that's my fault. He asked me to join him yesterday at brunch. He must have forgotten to tell you after all the excitement with the bomb at St. Rose."

Maggie nodded. Just like a man to forget something like an extra dinner guest. But of course things *had* been crazy yesterday.

"I'm so sorry. I was at a crime scene and it took longer than I expected. I told him to come without me."

"Don't be silly," Maggie reassured her. "I'm glad you're here."

Kimi pulled the required flatware from the drawer and closed it. "Michael is working the explosions case, but he's such an outdoor person, he feels trapped inside. He's been following up leads, but you know how those go. Most of them are just crazy suggestions."

Michael appeared in the doorway just as Maggie took the cover off the pot containing his favorite pot roast. He sniffed appreciatively before speaking.

"I can hear you two whispering in here, you know." He pulled out a chair and sat. "As if I don't know who you're talking about."

"Kimi tells me you're working on the explosives case. I thought they might not want you involved since you were injured by one of the devices."

167

"I'm just following up on phone calls."

He didn't sound happy, but Maggie chose to ignore the sullen tone.

"Are there a lot?"

"A lot of calls?" He sighed. "Hundreds. Most of them not worth a damn, but of course we have to follow up on all of them."

Maggie could see his frustration, so she carried the large platter to the table and set it in front of him. "I made pot roast," she said. She always made his favorites on Monday evenings when he came to dinner. "I hope it hasn't dried out, but I did turn the heat down an hour ago."

"Smells great, Ma."

"I'm sure it will taste great too," Kimi added.

"Sure. She's just fishing for compliments," Michael said, winking at his mother. "Her food is always terrific."

Maggie smiled at her son as she took her own seat. "I keep telling you — it's easy to make. You could make it for yourself — just put everything in the crock pot before you leave for work."

"I'd love a simple crock pot recipe," Kimi said. "They're so handy when you work all day. And this smells delicious," she added.

Maggie nodded, pleased to have a taker. No matter how easy she tried to make it sound, she couldn't seem to interest Michael in cooking. Eating, however, he enjoyed. "I've been trying for years to get Michael interested in cooking some simple meals for himself. I think he eats too much fast food."

She frowned at her son, but Michael merely shrugged. "I'm in great shape, Ma, you don't need to worry."

Kimi shared a sympathetic smile with Maggie. The young woman already knew how men could be, Maggie realized. Then she wondered if she planned to invite Michael over for pot roast made in the crock pot. That could work out just as well as having him cook it on his own. She'd make sure Kimi left with the recipe tonight.

"Is there any news about the explosions, or the people causing them?" Maggie asked. She passed a basket of buttermilk biscuits to her son, who had a generous serving of meat on his plate and was adding a spoonful of carrots and potatoes. "This whole thing has gotten crazy. It started with the Rivera boys and their friends setting off some leftover firecrackers. And now there are explosions all over the valley. You were injured, Paul Tipton is dead, and Deacon Adam almost lost his right hand. What's going on?"

Michael broke open a buttermilk biscuit and added a generous dollop of butter. "I don't think anyone knows right now. And everyone is getting into it, so it's gotten complicated. The FBI and ATF got involved right off because of the explosives, and after the power station was hit Homeland Security got into it. And now there are several police jurisdictions involved. There was an explosion in Phoenix last night — this morning, I guess. Similar to here, a loud noise and a mailbox destroyed. There's been trouble in Glendale, and in a county area. It's a mess."

"You know Edie is going around telling everyone that there's a terrorist cell operating in the neighborhood. She figures they're perfecting their bomb recipes. Either that or meth dealers making meth and causing lots of explosions. The ingredients are extremely volatile, you know."

Kimi laughed. "Is she serious?"

Maggie was surprised by the laughter since they were discussing such a serious matter, but then she realized that it probably would sound ridiculous to an outsider.

"You'd have to know Edie," Michael told her.

"She's very serious," Maggie said. "I guess you haven't seen her on TV. The news anchors love her, and she's been interviewed more than once. I'm afraid she's got other people at the church believing her now."

Michael winced. "Is that media circus still set up around the church?"

"After yesterday, it's worse than ever," Maggie replied. "All the Senior Guild members were accosted trying to get into the building this morning. Do you think this whole thing might be resolved soon?"

"I wouldn't count on it," Michael said.

"I've taken photos at most of the scenes here in Scottsdale," Kimi said, "and I have to tell you, I suspect there are several different groups involved. Or several people anyway."

"Why is that?"

"They're all so different. The techniques are all over the place. And I'll be surprised if the same explosive was used every time. I'm no expert, of course. It's just an impression, but after viewing so many of these, you kind of pick things up."

Maggie thought for a moment, recalling the various episodes and the reported damage. "That makes sense. We've talked about it over quilting. The first explosions weren't all that loud. They disturbed a few households, but only for a few blocks around the scene of the explosions. Then the next were extremely loud and started damaging property." She frowned. "I guess if different people were involved, then it makes it more difficult to catch them."

Michael and Kimi both nodded.

"You don't think there really is a terrorist cell?" Maggie asked. Michael looked at her in surprise and Maggie sighed. "When Edie first brought it up, we all thought she was crazy. But now there have been those attacks against the power station and the school. And they've called in Homeland Security."

"I hope not," Michael replied. "But I don't know if you can rule out anything at this point."

Michael reached out to help himself to seconds. "Great pot roast, Ma."

Maggie checked the contents of the bread basket and got up to refill it. Michael spoke as she seated herself once more.

"The Rivera boys have been in several times to answer questions." He reached into the basket for another buttermilk biscuit. "I don't think they'll ever stray from the straight and narrow again."

"Scared straight?" Maggie asked.

Michael nodded. "I'm glad you had them turn themselves in — and that you set them up with Walter. Otherwise, they would likely be in jail right now."

"Raquel told us they were called in after each of the newer incidents. But you did believe their story about just setting off some fireworks for fun?"

Michael nodded. "Yes. They've been co-operating. They named all the other kids who were involved and they all came in too. Some of them weren't happy, I can tell you. But some of them admitted to continuing to play around with firecrackers after Ramon and Angel backed off."

Maggie sat up straighter at this. "Did one of them cause the explosion that killed Paul Tipton?"

"Not that they are admitting," Michael said.

"They would have to be pretty dumb to admit that, since a man died," Kimi said. "They could be charged with murder."

"Speaking of that," Maggie said, "I got a call from Clare. She apparently stopped by the Tipton house this evening and volunteered to take the little boy and his grandfather's dog out with her when she walked Samson. She said Shannon — that's Paul's daughter — told her she hasn't planned the funeral yet because they haven't released the body. Clare really wants to know why that is."

Michael frowned. "You know I can't talk about ongoing cases. I've already said too much."

Maggie caught Kimi hiding a smile. She did know that Michael shared more than he should with her, but she also knew how to keep a secret. But this was their own neighborhood involved in these horrible events. It was important that the people be informed.

Then it occurred to her what he was not saying.

"Aha, so there is something suspicious about it." She smiled placidly at her son. "Clare has already been talking about a book she read where the heir arranged for a convenient accident. Something about a tree falling on the roof, and the inner supports sawed through."

For a moment, Maggie was sure that Michael appeared startled. Then he merely shook his head. Kimi watched the interplay with interest.

"I suppose his daughter, or her husband, could easily arrange to set an explosive under that old palo verde. Though it seems there must be a lot of math and physics involved to make certain it would hit the roof and fall in just the right place." Maggie frowned. "From what I've heard so far about Shannon and her husband, neither of them seem that intelligent."

"The husband?" Michael quickly jumped on her use of the word. "I thought Tipton had his daughter and her child living with him. I don't recall anything about a husband."

"We heard it at church this morning," Maggie said. "From Raquel Moreno — the Rivera boys' grandmother. She heard from her daughter that there was a man living there now and said there was a big fight at their front door this morning. Apparently Paul's wife is back and paid a visit. The neighbors think she's looking for her inheritance. They never divorced as far as anyone knows. Anyway, there was evidently quite a ruckus, and everyone was paying attention. The neighbor across the street called the police. She told Raquel's daughter that she looked out when she heard the yelling and that the man over there was waving a gun around."

Maggie realized that Michael had what she called his "cop face" on. Either he already knew about this and didn't want to tell her more, or he was just hearing it and wanted to check it out.

"I did the photos at the Tipton scene," Kimi said. "It was very sad. The old man was barely touched, but there was some heavy lumber sitting right on his chest."

"I understand it was the grandson who found him," Maggie said. "The poor boy."

Michael raised his right brow. "And you know this how?"

"Clare told me. Brad, that's the grandson, told her while they were walking the dogs. He said he went outside to call his grandfather for breakfast, but he was under all the wood and wouldn't wake up." Maggie sighed. "Though I don't know why his mother didn't see that the ramada was down from the house. That does seem odd." Maggie pushed at a carrot with her fork but didn't spear it.

"You know, Michael . . ." Maggie began.

Michael sighed. He knew that his mother was going to suggest something he should do. And probably something he did not *want* to do.

"You should recommend that the police hold a community forum, to talk about what's happening. You know, to help ease worries in the community. They could probably have it at the church or the high school." Having shared her idea, she now speared the carrot, put it into her mouth and chewed.

"That's not a bad idea," Michael agreed.

"They may have already thought of it and just not made the announcement. It's the kind of thing the police department does when there's a neighborhood issue."

"Except that this has gone way beyond a neighborhood issue," Kimi pointed out.

"True." Maggie frowned. "Do you think it's gotten too big for one of those talks? Maybe we could have Father Bob request someone come to the church and talk to the parishioners. That flashlight thing has people spooked. The rest of the donations were taken by the ATF, I guess, and everyone is too nervous to have another drive. So we won't be able to help many people. And a lot of people aren't even coming to the Senior Guild because of it. They're scared."

"I bet you haven't had a problem with the Quilting Bee." Michael smiled. He knew how they loved to solve mysteries. "I don't want you or your friends involved in this any more than you already are," he warned. "This is a lot bigger than teenage pranks or an heir arranging the death of his father. I'd hate to think Edie is right about terrorists, but they can't be ruled out at this point."

"Do you think it's dangerous? Clare won't walk Samson after dark because she's afraid to go out. Even though all the explosions have been in the wee hours when she would be in bed." She heaved a heavy sigh. "You realize this has been going on for over three weeks."

"Oh, I know. Believe me, I know. We've upped patrols in the area, but all those alleys make it difficult. They're dark and narrow, and sending motorcycles back there late at night would be noisy and disturb people. And I don't think the bicycle patrol would be much use in the dark. There aren't any street lights in the alleys."

"And it would be extremely dangerous for them, too," Kimi added.

Michael nodded. "Most of the explosions have been in the alleys. Let me tell you, it was a good thing when those alleys went out of style. They make it much easier for mischief-makers — easier for them to break into places, and easier for them to get away."

Maggie nodded. "The alleys were a good idea at the time the houses were built. The trash collection was back there, so they kept the cans off the street. And the heavy trucks didn't have to use the streets either with all that stopping; that was a good thing for both neighborhood traffic and the road surface. But once they got those trucks with the automatic arms, they couldn't operate in the narrow alleys."

"I wondered why those alleys were allowed," Kimi said. "It would make sense if they led into garages, but they don't. I've always thought they just make it simpler for burglars to operate. But now I understand the reasoning."

"Better for security when they did away with them and people started fencing in their entire property," Michael said.

Michael used one of the biscuits to mop up his plate. "Your pot roast is the best, Ma."

Maggie figured it was his way of getting them off the topic of the explosions.

"Did you make dessert?" he asked.

"As if I would forget to make dessert when you're coming over," Maggie scoffed. "I seem to recall a special request." Rising from her chair, she approached the oven and opened the door, reaching for pot holders at the same time. "What do you think?" she asked, turning around with a pie pan in her hands. Golden brown crust latticed the top of the pie, juicy peaches showing through. The smell of the sweet fruit overlaid with a bit of cinnamon permeated the kitchen.

"Mmm. Bring it on," Michael grinned as he sniffed appreciatively. "Smells as good as it looks."

"Why don't you get the ice cream?" Maggie suggested.

As they indulged in warm peach pie a la mode, Maggie turned back to the main topic of interest to everyone in the neighborhood.

"Everyone at church is terribly upset. It's not just the noise waking people anymore, it's your injury, the death of Paul and the bomb at the church. Everyone is scared. Deacon Adam is very well liked, and people are outraged about his injuries. Has there been any progress at all in finding who's responsible for the explosions? Paul's death and Deacon Adam's injuries have to put more of a priority on it."

"Oh, yeah," Michael agreed. He took a moment to savor another bite of pie before continuing. "It's pushed finding the culprits way up the line. But there are all kinds of complications, as I said."

Michael ate the last bit of crust and glanced over at the pie.

"Would you like another slice?"

"Thanks, Ma."

"And you didn't want to come tonight." Maggie couldn't resist chiding her son. "Honestly, sometimes I think you don't eat at all between your meals with me." Maggie shook her head, but she glanced fondly at her youngest son.

"Good thing you work out," Kimi said with a smile.

"Hey, I saw the size of that slice you put away," he teased.

"I work out too." Kimi's smug smile as she patted her flat tummy made Maggie laugh.

Michael pretended not to notice them, merely smiling as he accepted his refilled plate.

"So . . ." Maggie said. "Are there gangs in the Tipton neighborhood, and do you think they could be responsible for all this? Making meth maybe?"

"There could be. But the teens who started all this are not gang members or even wannabes."

"I didn't think they were," Maggie said.

Michael continued, between bites. "It's an older neighborhood and a lot of the residents are elderly — like Clare and Paul. But there are younger families moving in, especially as the housing prices have fallen. But more and more of the homes are owned by absentee landlords and rented out. Not too long ago a house full of illegal immigrants was found right near there. The smugglers were waiting to move them farther north when they were busted."

"I remember that," Maggie said. "It was

181

only a block from Edie, so we heard a lot about it," she added with a sigh.

"I can imagine." Michael grinned, glad he hadn't been there to hear it. "Unfortunately, we still have lots of people moving into the valley every year. And when they come from big cities, they bring the city problems with them. Like gangs and drugs."

"Edie says more or less the same thing." Maggie frowned. "I thought it was just more of her paranoia."

As Michael ate the last bit of pie, Maggie stood to clear his plate. "So is that a yes or a no about local gangs?"

"It's a 'we don't know yet'." Michael shrugged. "The school officer over there says there are some loosely organized groups that could be gangs or gang wannabes. He hasn't seen any signs of organized national gangs. The bomb at the high school puts that probability a little higher on the possible scale. The thing that bothers me," he added with a frustrated sigh, "is the idea that someone planned ahead enough to get the fireworks when they were widely available over the holiday but then didn't set them off. They saved them until now, just to cause trouble. It's some major mischief."

"And it's definitely fireworks, not gun powder taken from someone's hunting ammunition?"

"In the beginning, it was fireworks," Kimi said.

"The thing is," Michael said, "they could have just set them off in the middle of the alley. The noise would wake people and upset them, but there wouldn't have been any property damage."

Maggie nodded. "You're right — the fireworks have been placed to cause the most damage. It's why there's been so much talk at church right from the start. And why people are so worried." A slight smile tugged at her lips. "You know, if Clare was herself she would be saying that it was a very smart plan, leading up to a murder. Cause a lot of panic with the explosives, cause as much damage as possible — then when you kill someone by knocking a tree onto a roof . . ." Maggie sighed. "It sounds like just the kind of complicated mystery plot she enjoys."

Maggie wrapped the leftover pie in foil for Michael to take home. "It's that flashlight that has really scared everyone. It was so unexpected. Really a horrible thing to do."

"Maybe something a terrorist would do?" Kimi suggested.

Maggie nodded, her lower lip trembling. She was trying to keep up a brave front, but she was scared too. Not just for herself, but for Michael and all of her church friends. "A lot of people were injured. It could have been so much worse."

Michael picked up his empty coffee mug and took it to the sink. After rinsing it out, he set it in the dishwasher and put his arm around his mother. "I wish there was more we could do, Ma, I really do. I know everyone living there is terrified, especially now. But these things take time. And with three federal law enforcement groups involved now . . . who knows?" He leaned down to place a kiss on her cheek. "But don't worry, we'll find out who's responsible."

Yes, but how long will it take and how many more people will get hurt? Or die? Maggie determined to take her rosary to bed with her that night, even if she wasn't clear on exactly what it was she wanted to pray for.

CHAPTER 16

Clare was much more her old self on Tuesday morning, regaling the bee with her experience with Paul's daughter.

"She never even thanked me for the chicken and rice casserole I took over." She pulled a length of thread from the spool and clipped it off, quieting as she threaded her needle. But as soon as she began to stitch again, she was off once more.

"She did thank me for taking Brad out. She said he's hardly laughed at all since Paul died and he laughed twice before we even left the house. Can't blame him, poor child. He's a sweet little guy too. And Raquel was right about Shannon's husband turning up."

"*Is* it her husband?" Edie's arched tone implied she didn't believe they were married.

"He must be. Brad told me that Seth is his daddy but they said he could call him

Seth because Brad didn't want to call him daddy. He said he never had a daddy before. He told me himself. Said there were other boys at school without daddies but that daddies did fun things with their sons."

"He said that?" Anna shook her head in dismay. "Poor dear."

"Oh, yes, he did," Clare continued. "He also confided that Seth doesn't like him. I tried to say he must love him as he's his daddy. But he said Seth yells at him a lot, and that Seth thinks he's too noisy and leaves his toys all over to get in his, Seth's, way."

Anna sighed.

Maggie felt about the same, but refrained from joining in the "poor dear" refrain.

"Brad said that Seth yells at Max all the time too, and makes him stay outside for the most part. He said Max doesn't like him."

"Animals have good taste in people," Theresa said. "They can see inside to the real person."

Maggie agreed. "I do think dogs can be trusted when it comes to judging people."

"They're so good for watching out for their owners too," Clare said. "I don't know what I'd do if I didn't have Samson to let me know if someone is around the property.

He hears everything. And with all this funny business going on . . . Well, it's a comfort to have him."

"Did you get to meet this Seth?" Louise asked.

"No." Clare was obviously disappointed that she had not. "Shannon never really invited me into the house, though I did step into the foyer for a bit. It's an odd setup; the kitchen and the living room are on either side of the front door. Isn't that strange? All the houses we've had had the kitchen at the back of the house. That makes it nice to watch your children play in the yard."

Ah, Maggie thought. That explained a lot.

Clare's face clouded. "Did you know Brad was the one who found the body?"

"Oh, no." Anna looked close to tears thinking about a five-year-old discovering his beloved grandfather's dead body.

Even Edie shook her head sadly.

"I just wanted to cry when he told me," Clare said. "But of course I had to be adult about it because he was right there beside me."

"I'd wondered how it happened that he discovered the body," Maggie said. "I mentioned it to Michael and Kimi last night. I assumed the kitchen window would look out over the yard, as they usually do, so I thought Shannon would have seen that the ramada had collapsed."

"Michael *and* Kimi were at your house for dinner last night?" Louise asked, a smile on her face.

"Is it getting more serious, do you think?" Theresa asked.

Maggie replied that she didn't think so. "They spent quite a bit of time together over the weekend and he just invited her to come along with him. Maybe he felt it was a thank you for keeping him company after his hospital stay. But I was glad to have her."

Clare, looking impatient with this digression in the conversation, returned to telling them about her walk with Brad.

"Brad did not look excited about going back home. I noticed that his pace got slower as we got back on his block, and he was dragging his heels when we got to the front of his house."

"In that case, it's nice that you were able to take him out with you," Anna said. "It sounds like he really enjoyed it."

Clare nodded. "As we were going back down the front walkway, Samson was frightened by a noisy motorcycle."

"Noisy motorcycle is redundant," Edie observed.

Clare frowned but otherwise ignored Edie's comment. "The motorcycle went into the driveway and must have gone into the garage. So I think it was Seth just getting home."

"It's a shame you didn't get to meet him," Edie said.

"But what about them not releasing the body, Maggie?" Clare asked. "Did you ask Michael?"

"They haven't released the body?" Louise said. "That's interesting."

Clare nodded vigorously. "I asked Shannon when the funeral would be, and if it was going to be at St. Rose. Of course it will be at St. Rose, but she said she's waiting for them to release the body. She said something about a backup at the medical examiner's. Do you think that's true?"

"Maybe," Louise said. "There's always a backup there from what I understand. Too many bodies and not enough doctors."

"Michael wouldn't say anything about it," Maggie admitted. "He said he couldn't talk about ongoing cases. When he gets that way, it's no use trying to pry any more information out of him."

Still, hearing this excited Clare. "So they must think there's something odd there." She stopped stitching for a moment. "Oh,

189

this is so exciting. Maybe it wasn't an accident after all."

"How can you say it's exciting if it might be a murder?" Anna asked.

Clare's expression saddened. "I guess I used the wrong word. But don't you see, if he was murdered, it wasn't such a senseless death. The idea that someone set off a firecracker, or whatever it was, and a tree fell over and he was under it . . . That's just so senseless, don't you see? But if it was planned, if someone killed him for whatever reason, it might still be senseless, but it's not just a silly accident." She frowned. "I'm not explaining it properly."

"You're doing just fine," Victoria assured her. "I understand what you're getting at."

"You'd just like to find a proper reason for this happening, right?" Louise said.

Clare nodded, looking relieved that her garbled explanation had been understood.

"How's Vinnie, Louise?" Victoria asked, turning the conversation away from Clare and her awkward explanations.

"Good. The whole episode bothered me more than it did him." Louise shook her head.

"Men are tough," Maggie said with a chuckle. She should know, having four sons. Look at how Michael had bounced back after his head injury.

"Has anyone heard anything more about that?" Theresa asked. "That flashlight business." She shuddered. "It's just too frightening. Imagine picking up a flashlight and turning it on — and bang!"

Maggie shook her head. "If they know anything, Michael didn't pass it on. He said it's gotten to be very complicated. All the federal agencies are involved now — the FBI, ATF, even Homeland Security."

"That's because they realize now that it's terrorists," Edie informed them.

"Maybe they'll tell us about it at the meeting tonight," Louise said.

"Yes, I saw the signs when I came in," Anna said.

"I'll be there," Edie announced. "But I'll bet they won't tell us much."

"Let's hope for the best," Maggie suggested. Edie could be tiresome. She could even be right. Maggie just hoped she was wrong this time.

CHAPTER 17

As the women left the bee room just after noon, Maggie and Victoria almost literally bumped into Raquel coming from the embroidery room upstairs. Digging in her purse — probably looking for her keys, Maggie thought — she didn't see them step into the courtyard in front of her.

During an exchange of apologies from both sides, Maggie couldn't help noticing the stress lines on Raquel's forehead and around her eyes, lines she felt sure had not been there last week.

"How are Ramon and Angel doing, Raquel?" Maggie asked. Her voice carried her concern for both Raquel and her teenage grandsons. "I heard the police have asked them to come in to talk to them again."

Raquel's face crumbled, and she seemed to be making an effort not to weep. "It's been very hard for them — for all of us.

They are good boys; they are. They told about setting off the firecrackers, didn't they?"

"Of course they did," Victoria said. Her soothing voice usually had a calming effect on others. In this instance, however, it didn't seem to help. Raquel appeared as distraught as ever.

"We were just going to treat ourselves to lunch out, Raquel," Maggie told her. "Why don't you come with us? We can talk."

Raquel nodded her acceptance, looking grateful for the inclusion. She even asked to ride along. "If you don't mind dropping me back here afterward, to pick up my car."

"Of course not," Victoria assured her. "It's right on the way home. We're going to the Sugar Bowl. With all that's been going on, we thought an ice cream treat would be just the thing."

For the first time since they'd almost crashed into her, Raquel smiled.

They had a comfortable visit over soup and sandwich lunches and spoke only of minor things until their ice cream treats arrived. Sundaes for Victoria and Raquel and a Golden Nugget — the restaurant's specialty orange-flavored milkshake — for Maggie. Using her spoon, Maggie took an experimental taste, declared it delicious, and turned to Raquel.

"How are your daughter and her family? Has it caused any problems, that the boys confessed to the initial incidents?"

"*Has* it?" Disgust colored each word. "They've had graffiti on their house and nasty phone calls." She sighed. The initial pleasure achieved by the gooey caramel sundae seemed to have fled. "They are doing everything they can to help the police and they are being harassed. My son-in-law wants to take them all out of town for a while, but he can't get away right now. And the police keep asking the boys to come in for more questions."

Maggie put a comforting hand on her wrist. It was obvious that she was tormented by the rude behavior being inflicted on her grandsons, and on the continued pressure by the police.

"Where would they go?" Victoria asked.

"We have relatives in Casa Grande, and they have offered to have them stay for a while. It's not too far away, but at least they would be out of Scottsdale."

"Sounds like a good idea," Maggie said. "Though you'd better let the police know that they may be leaving."

Raquel nodded as she took in another

mouthful of her sundae. The cold creamy treat seemed to work its magic as she closed her eyes to savor the mixture of sweet flavors.

"Thank you for asking me to join you. This is just the break I needed." Raquel looked from Maggie to Victoria, her eyes bright with tears. "I just hate this whole thing. Ramon and Angel and their friends thought they'd have some fun setting off a few firecrackers, and look at what it's turned into. I know it's illegal to set off most types of fireworks in Scottsdale, but this still should have been a minor infraction." She sighed. "If my son-in-law buys any fireworks next July, I'm going to slap him upside the head."

Maggie believed she would too.

As they left the Sugar Bowl, Maggie suggested a walk. The day was overcast, so it wasn't as hot as it had been and everyone was hoping for a monsoon storm. Some rain would be welcome, and might even discourage the bomber — or bombers. They strolled along the sidewalk, passing small shops that aimed to attract tourist dollars. At the end of the street, they crossed over to the Scottsdale mall. They continued on the grass until they came to a low stone wall, shaded by overhanging trees.

"This is nice," Raquel said. "I keep meaning to get up early enough to have a walk before it gets too hot, but somehow it never works out."

"I know what you mean," Victoria agreed. "Though Maggie often gets up early enough to drive north and have a ride in the desert before Senior Guild."

"That's nice." But her voice had changed. Maggie was sure her mind was a million miles away from the conversation about getting some exercise during the hot summer months.

Raquel smoothed a wrinkle in her full skirt and heaved a heavy sigh. "This whole thing is more than I can cope with at this point."

Victoria patted her arm. "You're doing just fine. Do you think they might arrest your grandsons after all?" she asked. "I thought they decided that they were telling the truth about just setting off a few fireworks once or twice. Didn't I hear they were getting off with some community service for disturbing the peace?"

"Yes, yes, that's correct." Raquel was still agitated, alternately twisting her hands in her lap and twiddling with the fabric of her skirt. "Walter has been wonderful helping them out."

"What is it, Raquel?" Maggie asked. "Is there something else bothering you?"

Raquel sighed again. "It's our neighbor behind us," she said. "He talked to us last night, since he knew about the boys. He thought we might be able to advise him."

"Your neighbor in the back?" Maggie prompted when Raquel remained silent.

"Tomas Favela. He's a good man, but he lost his job a year ago and hasn't been able to find work. His wife works as a cleaner at one of the resorts on Scottsdale Road, and she's been taking extra work with their catering service in the evenings. But they still lost their house."

"They live behind you, but are losing their house?" Victoria asked, confused by Raquel's disjointed recitation.

Maggie wasn't sure where this was going, but she could see the situation was upsetting Raquel.

"No, no, not the house behind us." Raquel looked at Victoria, shaking her head at both her words and her inability to explain properly. "We've known Tomas since he was a boy. His family lived nearby when he was young and he would play with our children. He had a house over near Pima, but when he lost his job they couldn't keep up the payments. That was just about the time we heard the house behind us was for rent. The owners had been trying to sell it for some time, but it just stayed on the market, so the owner decided to try renting it. We told Tomas and they moved in. It's been nice for all of us, until now."

"And what's happened now?" Victoria asked.

"Tomas has three children, a teenage son and eight-year-old twin girls. His son is fourteen, Alberto, though he likes to be called Bert." Raquel sighed and Maggie wasn't sure if it was because of what was to come, or because of the young people's disregard for the culturally distinctive names chosen by the older generation. "Bert knows my grandsons. He's a lot younger, but sometimes they let him hang around with them."

Suddenly Maggie saw where this might be headed. "He was with them when they set off the fireworks?" she asked.

Raquel nodded. "Yes. He's younger than the other boys, but he trails around after them and they often let him." She shrugged. "I told you they're good boys. But I guess he got ideas. Bert, I mean." Raquel quieted, staring down at her skirt where she folded then unfolded a crease into the fabric.

After a moment of this, Maggie put her hand over Raquel's, stopping the compulsive movement of her fingers. "What happened?"

Raquel looked up. "Tomas just learned about what Bert has been doing and he came to ask our advice." There was another heavy sigh before she continued. "It seems Alberto had a brainstorm after he saw the fireworks go off, and he decided to take it further. He got hold of some fireworks and some shotgun shells." She paused for a moment to explain where he would come by that. "Tomas hunts sometimes during dove season," she said. "Then Alberto, he went on the Internet and figured out how to make the fireworks and the gun powder into something that would explode and cause damage to things like fences and irrigation lines. You see, Tomas has been working as a handyman until he can find something more permanent. So Bert hears his parents talking about their worries, about money, about his father's work . . . And so he decides to help out."

"He set off the explosions that caused minor property damage so that his father could repair it," Maggie said.

Raquel nodded. She seemed relieved to share her knowledge of the situation. "Tomas is a good man. A moral man. He was *very* upset with his son and told him he would have to go to the police. Alberto was so afraid, he said he would kill himself because he didn't want to go to prison. Tomas said it was very dramatic. He thinks his son has too many ideas from TV shows. He's thinking he'll have to cut back his TV time, maybe as punishment for the way he acted."

"Did he turn himself in today?" Victoria asked. "They said something on the radio about breaking news."

"I'm afraid it may be about Alberto," Raquel admitted. "But he didn't place bombs at the power station or at the high school. It never occurred to him to damage important places like that. He was just causing minor damage, then going around the day after and leaving flyers advertising his father's business. Tomas said he did get some jobs from it, but many people just fixed whatever it was themselves. If Bert was a little older, he would have realized that's what would happen."

"What about the Tiptons' fence?" Maggie asked.

Raquel blanched. "I didn't even think of that," she said. "Oh, no." She put her hand up to her mouth, as though she was responsible for what the boy had done. "I told

Tomas about Walter. Tomas goes to St. Rose too, so I told him to call Walter, that I was sure he would be willing to help. He was supposed to go in with them this morning. His wife wanted to go too, to stand by her son, but she was afraid to take the time off from work. They've had so much bad luck recently, she just doesn't want to take a chance she might lose her job."

"I'm sure it will be all right." Victoria patted Raquel's arm.

Maggie hoped so. But it would all depend on whether or not Bert had toppled the Tiptons' fence.

CHAPTER 18

Wednesday morning found the bee members rehashing the previous evening's community meeting with the police spokesperson.

"We were so lucky a storm didn't develop, with all those dark clouds we had," Clare said. "A lot of people would have stayed at home if it hadn't cleared up some yesterday evening."

After an overcast day, blue skies had appeared late in the day. An amazing sunset closed the day, with peach and pink, purple and gold painting the western sky.

"I found the meeting very disappointing," Edie commented. "I told you they wouldn't say much. They don't want to scare us by telling the truth about the terrorists."

"Disappointing!" Clare turned to stare at Edie. "How can you say that! They told us about the Rivera boys, and about Bert Favela — even though he didn't give any names. But the news about Paul! How can you say it wasn't something new and amazing — to learn that he was murdered!"

"He didn't say murdered," Maggie protested. "He just called his death suspicious."

"And cleared all the teenage boys who have already come in," Victoria noted.

"Sometimes I worry about how much you seem to like hearing about murder," Louise told Clare.

Instantly, Clare's face lost its glow and her eyes grew moist. "No," she said. "It's not that way at all. It's not murder that I find exciting. It's solving the puzzle of how it was done and who could have done it. That's what I find so interesting. I've always liked puzzles," she said, her voice growing small and almost embarrassed.

"We know," Louise said, patting her arm. "And I know you liked Paul. But you did seem unnaturally excited for a moment there."

"It's good of you to pull me back to earth." Clare pulled her needle through one last time and cut her thread. "I was so shocked when I heard them say they're looking at it as a suspicious death that I barely heard the rest of it."

"I know what you mean," Theresa said. "It was quite a shock to me too. Paul didn't

203

have many friends, but I don't think he had a lot of enemies either. You don't kill someone because you don't care for his personality." She finished traveling her needle to its new site before looking up and around the quilt frame. "Do you?"

"Well, I've heard of instances where someone kills a person in a moment of fury," Maggie offered. "I guess that could be considered a case of not liking the other's personality."

Theresa thought this over as she pushed her needle into the quilt, starting another line of stitches. "I guess."

"People kill for many reasons," Edie declared. "And many of them are senseless."

"Power, money, sex, revenge . . ." Louise named the most common motives for murder. "Aren't those the most common motives? Which do you think it might be with Paul?"

"Well, he didn't have a lot of money," Clare said, taking Louise's question at face value. "And power and sex are out too. So it must be revenge," she finished with a triumphant grin.

"Revenge for what?" Louise asked.

"That's the question, isn't it?" Edie said. "If we knew that, we'd know who wanted him dead."

"Well, I for one still feel apprehensive about all this, even after that meeting last night. It was supposed to reassure us, wasn't it?" Anna asked. "But telling us Paul's death was suspicious isn't exactly reassuring." She frowned. "They didn't say very much, did they, except about finding out the teens had set off some fireworks."

"And the teens all turned themselves in, so the police didn't even find them," Edie remarked.

"It shows that there's a lot of good in our young people," Victoria said. "No matter how the media tries to paint them all as troublemakers verging on criminals, there are a lot of good kids out there."

"That might be true," Louise said. "But they still did start the mischief. And Bert was deliberately causing property damage."

"Nothing was said about terrorists," Maggie mentioned. She pulled her thread through the quilt layers and tugged lightly as she checked the line of stitches. She did not look at Edie, though the side of her mouth twitched and Victoria's elbow poked lightly at her side.

"Of course not." Edie was calm as she addressed the implied criticism of her theories. "Like I said, they wouldn't want to scare everyone by saying they suspect there are terrorists at work here. And besides, none of the federal agencies looking into that part of it were represented, were they?"

There was nothing to be said to that, and nothing was.

"When Carl heard about them finding another flashlight bomb, he suggested we go to San Diego for a vacation, starting now," Theresa said. "He didn't actually say it, but I know he wants to get out of the area until they catch whoever is causing so much trouble."

"Last night's speaker said they suspect copycats around town," Louise commented. "So it's not just a question of finding one person. But hearing about that second flashlight did make my heart pound."

Victoria nodded. "It was lucky that the man who found it knew about the one that exploded here and called the police right away."

Clare nodded. "It was Charles Higgins, you know. He and his wife always go to the nine o'clock mass on Sunday and he'd heard all about the trouble here, and how Deacon Adam was injured."

"How is Deacon Adam?" Anna asked. "Has anyone heard how he's doing?"

Once again, Clare was the one who knew. "His wife says he's doing well. He lost most of his fingers, but she said his spirits are up. He's always been an upbeat person and that has to be a good thing in this situation."

There were nods all around the frame.

Edie paused in her stitching, looking at her companions as she recounted the situation. "Those first explosions were set off by the Rivera boys and their friends, using firecrackers. Then we learned about Bert trying to drum up business for his father with fireworks and gunpowder. But these later ones at the substation, the high school and here at the church — they are something else entirely. And these were the worst of them, and the most frightening. I'm telling you, terrorists are the logical answer."

"I wonder if they used plastic explosives in that attack on the power plant," Clare said. "In books and movies, they always use plastic explosives for things like that."

Clare's speculation brought a gleam to her eyes. Maggie hid a smile as she nudged Victoria. It was too serious a subject for smiles, but she was happy to see Clare back to her old self. Victoria nodded back, understanding what Maggie had silently conveyed. They had recently discussed their concern about Clare, who had not been herself these past weeks. The interrupted sleep, the loss of her friend, but mostly the fear — it was affecting them all, but especially Clare.

"Plastic explosives?" Anna shrank back into her chair, her hand stilled above the quilt top.

"It's fine, Anna," Maggie reassured her. "I'm sure it wasn't any such thing. Where would someone in the neighborhood get plastic explosives?"

But Edie refused to give in. "From working in a mine, or in construction. Or from ordering it off the Internet."

"I doubt you can order plastic explosives off the Internet," Victoria said, shocked.

Maggie shot a warning look toward Edie. If Edie hadn't been seated so far from her, Maggie might have kicked her under the table. "The FBI and the ATF have things well in hand, Anna. They just aren't very good at sharing with the public."

"Why didn't the Scottsdale police have someone from ATF to talk to us?" Edie asked, then answered her own question. "Because they don't want all that scary information getting out."

"I'm sure the ATF people are all busy investigating," Maggie said.

"Hmpf." Edie sniffed. "We're the ones in danger. We should have some answers."

"On TV the feds never like to share information," Clare said.

"Do you think that's really true?" Anna asked.

"Wouldn't surprise me," Maggie said.

"And that could be why the local police don't have answers." Edie nodded in satisfaction.

"Perhaps a good heavy rain tonight would help," Louise said. "Drive the crazies inside for good maybe. The weather person on the TV morning show gave a seventy percent chance for a monsoon storm tonight. And she thought it might be a doozy."

"It won't tell us who killed Paul," Clare said, her voice sad.

"No, but we could use the rain," Maggie replied. "And if it stops all these idiotic copycats, then I'll say a few prayers for a storm."

Edie pulled out her smartphone and began typing something in, then pressed her finger against the screen several times. Maggie was getting ready to ask her what she was searching for when Edie looked up.

"St. Genevieve," Edie said. As everyone looked at her, trying to imagine what she was talking about, she elaborated. "St. Genevieve is the patron saint of excessive rain. That's who you should pray to."

Maggie laughed. It felt good.

CHAPTER 19

Maggie eyed the ever darkening sky as she sewed that evening. The weather people on the news predicted a big storm, running on about the luck that it still hadn't hit during the height of the evening rush-hour commute. Their prayers to St. Genevieve appeared ready to be fulfilled as the clouds loomed lower and the wind increased. So she was surprised to hear her doorbell ring. She rarely had unexpected company, and especially on such a gloomy night. The sun shouldn't be setting for another hour or so, but it was already dark indoors. Spoiled by their usually sunny weather, the locals didn't favor going out in the rain. She headed for the door wondering who it could possibly be.

"Frank!" Maggie hugged her son in delight. "What are you doing in this neighborhood? And in this awful weather! Is Megan with you?" As she peered around Frank, hoping for her only granddaughter's presence, she discovered Michael standing behind him, still in his uniform. "What's going on? Is everything all right?" Worry crept into her voice. The weather seemed to pick up on her change of mood, the low boom of thunder rolling across the sky just as she finished speaking.

"Everything's fine, Ma," Michael said, stepping forward and ushering his mother back into the house. Frank followed. "Except for this weather," he added.

As they moved toward the living room seating area, Frank spoke. "We've been talking," he began.

"We being . . . ?" Maggie asked.

"Hal, Frank, Bobby," Michael said with a smile. "And me."

Maggie frowned. "Are you all ganging up on me about something? I don't want to leave town, if that's what it is. I know a lot of people are talking about it, but I like it here. I have a lot to do here." She eyed her sons. "It certainly wasn't the best idea coming out on a night like this. You should get home before the storm hits."

Frank quickly reassured her. "It's not that. It's just that with all that's going on around here right now, we're concerned for you, being here all alone."

"And?" Maggie was curious now. Was Michael going to suggest moving back in temporarily? As her sole unmarried son, he was the only one she could think of who might entertain that kind of inconvenience. Still, much as she'd enjoyed having him for those few days of his recovery, she liked living on her own. "I won't move in with any of you," she warned.

"We know how much you enjoy . . ."

But Maggie wasn't to learn what it was she enjoyed, as the door opened and Frank's wife April stuck her head around the jamb. "Are you ready?" she called.

"Ready for what?" Maggie asked, moving toward April. She was definitely curious now. What were her boys getting her into?

"Not quite," Frank replied, "but you might as well come in. We need to hurry anyway if we want to beat the rain home."

April entered the foyer, seven-year-old Megan trailing behind her. Maggie's exclamation of joy at seeing her only granddaughter was halted when she saw what she carried.

"Why, Megan, did your parents get you a dog?" They already had a family dog, a lovely red and white Aussie, but she was getting older and Maggie could understand if they wanted to add a younger dog to their family. Megan was certainly old enough to look after a dog herself. And Maggie knew how she loved animals.

"No, grandma, we picked her out special for you." With that, she thrust the fluffy puppy into Maggie's arms.

"For me?" Maggie didn't know whether to be flustered or honored. She liked dogs, of course, but had never considered getting herself a puppy. She got her dog fix when she rode out at Hal's ranch and Goldie, their Golden Retriever, followed along to keep her company. And this little ball of fluff didn't look tough enough for romping through the desert.

"We know how you enjoy Goldie," Frank began.

So *that's* what he had started to say when April interrupted, Maggie thought. The puppy wriggled closer to her heart, and she ran her hand over the soft fur.

"After you left on Sunday we talked about getting you a dog, so that you'd have some idea if anyone was around your property. Dogs are great at letting you know about anyone in the vicinity," Frank added.

"And we were at the store this evening getting dog food and they had puppies up for adoption," April said.

"You must have been desperate to go out

on a night like this," Maggie commented.

Frank shrugged. They led busy lives. Sometimes, things ran out.

"As soon as I saw Rosy, I told Mom and Dad that she would be perfect for you," Megan chimed in. "Isn't she beautiful? I named her Rosy because her fur is a rosy color."

Maggie looked down at the puppy in her arms. A pink tongue came out and licked at her chin. She had to smile. Who could resist a puppy? She was a small dog, probably around four or five pounds, and appeared to be a poodle mix. Her fur was long and fluffy, a pale beige with that rosy tint Megan had noted.

"You do like her, don't you, Grandma?"

Megan's concerned voice settled things in Maggie's mind. "Of course I like her. She's lovely. It was very nice of you to think of me."

Megan bounced in glee at her grandmother's words, and she grabbed her uncle's hand and rushed to the door. "We got you all the things you need for her too," she said.

As soon as the door closed behind Megan and Michael, Maggie turned to Frank. "It would have been nice if you'd asked me first, you know."

"I told them they were putting you in a

spot," April told her. "But you know how they all get."

"Yes, I do." Maggie frowned at Frank, but she immediately smiled as the pup inched her paws up to her shoulder and licked her chin again. "She is a cute little thing."

"We knew you wouldn't be able to resist." Frank smiled. "I checked her out, and she's in good health. She could probably use a bath, though."

"When we talked about it," Michael said, "we planned on a Lab or a Doberman. Something that could be protection for you." He frowned at the bundle of fur in Maggie's arms.

"But then Megan saw Rosy here," Frank said. "She'd heard us talking, and she decided this was the perfect dog for her grandma."

Maggie looked down at Rosy. "She's right, you know. What would I do with a Lab or a Doberman in this small place? Large dogs like that need room and more exercise than I'd be likely to provide."

"We got everything you'll need, even piddle pads," Frank told her. "She's almost three months old and a poodle mix — maybe part Schnauzer or Bichon. Someone's pedigreed dog got out of the fence before they could get her mated with another poodle, and they just brought all the puppies to the shelter. So they don't know about the sire. I figure she won't be more than ten or fifteen pounds fully grown."

Megan burst back into the room, her arms full of bowls, a collar and a leash. "Look at the pretty collar, Grandma. I chose it myself." She held up a bright pink collar decorated with flowers. "And don't worry, Grandma. If you want to go away on another trip to quilt with your friends, I'll watch Rosy for you."

Maggie sighed. It looked like she was the proud new owner of a rescue puppy.

A loud crash of thunder had Rosy cowering against Maggie's chest.

"You'd better get going," she urged her sons. "All the weather people have predicted a huge storm, and it sounds like it's almost here."

She stopped short of shoving them out the door, but she didn't fully relax until they were gone. She sent a quick prayer skyward when the rain didn't begin pounding down for a full fifteen minutes after they left — plenty of time for her boys to get home.

CHAPTER 20

The huge monsoon storm the previous night was the main topic at the Quilting Bee the next morning. There were a lot of branches down on both Louise's and Clare's streets. Edie's cul-de-sac was completely flooded the night before as the rain came down faster than the water could move through the washes. As a result, she'd lost her cable television signal for several hours.

"But it's really brought the temperatures down, which is nice," Theresa commented. "Though the humidity is so high, I feel like I'm back in Hawai`i."

There were a few nods of agreement. It had been extremely humid at the bed and breakfast where they had stayed for a special quilt seminar earlier in the year. But there they had been right near the ocean — close enough to enjoy the lovely briny scent through the open windows.

As they settled in for some serious sewing, Victoria smiled, amusement in her eyes. "Maggie has news about a new family member," she said.

Maggie was immediately bombarded with questions about which of her sons' wives might be expecting.

"You've got it all wrong." Maggie explained about her sons deciding she needed some form of an early-warning system. "I'm not at all sure I wanted a dog," she said. "Don't get me wrong, I love dogs. But a puppy is a lot of work, even an older one who is partially housebroken."

"Don't let her fool you," Victoria said with a laugh. "She's already in love with the little fuzz ball."

"What kind of dog is it?" Clare asked.

"Frank and April were told that she's a poodle mix, maybe Schnauzer or Bichon."

"I think it's really sweet that your granddaughter picked her out for you. And named her too." Theresa rethreaded her needle and quickly made a knot at the end of the thread. "I'd do the same thing if my granddaughter brought me a dog." Then she tapped her knuckles quickly against the wood of the quilt frame. "Knock wood she doesn't. I don't think Precious would like it much, especially at her age."

The others had heard about Precious

before — a haughty Himalayan cat who ruled the Squires household. And although her husband Carl had disdained her choice of pet, and her frou-frou name — Theresa always said they'd gotten her during her Tolkien period — the charismatic cat had quickly won him over.

"You'll have to take Rosy for walks," Clare said. "It's a shame you can't come along with Brad and me. Walking the dog is such a relaxing thing to do, especially now that most of the explosions have been explained."

"What do you mean, the explosions have been explained?" Edie asked. "The two largest, most important ones haven't been. Neither have they found the person responsible for the exploding flashlights."

Clare blushed at her faux pas. "I said 'most.' I meant the neighborhood ones have been explained. The bombs at the substation and high school are in a totally different class, don't you think? The flashlights too. I'm sure they aren't related to those first explosions. I just walk on residential streets and I'd know to report a flashlight sitting on a street corner."

Maggie hid a smile at Clare's ironic finale. Most of them agreed with Clare, but not necessarily with Edie as she once again stated her opinion of the attacks.

"Of course, the larger explosions are much more like terrorist actions," she declared. "The flashlights too. Very scary to think any flashlight might blow up in your hands. In fact, it's just the kind of atmosphere these extremists want to create."

No one was going to argue with that statement.

"Wouldn't it be wonderful if we could figure out what's happening?" Clare asked, eagerness in her voice. "I heard there's a reward. We could donate it to the church along with the money from the quilt auction."

"A worthy goal," Louise replied. "But how do you suggest we go about it? The police and a bunch of federal agencies are working on the case and haven't caught anyone yet. They haven't even announced any persons of interest. The only ones who have been 'caught' — if you want to call it that — are the kids who turned themselves in."

"We could try it the way we did in Hawai`i," Theresa suggested. "Remember? We talked about each of the possible suspects and eliminated them one by one."

"That's a good idea," Maggie said. "Except that in Hawai`i we had a limited number of suspects. We knew it had to be someone who was at the luau with us, and most likely someone right at our table. It was like one of those house party mysteries that Agatha Christie used to write with the group of houseguests. But in this case, almost anyone in the entire valley could be the culprit. There have been episodes all over the valley."

"Well . . ." Louise looked thoughtful as she clipped her thread and reached for the spool. "We do know that most of the new incidents in other parts of the valley have nothing to do with the original explosions that began here. The ones all over the valley are copycats, and several of those people have been caught."

"And by 'original explosions' you mean the ones here in our neighborhood?" Clare asked, but they all knew the question was fairly rhetorical.

Louise nodded anyway. "We know it all began with the Rivera boys and their friends."

"Then the first copycat was that young man trying to get some handyman work for his father," Theresa said. "What was his name again?"

"Bert Favela," Victoria said.

"Oh!" Clare suddenly looked excited and eager to share something. "I ran into Raquel earlier. She told me Bert's father got a job."

"He did?" Maggie said. "That's good news."

"And we could use some," Louise muttered.

"Yes." Clare smiled, happy to have good news to share. "K.C. Gilligan heard about him and his son and their situation and he asked him to come in. He was impressed with Tomas and offered him a job right away. You should have seen Raquel — she was beaming. Tomas is almost like a son to her and Rodrigo. Kind of like you and Jonathan Hunter, Maggie," she finished. Jonathan Hunter was the murder victim who had first drawn the Quilting Bee into crime-solving.

"I'm not surprised that K.C. did that," Theresa said. "He's a good man. And he likes to help parish members."

"We still have the most serious explosions unexplained, and with no suspects that I can see," Maggie stated. "The substation, the high school, and the flashlights."

"Terrorists," Edie stated.

Maggie sighed. She was utterly weary of hearing Edie expound on the subject of local terrorists.

"We all agree the two incidents at the substation and the high school were prob-

222

ably caused by the same person," Louise said, ignoring Edie's view. There were nods all around.

"But that's about as far as we can go with it," Victoria said. "We just don't have enough information."

"Or for the incident with the flashlight," Anna said. "I'm sure Deacon Adam did not have any serious enemies, so it's unlikely it was aimed at him."

"But surely it was pure accident that he was the one who picked it up," Louise said. "It could just as easily have been Vinnie or any of the others helping sort the contributions."

Edie wasn't ready to give up. "So much like a terrorist bombing," she said. "Any random person can be the victim. That's part of the *terror* factor," she added.

Once again the others tried to ignore her. Maggie was sure everyone else was as fed up as she was over the whole terrorist concept.

"And then there's Paul's death," Clare reminded them. She sighed in frustration.

"Of course," Maggie conceded.

"None of the teens admitted to toppling that tree, the one that knocked down the fence and the roof and killed Paul." Edie pulled her needle through, looking around at the faces of her friends as she did so. "But of course they wouldn't, would they? None of them want to admit to killing Paul — or being responsible for his death. Even if they weren't charged with murder, manslaughter is still pretty darn serious."

"It sure would be nice to know exactly what killed him," Louise said.

"What do you mean?" Clare asked. "The roof fell on top of him."

"Yes, I know," Louise replied. "But the cause of death has to be something more specific. Did he have a heart attack because of what happened? Did the boards from the roof knock him on the head and cause a concussion, or bleeding in his brain? Did a board hit him on the throat and cause a kind of instant suffocation? There are a lot of possibilities."

The others stared at Louise. "See what I mean?" she said.

Edie nodded. "An excellent question." She turned toward Maggie. "Any chance you can find out from Michael?"

Maggie shrugged. "It depends on how the department is treating it. I can always ask. But don't get your hopes up. I tried to ask him about the body not being released back at dinner on Monday night and he wouldn't say anything about it. No reason to believe he'd answer this either. He'll give me the standard 'ongoing investigation' line."

"But don't you see?" Clare asked, almost bouncing in her chair. Maggie couldn't determine if it was due to mere excitement or if it was caused by anxiety. "Some of those possibilities leave the way open for murder. If he died from a concussion, for example, anyone could have hit him on the head. It doesn't mean it was really the boards falling that did it. Having all those boards fall on him would just mask the original cause of death."

"That's a point," Theresa agreed, looking fairly excited as well.

"Another possibility is that someone might have arranged the bomb and subsequent damage to cover up an accidental death," Victoria suggested.

Maggie raised her eyebrows at that, but she had to admit it was an interesting theory.

"However," Maggie said, "we never did determine if there was a motive there for killing him — if he was murdered. He didn't seem to have any enemies that we've been able to uncover and his estate doesn't seem large enough to tempt anyone into committing such a heinous crime."

"A mortal sin," Anna reminded them.

"Only to a Catholic," Edie said.

"No, it's one of the Ten Commandments and I believe all Christians and Jews adhere to those," Victoria said. "We Lutherans certainly do."

"There's something not quite right about the whole business with Paul." Clare sighed. "He died about the same time the teens were setting off their fireworks. But it seems like it would take more than a bit of fireworks to topple that big palo verde into the fence and the ramada roof. Wouldn't you think it was more like the bigger bombs that damaged the substation and the high school?"

"You may have a point there," Louise said. No one looked at Edie. No one wanted to tempt her to come up with something outrageous to explain why terrorists might want to kill an elderly Scottsdale man.

"I was shocked to hear the police say his death was suspicious," Theresa admitted. "What does that mean exactly?"

"It means he didn't die a natural death," Maggie replied.

"It could still be death by misadventure, or an accident," Louise said. "I like your idea of a cover-up," she told Victoria.

"It could also be manslaughter by whoever set off the explosion that toppled the tree,"

Maggie said.

"On television, the cops always look at the family first," Theresa reminded them.

"That's true," Victoria agreed. "Most murders are committed by someone known to the victim; that is a statistical fact."

"Maybe we can try to see what Shannon and her husband are like at the funeral. I found out last night that Shannon has set a date for the funeral," Clare told them. "It will be on Monday. She told me when I dropped Brad off this morning." She pulled her thread through and paused before taking another stitch. "Louise, aren't you on the bereavement committee? Will you be calling on Shannon to discuss the funeral?"

"Probably not. Most of the talking is done on the phone. And it's a big committee, so there's no telling whose turn it might be to take care of the consultation. But I don't do much of that anyway, unless it's someone I know from Senior Guild. I usually just help with details at the church, and if they want to have a reception here afterward. I haven't heard from anyone about a reception at the church next week."

Clare shook her head as she pulled her needle through the quilt. She spoke again as she inserted it for another line of stitches.

"She's having the reception at the house.

Surprised me, after all we've heard about her. She wasn't all that friendly when I first asked if Brad and Max could walk with Samson and me. But yesterday she was practically bouncing on her toes, telling me she had to clean and cook to get ready. Brad said she was in her work mood and she'll work like crazy for days. Then she'll be all tired out and she'll sleep for days."

Louise raised her eyebrows. "Sounds like manic-depressive cycles. Is she bipolar?"

"No way for us to know, but it sounds like she might be," Maggie said.

"It would explain some of her previous outbursts too," Louise said. "Those shouting matches the neighbors have heard." She finished sinking a knot and reached for the scissors and the spool of thread. "It's a shame the reception won't be here. I could have arranged to go over to talk to her about it. That could have proved interesting."

"Well, we'll have that opportunity at the funeral," Edie stated. "We can all observe the family there and at the reception."

"Do you think Michael will go?" Clare asked. "On television the police always go to the funeral. They say the killer always attends, so we should pay attention to who is there."

"I think that's a fictional conceit," Victoria

228

said with a smile. "Still, it's always a possibility, especially if it is a family member."

"Gosh, I wish the funeral was tomorrow
instead of Monday," Clare said.

CHAPTER 21

As soon as they were all settled in place around the quilt frame on Friday morning, Edie spoke up. "This isn't to do with Paul, but I had a thought as I was falling asleep last night."

No one spoke, waiting to hear what she might say. Maggie hoped it wasn't going to be more about hidden terrorists.

"Do any of you get gas at that convenience store near the high school?" Edie asked.

The store mentioned was the closest gas station to the St. Rose campus, so most of the women nodded.

"Do you recall seeing a homeless man hanging around?" Edie continued.

Once again, there were many nods. And the others began to see where she was headed with her questions.

"You're thinking he might know something," Clare said, smiling brightly at being one step ahead of Edie.

Everyone was paying close attention now. Maggie wondered how none of them could have thought of the man before this. There were few homeless people in their neighborhood, and Maggie knew some of the parishioners looked out for him and provided him with water and meals.

"I stopped for gas last night on my way home," Edie said. "It was my evening to help out at the homeless shelter," she continued. "And it wasn't until I left there that I realized there was something missing. But it took me until bedtime to figure out what it was. I used to see him there by the store and I'd give him some money for food, you know. And I realized I haven't seen him since the explosions at the power station and the high school."

"I heard he was a veteran with some mental problems," Louise offered. "Probably suffering from PTSD."

"Are you saying you think he caused the explosions at those two sites?" Theresa asked.

"No, not at all," Edie said. She frowned. "No. I wondered if he might have seen something and been scared off. Don't you think it's interesting that he's been hanging around there for years and then suddenly no one's seen him since the substation explosion? I asked inside the store," she added.

There was real interest now.

"Oh, my," Clare exclaimed. "You're thinking he saw what happened before those bombs went off? Maybe saw the bomber?"

Edie nodded. "He hung around that same area all day and all night. And then he disappears just after something momentous happens practically across the street? Don't you think that's odd?"

"If he does have PTSD the explosions probably scared him badly," Louise said. "It could bring back the kinds of memories he's trying to avoid."

"But if he's not there anymore . . ." Anna said, her voice dropping off.

"Is there a shelter for veterans that he might apply to?" Victoria asked. She looked toward Louise, who was the most likely to know.

"There are a couple of places that try to help the vets, but I don't know if any of them have beds available." Louise frowned. "It's a big problem and there isn't a lot of money for facilities. And many of the men don't want to take advantage even if there is something available. The St. Vincent de Paul group here helps him out," Louise added. "I've heard Vinnie mention it."

Edie checked her watch. "Let's go ask in the break room if anyone knows him. There should be quite a few people in there about now."

With Edie leading the way, the entire Quilting Bee walked over to the break room.

"Are you investigating the explosions?" one of the women asked immediately. It was unusual for all of the quilters to arrive together — unless they were on one of their investigations. The break room was a great place to search out information.

Edie explained about getting gas the previous evening and missing the sight of the homeless veteran. "He's always there, you see, and it's so close to the explosions at the substation and at the high school."

"You don't think he caused those explosions?" someone asked. The question was carefully voiced, but Maggie could hear the anger that underlay the words. She knew the speaker was a veteran himself and had a lot of sympathy for other vets, especially those who suffered from PTSD.

"No, we don't," Maggie hastened to explain.

"We wondered if he saw something that scared him away from his usual spot," Louise said.

"I used to know him," someone offered.

233

"Nice guy. Went to school with him actually — we both grew up in this neighborhood. Was never the same after he returned from Vietnam. PTSD, or whatever they called it back then. Just never recovered, couldn't stand to be indoors. Camped out in his backyard until his wife couldn't take it anymore and divorced him. A real shame."

Another man nodded. "I talk to him sometimes. Some people think he's crazy but he's not. He chose to live like that. He likes to be out in the open; can't stand being closed in. I take him food and water now and again. I offered him a bed one freezing night. That's when he told me about his claustrophobia. I think he was a POW. Must have been a horrible experience. Anyway, I took him a couple of blankets instead."

"Do you know where he might be?" Maggie asked.

"You don't think he's the one responsible for all these explosions?"

"He's a vet; he might know about explosives," Edie ventured. The comment drew a lot of frowns her way. It was obvious that the parishioners liked the homeless man and didn't believe him capable of causing the recent events.

"Where would he get explosives?" It was the first speaker, the anger more evident in his voice.

Edie shrugged. "Find them. Steal them."

As those who professed to know the man began to object, Maggie raised her voice. "Please! Edie is just playing devil's advocate." She shot a speaking look toward Edie, letting her know she'd better not disagree. "We never meant to suggest that this man was responsible for anything. We only remembered how he always hung out around the convenience store, which is right next to the substation. We thought he might have seen something. If he did, it might be important. We just wanted to talk to him. *That's* why we're wondering what has happened to him."

"Yeah." One of the men who professed to know the homeless man, pursed his lips for a second. "If he did see something that night, I'm sure it scared him off. He's emotionally fragile. The explosion at the power station alone could have scared him off, but if he saw the person do it . . . I don't know."

"So no one has any idea where he might have gone?" Maggie asked.

No one replied, and there were numerous head shakes. With a sigh, the women finished their tea and started back toward the Quilting Bee room. As they reached the door, one of the Senior Guild men who had been in the break room with them approached Maggie. She and Victoria stopped in the courtyard, while the others went inside. Maggie had to stare at Edie when she hesitated, but she did finally follow the rest of the Quilting Bee members.

"I think I might know where Joe might be."

"You said you knew him in high school," Maggie said.

He nodded. "His name isn't Joe, but that's what everyone started calling him out on the street."

"G.I. Joe," Victoria said, and he nodded.

Maggie had a sudden insight. "Do you think he's gone back to his childhood area?"

His eyes brightened. "That's what I'm thinking. Look, he's pretty skittish about strangers. If you gals try to find him, he might just run again. Same if you send your son. He's a big guy and he wears that official uniform. Let me see if Joe is where I'm thinking. I'll try to talk to him, see if he saw anything. Okay?"

Maggie nodded. "Let me give you Michael's cell number. I'll tell him about this conversation and let him know to expect your call."

He entered the numbers into his phone,

then moved off toward the wood crafting room.

"Well, let's go tell Edie," Maggie said with a heavy sigh. Edie was sure to be upset about being left out at the end when it had been her idea to check on the missing Joe.

Victoria put her arm around Maggie's shoulders. "Buck up."

That brought a smile, which was bolstered when they entered the Quilting Bee room. The sight of the Bright Hopes quilt always made Maggie smile. Its colorful fabrics and inspirational name did have the uplifting spiritual effect Victoria had hoped for when she brought it in.

"So what happened?" Edie demanded.

CHAPTER 22

The Browne family brunch was a more cheerful event that Sunday. For one thing, Michael wasn't fresh out of the hospital with a concussion. For another, they had had another night free of explosions, making six whole blast-free days in the neighborhood. Everyone hoped that the big storm on Wednesday evening marked the end of the explosions. With the heavy media coverage, police presence was high. Everyone hoped that and the presence of so many federal agents meant the end of the mischief.

Finally, Maggie had returned home after mass to collect Rosy, and the little pup was inserting a lot of fun into the day. All the grandchildren loved her, and enjoyed running and playing with her. Megan recounted how she'd seen Rosy and known she was the right companion for their grandmother. Rosy herself had taken an instant liking to

Goldie, Hal's elderly Golden Retriever, and was currently curled up against her side, exhausted by all her activity.

As soon as everyone was seated with their food in front of them, Maggie turned to Michael. "Have you heard from Pat? Was he able to find that homeless man we talked about?"

Michael nodded. "He called me yesterday afternoon."

Bombarded with curious questions, they had to take time to explain to the others while Maggie fidgeted, anxious to hear what Michael might have learned.

Finally, explanations were done and Maggie looked at her youngest son. "So . . . ?"

"He told me that Joe did see someone at the power plant, in the same place where there was an explosion soon afterward. He got out of there fast, and hasn't been back. Brought back too many memories, he said. And he didn't want to talk to the police or the feds about it," he finished with a frown.

"Did he see the person who did it enough to identify him?" Sara asked.

"He saw him all right, but that isn't going to help anyone much." Michael heaved a sigh. This was pretty much the story about all the so-called leads they got in this crazy case. "The guy wore a hoodie pulled up over his head, and tinted glasses, even though it was dark out. Said the guy looked like the Unabomber."

"Oh, my . . ."

Michael nodded. "Joe told Pat it traumatized him all over again. Pat doesn't know if Joe will ever return to the convenience store, even though a lot of people looked for him there and helped him out."

"So, after all that, there isn't really anything to go on." Maggie frowned.

"No," Michael agreed. "And we already had that description of the bomber from video surveillance at the high school. Same thing. It's a figure wearing a hoodie. Can't see anything of his or her face."

"You think it could be a woman?" Maggie asked.

"No way to tell if it's a man or a woman. About all we've been able to get from the video is the person's approximate size. It's a lightweight man or a woman. Period."

"So this new information merely confirms that it's the same person," Hal said.

Michael nodded. "That means it isn't new information. And that means there's no need to further pursue that avenue of inquiry."

"It isn't good for the investigation, but it

is good news for that poor man," Maggie said.

As the adults pondered this in silence, Megan called over from the children's table.

"Grandma, Jason says Rosy isn't pink. But *I* think she has a pinkish, rosy color. You do too, don't you, Grandma?"

Maggie was glad for the distraction of a spat between cousins. Hearing her name, Rosy looked over to the children's table, got up and stretched, then trotted over to Megan. Her tail wagged furiously back and forth.

"She's really smart, isn't she, Grandma?" Megan asked.

Even as Maggie agreed with Megan, the other children began to argue that their own dogs were the smartest. This caused the adults to interfere to keep things from escalating into a scrap. Maggie hoped they could keep to such familial topics for the rest of their time together that morning.

However, as the meal wound down, Michael asked Maggie if she would be attending Paul's funeral the next day.

"Of course. The entire Quilting Bee will be going. Probably the entire Senior Guild."

"I'll see you there then," Michael told her.

Maggie's eyebrows shot upward. "Checking to see who will be there?"

Frank laughed. "The old 'seeing if the killer attends the funeral' trick."

"But was he killed?" Hal asked. "So far 'suspicious' is all we've heard."

"That's true," Maggie replied. "What exactly killed him, anyway? Did he get conked on the head by the roof beams?" Pool-side ramadas were usually made with a crisscrossing of heavy wooden slats. The shade was enough to provide comfort in high temperatures as it kept out direct sunlight.

Michael frowned at his family. They were always asking him for information that hadn't been released. Still, he didn't have an answer to this particular question, so it was safe enough to answer it.

"The medical examiner says he was already dead when the roof caved in. Other than that, I think he's waiting on various tests."

"So he doesn't know exactly how he died?" Sara asked.

"As far as I know," Michael said, "not yet."

"That's important," Maggie said, frowning at Michael though she knew it wasn't his fault they didn't know. "How he died might point to motive. So far the only motive we've been able to come up with is inheritance, but it seems unlikely there was much involved in his estate. Just the house probably and it doesn't seem worth killing for."

"You forget, murders have been committed for just a few dollars from a cash register, even for a pair of shoes. A small inheritance doesn't eliminate the heirs as suspects."

"We've been debating whether Shannon — his daughter, you know — might be bipolar. She seems to run hot or cold with little in between."

Michael stared at his mother. "Is that why you asked if the figure on the security camera could be a woman?"

"Yes. We've been talking about that at the Quilting Bee," she told him. "Wondering if Shannon might have been able to manage killing her father for her inheritance."

"But explosions like that?" Sara asked. "You think a woman could do that? And why on earth would she want to bomb the substation and the high school?"

"The latter is easy," Hal said. "Misdirection."

Both Michael and Maggie nodded.

"And at quilting we decided sex and even age don't matter here, because anyone could learn enough to make a bomb from information online."

"Unfortunately," Michael agreed.

"The motive is the thing that's eluding us so far," Maggie said. "I hope talking to people at the funeral tomorrow will help."

CHAPTER 23

The Quilting Bee met as usual early on Monday morning, though they were all dressed more formally than usual. Paul Tipton's funeral would be later that morning, and they all planned to attend.

After several days of blessed quiet, there had been another of the loud blasts before dawn. The police quickly discovered the site of the explosion, behind an empty, bank-owned house. There was a slatted wooden fence and a large palo verde tree; the force of the blast had toppled the tree and one section of fence. Two other sections were tipped and hanging precariously inward.

News of this latest damage raced through the church community. The similarity to the blast that killed Paul was too close to ignore. The bee women speculated on this as they stitched on the Bright Hopes quilt top.

So much for her bright hopes that the spate of explosions had ended with the monsoon storm, Maggie thought.

"It's too strange that this new explosion is so much like the one that killed Paul," Clare said. "I got goose bumps when I heard about it."

"We don't know that that explosion killed Paul," Edie reminded her.

"Still . . ." Clare shuddered delicately. "It's eerie."

Edie didn't bring up any theories of terrorists, but her mouth, turned down at one corner, spoke volumes about what she thought of Clare's pronouncement.

Instead of dwelling on this most recent incident and its similarities to the Tipton one, Maggie told everyone about Michael wanting to meet her for the funeral. Clare, Louise and Theresa would be meeting their husbands at the church as well, as they all knew Paul through the St. Rose men's group. They expected a large crowd. The new explosion brought the media back to the area in full force, and there were trucks from all of the major networks already parked near the church. The anchors would probably be saying something much like Clare had about the eerie coincidence of this recent episode.

There was also plenty of time to discuss the similarities of this new explosion to the one that killed Paul. Or didn't kill him, Maggie thought. She had to bite her tongue not to reveal the tantalizing news Michael had shared with the family the day before. But he'd requested they not share the information.

"It was *just* like the explosion that killed Paul," Clare told everyone. "I can't believe he got away with it *again.*"

"I saw Rose Paladini as I arrived," Louise said. "She told me the noise woke them just before the sun came up and they called nine-one-one right away. She said the police arrived in five minutes — maybe less. They live next to that vacant house, you know."

Clare nodded. "That was where Yvonne Benedict's daughter lived, but they lost the house when her husband was stationed in Iraq for so long."

Several of the women shook their heads at this injustice.

Before anyone could begin a dialogue about how something needed to be done, Clare spoke. "I walked by the alley this morning with Samson. I wanted to see how it looked, if it really was just like over at Paul's."

"You did?" Anna stared at her wide-eyed.

"And no one stopped you?" Maggie asked. "I should think it was a crime scene."

"Oh, it was. But they barely noticed an old lady walking her dog. They just told me to move on. There were lots of people there wearing jackets with initials on them. ATF, FBI, DHS." Clare paused. "What does DHS stand for, anyway?"

"Department of Homeland Security," Edie supplied.

"Oh." Clare was momentarily brought to silence as she processed this.

"We talked before about Homeland Security being brought in after the transformer was bombed," Edie reminded her.

"Yes, of course. It's just that I was trying to remember something." Clare's forehead wrinkled in thought.

"Were you able to see anything?" Edie asked. Maggie had the distinct impression that Edie wished she had thought to walk past the latest crime scene.

"A little," Clare admitted. "I could see the tree. It was a little smaller than the one at Paul's. It was lying on top of a whole section of wooden fence that was flat on the ground. And the two sections on either side were hanging there, like they might topple over at any moment."

"So this was on the back of the property, in the rear alley?" Louise asked.

Clare nodded. Just like Paul.

"It was even behind the pool, like at his place. I wish I could have had a better look," Clare said with a frown. "But I only got a quick peek before I had to turn around."

The church was fairly quiet when Maggie, Victoria, Edie and Anna slid into a long pew about halfway back from the altar. The other bee members took the pew in front of them, watching for their husbands to arrive and join them. Paul might not have had close friends, but many people in the parish came to pay their respects. Also, people from the neighborhood and those who had worked with him at Gilligan's. Clare also pointed out some faces she recognized from local television.

Maggie wasn't surprised when Michael slid quietly into the pew beside her. He wore khakis and a neat polo shirt in a mellow gold. "Undercover?" Maggie asked. The softly voiced question was heard only by Michael and Victoria on either side of her.

"Coming back from the doctor," he replied in a similarly low tone of voice. "Thought I'd come support my dear mother," he added. Then with a smile he told her, "I'm all cleared health-wise. No more deskwork." His big smile brought a smile to his mother's face as well.

"I'm glad," Maggie told him. She knew how frustrated he'd been cooped up indoors for the past week.

Within minutes of Michael's arrival, the music began and the casket moved up the aisle, accompanied by Father Bob, Deacon Adam, his right hand still bundled in a thick bandage, and the family. There were pathetically few of the latter. A young woman who Maggie knew must be his daughter Shannon, holding the hand of a sobbing boy. Maggie stole a quick glance at Clare, who was dabbing at her eyes with a handkerchief. She was probably feeling poor Brad's pain.

Of more interest to Maggie — and probably the other bee members too — was a young man close to Shannon's age who slouched down the aisle beside her, his arm around her shoulders. He appeared to be whispering in her ear — offering words of comfort, perhaps. Personally, Maggie doubted that. From the strange expression in his eyes she wouldn't be surprised to discover that he was making fun of the solemn ritual. This had to be Seth Moody. Maggie wasn't impressed with his posture, or with his lack of respect for the man in the casket.

Maggie looked quickly toward Michael, noting that he, too, was checking out Shannon's companion. Of medium height, thin and wiry, Seth wore a dark blue golf shirt, dark jeans and black sneakers. In his way, Maggie supposed he had dressed for the funeral. Still, she couldn't help relating his posture to that of young teens who wished to show everyone how bored they were with the world. This man had to be in his mid to late twenties; he should be past the blasé rebel stage.

Shannon had at least made an attempt to dress properly. But her black dress was dated, too snug at her chest and hips and much too short. But she had added a short-sleeved black cardigan, which helped make the outfit more appropriate.

Behind the little family, but definitely separate, walked an older woman. Maggie recognized her immediately. Fay Tipton hadn't changed much, except perhaps to gain some self-confidence. She stood up-right and proud, looking straight ahead with her head held high. She was thin and pretty, her white hair styled in an attractive bob, and wearing an appropriately dark calf-length dress with a string of white pearls. She fingered the necklace as she moved forward, and Maggie wondered if they were her wedding pearls.

Maggie thought there was a certain resemblance to Shannon that could not be ignored. Of greater interest to Maggie was the tall, distinguished-looking man in a dark suit who walked beside her. They didn't hold hands, but every few steps the back of their hands brushed. It was a strangely intimate gesture.

Maggie and Michael exchanged a look. "The wife?" he mouthed.

Maggie nodded. "Yes. It's Fay."

"Who's the escort?" Victoria asked, keeping her voice low.

Maggie shook her head. Fay sent newsy letters every Christmas but she'd never mentioned having another man in her life.

Clare leaned back from her position in front of Victoria. "Look at how Seth is supporting Shannon. I guess he's not all bad. It's very romantic." Clare ended with a sigh as she dabbed at her eyes with her tissue once more. She loved romantic love.

Maggie moved her focus back to Shannon and Seth just as the family entered the first row of pews. Somehow they didn't strike her as romantic. To her it still looked more like boredom on Seth's part. Interesting how two people looking at the same thing could arrive at such different conclusions. Except for young Brad, no one appeared too broken up over Paul's death, although

Fay did project a solemn regret. Even after seating themselves, Shannon and Seth continued to whisper to one another. All of the bee members noticed — surely the entire church did — and there was much exchanging of dismayed looks at their rudeness.

Meanwhile, Fay had gone into the first row on the opposite side of the aisle. While suitably grave, she scanned the church as if seeing it for the first time. Or perhaps examining the changes that had occurred over the years she had been gone. Maggie wondered if she and her companion were holding hands. Something about the movement of his shoulder when they first sat down gave Maggie that impression.

There was no more conversation among the bee members as the requiem mass began and Father's voice rose in prayer. Maggie savored the serenity that fell over her, brought on by the familiar words of the religious ritual. She was sure the others were similarly affected. Well, she reminded herself, except for Victoria, who wouldn't be familiar with the Catholic rite. As much a part of the Quilting Bee as any of them, Maggie had to remind herself that Victoria was still an outsider here.

Afterward, they gathered outside. Shannon, Seth and Brad moved immediately to the car provided by the funeral home, but Fay remained near the door to accept condolences.

"I want to say hello to Fay," Maggie said, getting into line behind other parish members who were already waiting to greet her.

"Let's all," Edie suggested, joining her.

When they reached Fay, Maggie wrapped her in a hug. "Fay, it's so good to see you. I'm sorry about Paul. Such a sad situation."

"Thank you." She returned Maggie's hug with a tight squeeze. "I did try to contact him over the years. I wanted to get to know Shannon. But he wouldn't listen to me. Said I'd made my choice and to keep away from Shannon." Maggie could see tears gather in her eyes.

"Fay, these are some of my friends from the Quilting Bee." She ushered Victoria and the others forward and they all expressed their condolences.

"Paul and I had some good years together," Fay said, then turned to introduce her friend. "This is Leland Griffon. We work together in Los Angeles."

Maggie moved along to shake his hand. "I guess you didn't know Paul?"

"No. But I feel as though I do from all that I've heard from Fay."

Maggie noted that he said it in a perfectly straight manner, no sarcasm, no indication that he disliked the man his "friend" had left behind so many years ago.

"Will you be going on to the reception at the house?" Clare asked. The other bee members had followed Maggie and Victoria and were now greeting Fay and Leland.

"I'm afraid not. I don't think I'd be welcome there." Fay's droll voice told them all they needed to know.

"We heard there was an incident . . ."

Maggie couldn't believe Edie had brought that up, but to her surprise the dignified Fay did not turn away or dismiss it with a wave of her hand. She merely frowned.

"I'm sure the entire parish knows all about it. Shannon has never forgiven me for leaving. She doesn't understand how hard it can be losing a child. Especially when the marriage wasn't as strong as it should have been."

Maggie recalled Theresa's gossip that Paul's fellow workers thought Shannon's birth had been an attempt to save a floundering marriage.

Maggie thought Fay looked very sad, and her heart went out to the woman. How much did she know about the circumstances of Paul's death? she wondered.

"Will you be staying in the valley long?" Theresa asked.

"I planned on a week. I'll have to see," she said, then turned toward the next person in line, an elderly man who had worked with her husband many years ago.

The Quilting Bee women moved aside, waiting for the cars to line up for the procession to the cemetery. Their husbands excused themselves, not wanting to travel on to the graveside or the house afterward.

"Did you notice how they talked all through mass?" Louise asked. Even without names mentioned, everyone knew she referred to Shannon and Seth.

"Neither of them went up for communion either." Edie's voice indicated her disapproval. "No respect," she murmured.

"I think Seth came to offer his support in her time of grief," Clare suggested. "I think it's sweet."

"That would certainly be a fine thing," Victoria said.

If that's really what it is, Maggie thought. A thought echoed by Louise.

"Or it could be," Edie said, "that inheriting a house and whatever else Paul owned makes Shannon more appealing."

"Neither of them seems to be comforting Brad," Anna said, her voice reflecting her sadness. "And he's the only one who really seems upset at Paul's passing."

The others all agreed with her.

Edie scanned the crowd. Many people were already getting into their cars to leave. "Shall we go on to the graveyard and see what happens?"

Maggie turned to Michael. "Should we?"

"Definitely," Michael replied.

Maggie had seen the way he observed everyone in the church; his scrutiny had been unobtrusive, but thorough.

"There aren't many people here close to the daughter's age," Michael commented.

Maggie had noticed the same thing. "It's mostly people from St. Rose and from Gilligan's."

"And reporters," Edie added. She didn't seem as disturbed by this as the rest of them.

"It was nice of K.C. to come himself," Theresa said. "He's always been that kind of boss."

"Shannon went to school here in town," Clare said. "Isn't it funny that none of her old school friends came?"

"I guess she lost touch," Victoria said.

"It happens," Louise agreed.

"But she's been back here for two years," Clare persisted. "Seems like she would have picked up the acquaintance with some of them. She must have had some kind of life aside from Paul and Brad."

"Maybe that's what you should try to find out at the reception," Michael suggested.

The graveside ceremony was short and simple. Father Bob said a few prayers, sprinkled some holy water, then invited those present to leave flowers on the coffin. A basket of white carnations sat to one side.

Once again the women watched the family with interest. Young Brad was very upset, sobbing in a manner that made the bee women's hearts ache. He was too small to reach the top of the coffin to deposit his flower, and Father stepped in to lift him. Shannon held a tissue to her face as she placed a carnation on top of the casket, but it was hard to tell if she was crying or just hiding her expression. Seth Moody didn't seem upset, or even sad, Maggie thought. He still looked more bored than anything, as though he was marking time until he could leave. He dropped his carnation onto the casket in an offhanded manner, and headed directly to his car. Clare had told the others that she had heard people say his last name was indicative of his personality and that certainly seemed true. Maggie did notice that whenever he approached his grieving son, the boy shrunk back closer to his mother's side.

Fay walked solemnly past the casket, dropping her carnation with a momentary bow of her head, as though saying a prayer as she presented the flower.

The Quilting Bee members were among the first to pass by the coffin, leaving flowers, then stepped aside to watch until the lid was covered in green and white. As people began to leave Maggie looked around, wondering what had become of Michael — who startled her by popping up on her left flank.

"Michael, there you are. Will you be going to the Tipton home with us?"

"I'm afraid I have to get back to work, Ma," he answered. Then, lowering his voice, added, "Just note anything interesting that happens there and I'll check back with you, okay?"

Maggie saw a spark of excitement glow in Clare's eyes at Michael's casual statement. Thank goodness she was her old self, feeling the excitement at having a part in a police investigation, although a very minor one.

Before Maggie could say a word, Clare answered for all of them. "We will."

"Good. If you don't mind, I'll stop by the church in the morning and see what reactions you all have to the funeral and the luncheon." He turned toward Maggie. "I'll stop by your place in the morning and drive you over. It will look more natural, not that I think anyone is paying attention to what I do." Even as he offered the disclaimer, he glanced around the cemetery. "But it doesn't hurt to be careful and pay attention to detail. If you let me join you for breakfast, it will seem normal for me to drop you off at the church. You can ride home with Victoria."

So it was arranged.

Clare bubbled over with anticipation as they headed for their cars. "Maybe we'll be able to figure out who's responsible for all this," she said. "Aren't the killers supposed to attend the funeral?" With sudden seriousness, she glanced around her at the mourners getting into their cars.

"Only in the movies." Louise's dry voice cut through to her consciousness.

"Oh," Clare said, deflating somewhat. But

she quickly recovered. "But we shall see, right?"

Edie rolled her eyes, but followed her into the back seat of Louise's car.

CHAPTER 24

Shannon stood at the door of the Tipton house, the lean young man they'd seen beside her all day still standing at her side. She introduced him as her husband. "This is my husband, Seth. He's been working out of state," she added.

The phrase sounded so worn, Maggie assumed she'd repeated it to all of the people who had followed them home from the graveyard.

"Shannon and Seth." Clare was delighted. "Your names go together so well, don't they? It's like the two of you were made for each other."

Her wide smile seemed to startle Seth, who actually took a step back. Since they stood in a smallish foyer, he bumped into a long table, rattling a vase with a large floral arrangement. Maggie recalled seeing it at the altar earlier. Shannon must have brought it back to the house for the reception. She'd managed quite a lot of work, assuming she'd done it all on her own. The house looked neat and clean; and the table she could see in the kitchen was covered with dishes and bowls.

Since both Shannon and Seth seemed to be struck silent by Clare's effusiveness, Maggie stepped forward, offering her hand to Shannon. Paul's widow had been prominent at both the church and the graveyard, and Maggie thought it a shame she wasn't part of the reception line here. But she knew as well as Fay that she would have been persona non grata at her old home.

Pulling her thoughts back to the couple at the door, Maggie moved from Shannon to Seth. "Nice to meet you," she said, shaking Seth's hand. Limp, she thought.

"I'm sure Shannon and Brad are very happy to have you here during this difficult time," Victoria said, also offering her hand to Seth.

Seth appeared surprised at Victoria's kind greeting and mumbled something that none of them could quite make out. The man was obviously lacking in people skills. Something he had in common with his late father-in-law? Maggie wondered.

"Will you be returning to your job out of state?" Theresa asked, as she took her place before Seth. Maggie knew she really wanted to ask where exactly he had been working, but managed to contain her curiosity. They were all curious about where he had been and exactly when he arrived in Scottsdale.

"Will you and Brad be going with him now?" Clare asked, turning back to Shannon.

Seth looked a little shell-shocked at the barrage of questions. And not at all happy to be at the receiving end of them. Maggie also noted a flash of something in Shannon's eyes — she wasn't sure exactly what. Anger? Fear? Maggie could understand if she thought they were being too nosy, and that could make her angry. But why would she be frightened? Was Seth an abusive husband? Was she afraid of him? From what Clare had heard during her walks with Brad, Seth had a temper, but the child hadn't said anything to her about being hit. Of course abuse could take different forms, not all of them physical.

"I guess it was frightening being alone here in the house after the accident," Maggie suggested, watching carefully for Shannon's reaction.

Shannon seemed relieved, agreeing quickly that she was glad to have Seth there. "It *was* scary being here alone with Brad and those explosions still going on. The next time it could have been one of us injured or killed. And now the police are saying someone did it on purpose . . ."

Seth let out something between a grunt and a snarl. "Stupid police. How can they say it wasn't an accident? That kid was looking for a big score for his dad to fix up but he got more than he bargained for. And now the stupid police are trying to make out it wasn't him."

Seeing the startled looks on the faces of the women facing him, Seth shut up.

"Maggie's son was the police officer injured by one of the bombs," Victoria said quietly.

Seth had the grace to look embarrassed. Shannon blanched, but managed to squeak out a "sorry." Maggie wouldn't have been surprised if she'd run to the bathroom with nausea, but she stood where she was, grasping Seth's arm like it was a lifeline. Very interesting, Maggie thought.

"So were you already here before Paul died?" Maggie asked Seth. He certainly made it sound like he'd been around when it happened.

Seth's eyes moved rapidly from side to side, as though looking for a place he could escape these crazy old women. Maggie wanted to laugh at the expression on his face.

"Seth came when he heard about Daddy," Shannon said, her tone leaving no room for more questions about that particular topic. Her other hand joined her first around his arm and she hugged it to her. "He knew we'd need him here," she added.

"You don't think Paul's death was anything more than an accident then?" Maggie inquired. Seth certainly felt that way despite the police report. But what about Shannon?

"The police say it's suspicious," Shannon said. She shrugged her shoulders. "Whatever that means. I guess we have to believe them. But I don't understand how it could be. Who would have killed him? Daddy didn't have a lot of friends, but most people liked him well enough. You saw all the people at the church." She stared boldly at her, as though challenging Maggie to contradict her.

Maggie nodded, not wanting to tell Paul's daughter that the recently announced verdict of a suspicious death was bound to bring out a large audience, whether they had known Paul or not. Church members, neighbors, others who might know him in passing — all would be curious after hearing he might have been murdered.

"You told me he didn't get on with the neighbors," Seth mumbled.

All the bee women turned toward Shannon after hearing this juicy tidbit.

Shannon shot an irritated look toward her husband before offering an answer.

"He complained to the Riveras sometimes about noise. They have kids and you know how loud they like to play their music. And the guy on the other side is new, and he had some kind of complaint about the property line. But they're supposed to handle all that stuff before the sale goes through, so I don't know why he was all upset."

"What kind of complaint about the property line?" Edie asked. This was the kind of thing she found interesting. She even admitted to watching the television judge shows to listen to the remarkable — her word — cases handled on air.

"I don't really know," Shannon hedged. "Something about the fence being on his property. But it's been there since before I was born. I know that's the same fence. So I don't see how he can claim it's wrong."

"Hmm," was all Edie said, but Maggie could almost see the gears turning in her brain. She was sure they would hear more about this in the bee room the next day.

"You went to school here in town, didn't you?" Maggie asked. "Have you lost touch with all of your classmates? There weren't any young people at the church."

Shannon frowned and Maggie knew she wanted to tell her it was none of her business. "High school wasn't the happiest time for me," she finally said. "Besides, they're probably all at work."

After that answer, Maggie wondered if she'd had any friends in high school, but knew it would be rude to ask.

"I'd love to say hello to Brad," Clare said, as the others finally moved toward the gathering around the food-laden table.

Clare stood on tiptoe, trying to see into the other rooms, looking for the small boy. "Where is he?"

"He's probably outside with that dog," Seth replied.

Maggie cringed at the term "that dog" and knew that Clare must want to slap him.

"Should they be outside in this heat?" Victoria, who had already stepped past them, turned back, concern lacing her voice. It was past noon and the outside temperature was well over one hundred.

"He'll be in the shade on the patio and he's used to it," Shannon answered. "He's a real desert rat, Brad is. He loves to play outside whatever the weather. He and Daddy spent a lot of time outdoors. You might not know it, but Daddy didn't care for air conditioning. That's why he was sleeping outside. He had insomnia and he said it helped him sleep if he was out under the stars."

"Did Brad sleep outside sometimes too?" Maggie was glad Louise asked, because she was also curious about that.

"Now and then," Shannon responded. "But he does spend a lot of time in the yard, even more since Daddy died. He misses him."

The tinge of distress in her voice at this last sentence struck Maggie as the most motherly thing Shannon had said since their arrival. Seth, however, showed no signs of fatherly concern.

"I told him to keep that dog away from the guests," Seth said.

Clare frowned. Maggie knew she did not like the way Seth kept referring to "that dog." Maggie didn't much care for his tone either. But they couldn't create a scene at Paul's funeral reception.

"Max would never hurt anyone," Clare said. "I want to say hello to him too. He and I are old friends — he and I and my dog, Samson," she added.

269

Shannon was still hanging on to Seth's arm. Maybe she needed his support after losing her father, but Maggie thought it was more a case of "don't you dare leave me alone with these people." He definitely gave the impression of someone who wanted to flee to another room.

Shannon looked up at her husband. "Mrs. Patterson is the one who takes Brad and Max on walks."

Maggie almost laughed at the expression on Seth's face. It said "so you're the old biddy" much more clearly than "how nice of you to help out."

"Do the police have any idea who might have caused the damage that injured Paul?" Louise asked.

"If they do, they haven't shared it with us." Shannon looked at her husband.

"If you ask me," Seth said, "they should keep looking at those boys next door and his friends. That includes that idiot kid trying to drum up business for his father the handyman."

"Really?" Louise said. She didn't have to feign her surprise.

"Oh, yeah. There are two teenage boys next door, real punk kids. Hang around with a bunch of others just like them." Seth put his hand in his pocket, then abruptly pulled

270

it out. "That other kid is probably one of them."

Louise studied his fidgety fingers with their nicotine-stained tips and realized he was anxious for a cigarette. Nice of him not to pull one out inside. She looked over at Maggie, wondering if she had noticed.

"They were playing with firecrackers over there on the Fourth," Shannon said. "Dad and I thought of them right away when the explosions started. The first one was right here, in our alley, you know. Daddy saw them."

"Did you call the police?" Louise asked.

"As if they listen to what we have to say," Seth said.

Maggie thought he looked like a punk kid himself, with that sour expression on his face, though he was a bit old for the designation. What a disagreeable man. Paul may have preferred his own company, but he knew how to interact with people in ways that did not appear rude. Other people liked him. Maggie found it hard to believe Seth had many friends, if any.

"I still can't believe they got away with killing Paul," he continued. "Got a lawyer, I heard, and confessed to some minor thing. It's just a trick to avoid a manslaughter or murder charge."

Maggie raised her eyebrows. No wonder she hadn't seen Raquel or any of her family at the funeral. This looked like an instance where good fences did *not* make good neighbors. Unless the man was merely a bigot and didn't like having Hispanic neighbors. That would explain his attitude toward the Rivera boys whom Maggie had found polite and friendly.

He continued with his rant, though none of the bee women were interested. "None of the neighbors around here are any good."

To Maggie's surprise, a loud voice broke in — from right behind her.

"I agree. So, now that the old man is gone, maybe you'll listen to some sense. That fence is way over on my property — you know it as well as I do. Just because the old guy wouldn't admit it is no reason for the courts to say it's okay."

Shannon glared at him. "Daddy took you to court and he won. You can't come back now and try to start this up again."

"Look, whoever built that fence back in the dark ages just didn't know how to survey and that's not my fault. I don't know why the previous owner didn't complain, but the property is mine now, and I had it surveyed. If you don't get that fence moved in the next six weeks, I'm just going to take it down myself."

"You can't do that," Seth said, stepping into the other man's space, trying to intimidate him, Maggie thought. But the other man wasn't going to allow that. In fact, he stepped forward too, so that their chests almost touched. He was some five inches taller than Seth, and Maggie wasn't surprised when Seth broke the staring match by looking down. Then he stepped back.

"If you destroy any of my property, I'll call the cops," Shannon warned. "The court ruled that it's ours by eminent domain. It's been over twenty years and no one ever complained before. For God's sake, it's only six damn inches."

"It's *my* six damn inches," he declared, stomping from the house.

The funeral guests in the vicinity stared after him, all slightly shell-shocked from seeing such an outburst at a funeral reception.

"Who was that?" Clare asked.

Maggie was glad to see her face retained a sober demeanor because Maggie herself knew Clare was delighted that she hadn't proceeded outside to find Brad. Clare was sure to have some theories about the rude neighbor and Paul's "suspicious" death.

"Seems to be a new neighbor," Edie said,

looking to Shannon and Seth for comment.

"He bought the house next door." Shannon waved toward the east side of the house. "Then he started in on Daddy about the fence between the houses. Claims it's encroaching. But it's been there forever and no one ever challenged it. And there's been at least one other owner since the fence was built. I remember it selling when I was in high school. The new neighbors had a stuck up daughter who called me names."

Wow, Maggie thought. What did the kids call it — TMI, too much information. But perhaps it helped explain those rebellious high school years they'd heard about. And the lack of high school friends.

"And Paul took this new neighbor to court over the fence placement?" Louise asked.

"It was that guy who took it to court," Shannon almost shouted. Her face was red and her eyes flashed with anger. "But Daddy went, and he won too. The judge said it's been that way for so long, it can be considered part of this property. Eminent domain, it's called. It's only a measly six inches," she added.

Maggie wondered how she would feel if the problem had been the reverse. She could definitely imagine Shannon arguing vehemently on the other side if that was the position in her favor. The woman appeared to have anger management issues.

Theresa turned to Shannon. "I knew your father from Gilligan's, you know. I'm retired now, but I worked there for twenty years."

"Yeah," Shannon said. "I thought you seemed familiar. It's been a long time since I worked there, but I remember you. You were always nice to me."

"Why, thank you," Theresa said. "It was nice of K.C. to attend the services. Is he here?"

"No. He talked to me at the graveyard," Shannon replied. "He said he had to get back to the office."

"That's too bad," Theresa said. "I would have enjoyed talking to him. I'll have to see if there's anyone else here from Gilligan's."

"There's a few." Then Shannon surprised them all by continuing. "I think Daddy regretted retiring when he did. He liked going in, liked working, and seeing the other workers there."

"Paul wasn't a people person," Theresa said, "but we sure missed him after he left. He did wonderful work. I always knew he'd find the problem when I took my car in."

Shannon mumbled something appropriate and Seth frowned. It was clear that he hadn't much liked his father-in-law, despite his anger at the police about the investigation into his death.

"He tried hard to be a good father," Shannon finally said. She let go of Seth's arm and he shook it as if trying to eliminate the feel of her heavy grasp. Perhaps she'd impeded his circulation, Maggie thought.

"He was a wonderful grandfather," Clare added. "I often saw him with Brad and Max."

"Yeah," Shannon agreed. "The three of them made quite the trio."

Somehow, Maggie didn't think Shannon quite approved of the trio, however. Perhaps because she wasn't a part of the loving band. She certainly ran hot and cold, storming about the neighbor one minute then being so nice to Theresa the next.

Seth shook his arm once more, shrugged, then ambled into the kitchen mumbling something about getting a drink.

Shannon seemed to remember that she was the hostess and told them to help themselves to some food. "The drinks are on the kitchen counter," she added.

Maggie thought she looked relieved when they all moved toward the food-laden table in the kitchen. Maggie was amazed that the strange young woman had managed such a display. There was a nice spread of cold cuts and salads on the dining room table — just right for a hot summer day. The platters, which did not appear to be store-bought, had been beautifully arranged and garnished with olives, peppers and orange twists. There were several casseroles, though Maggie thought those may have been dropped off earlier as people learned of Paul's death. In fact, she recognized Clare's chicken and rice casserole. So Shannon wasn't quite as clueless as she tried to make out. She had had sense enough to hold on to donations for the funeral reception, plus she'd done a good job with the things she assembled herself. The dessert section included an interesting assortment of cupcakes, cookies, cakes and pies. Maggie wondered how much of those had been donated by neighbors as well.

"I'm going out to see Brad and Max first," Clare announced. She gestured toward the family room adjoining the kitchen. Maggie could see the sliding glass doors there that led into the backyard.

Maggie quickly offered to accompany her. "I'd like to see the backyard," she told Victoria, her soft voice carrying only to those immediately beside her.

"Good idea," Victoria responded.

Edie excused herself to find the restroom,

and Louise, Anna and Theresa continued on toward the food and the other guests.

Chapter 25

As soon as they passed through the sliding glass doors, Clare rushed over to Brad and gave him a hug. Max leaped into the air in greeting, his tail waving in a blur of love. As soon as Clare had greeted him with a pat and an ear rub, he turned his attention to Maggie. Standing before her, he propelled his little body upward, his tongue lolling, tail wagging.

"He likes you." Brad laughed at the little dog's antics. "He wants to say hi."

"Watch that tongue," Clare warned Maggie. "If you let him get close, he'll have your face washed before you can say boo."

"Yes," Brad agreed. "He loves to lick faces. That's how dogs kiss, you know."

"Yes, I do know," Maggie replied.

"This is Mrs. Browne, Brad." Clare gestured toward Maggie as she made the introduction. Maggie held Max, allowing him to greet her with several swipes to her chin. "She's one of my best friends," Clare told Brad.

Like a proper little gentleman, Brad held out his hand as he approached Maggie. They shook while he said "nice to meet you" and Maggie lowered Max to the ground.

"It's nice to meet you too," Maggie replied. "And Max, too, of course. I'm very sorry about your grandfather," she told him.

Brad hung his head. "I miss him. It's nice to have Max. We both loved Papa."

Maggie picked up the little dog again to give him a good head rub. "I just got a small dog of my own," she told Brad.

Brad wanted to hear all about her new pup, and he managed to extract a promise that she would bring Rosy over one day to walk with Max and Samson.

Once they'd talked, Maggie turned her attention to the yard. It was a nice size, not too large. About half the space was taken up by the swimming pool, not unusual in Scottsdale. As in so many of the older homes, the pool had been built directly behind the patio. A fence between the pool and the patio appeared to be a newer addition. Wrought iron railings filled the spaces between the patio's support columns, one of them fitted with a locked gate. Maggie assumed Paul had added the gate when Shannon arrived with her three-year-old. Access to the small lawn was through the final two columns, where the wrought iron fence bent at an acute angle to follow the shape of the pool.

The infamous ramada was at the far side of the pool, the stack of heavy wooden slats looking like a giant's set of toppled blocks. It lay on a concrete pad about twelve feet long by eight wide with a brick barbecue set up along the side fence. Behind that was the damaged wooden fence. It was inexpertly propped up with a few of the damaged slats — probably to keep Max from escaping the yard. Maggie could see the dried-out branches of a palo verde tree reaching above it. The tree must have been very large for the branches to extend so high. The EMTs must have pushed it back into the alley in order to reach Paul that fateful morning, just as they'd thrust aside the wooden beams of the ramada. At that time, there was no reason to believe that it was anything other than an accident. Maggie thought it odd that the side fences were both block, while the rear fence was made of wooden slats. Probably another aspect of Paul's stinting, Maggie thought. And it looked like it might have killed him. A block fence would never have buckled so easily.

Brad noticed Maggie's focus and came to stand beside her. "That's where I found Papa," he told her. "See, his chair is still there."

He pointed, but the motion was unnecessary. A very nice wooden lounge chair with fabric cushions in an attractive brown and gold stripe stood alone in a cleared spot to the right of the debris.

"Papa got a chair for me too, but Mommy didn't like me to sleep outside."

Just visible beneath the heavy wooden slats, they could see another chair. Of course they couldn't know how it all looked before the rescuers arrived, but Maggie thought it lucky indeed that Brad had not been lying in it.

Maggie gestured toward the side fence. "That's the east side, isn't it?" she asked Clare.

"Yes, it is." Clare looked at it, then the recent argument with the neighbor seemed to register. "Ohhh," she said, giving Maggie a significant nod.

"There's an alley back there, isn't there?" Maggie asked Brad, pointing toward the rear of the property. The wooden fence along the back was interrupted by a wide gate just a few feet from the damaged area.

And of course there was the damaged section behind the pool.

"Yes. That's where Papa said he heard the first fireworks go off. Over there," Brad added, pointing toward the area where the lawn met the back fence.

"So the Riveras must live on that side," Maggie told Clare, pointing toward the side fence farthest from the pool. She noted that the gate was closer to the east side of the fence. Not that she knew if that was significant or not. This whole thing with the explosions and Paul's death was the most complicated mess they'd ever dealt with.

Back inside the house, Theresa spent time talking to old friends from Gilligan's, who all remembered Paul fondly. They exchanged pleasant memories of time spent with him and caught up on one another's lives as well.

Meanwhile, Edie made her way to the bathroom, carefully checking all the rooms she could on her way. She didn't mind calling herself a nosy woman. She was curious about a lot of things, and the best way to appease that curiosity was to pay attention. It was often the little details that told you the most.

Like that bottle Seth was hiding behind a

detergent box in the cupboard, Edie thought, peeking quietly into the laundry room. He didn't know she was there until he turned. He jumped, causing the liquid in his glass to slosh dangerously close to the upper edge. He frowned at her.

"What are you doing in here?" His tone was less than polite.

Still, Edie thought he did a good job of controlling himself. She was sure he wanted to yell at her, perhaps call her a nosy old biddy.

She stood tall, facing him squarely. "I'm looking for the bathroom," she declared. "We old ladies need the facilities more than you young people," she added for good measure.

"Oh."

Edie could see that she'd caught him unaware for a second time. Perhaps those television commercials for adult diapers had him thinking anyone with white hair might be in danger of creating a bad situation. In any event he mumbled something that sounded like "down the hall, second door," took a long swallow of his doctored tea and left the room.

Edie smiled. She opened a closet door to peek inside — just the linen closet — then made her way to the bathroom. She was anxious to peek into the medicine chest. You could learn a lot about someone from peeking into their medicine cabinet.

CHAPTER 26

Michael appeared at Maggie's door early on Tuesday morning. She ushered him into the kitchen, finding that she enjoyed having someone to cook breakfast for. She didn't bother with much when it was just herself, but she'd gone full-out this morning. And it smelled great.

Rosy following tight on her heels, Maggie placed a plate of scrambled eggs, bacon, sausage and breakfast potatoes in front of Michael, then returned to the counter for the bowl of fruit and basket of warm muffins. She hadn't made the cinnamon-apple muffins in a long time, but she recalled Michael liking them. And what he didn't eat she could take to the church for the Senior Guild's break room. If there were any left, that is.

As she turned with both hands full, she almost tripped over Rosy. Maggie sighed. "It's been a long time since I've had an animal in the house. It's going to take some getting used to," she admitted.

"Aw, you're an old hand at it," Michael told her. "Just look at how you didn't fall or drop anything just now when she got in front of you."

Maggie sank into her chair, pulling the little dog onto her lap. "She is a sweet little thing," she said. Then laughed as Rosy took advantage of her new position to steal a mouthful of scrambled eggs from Maggie's plate. Michael grinned at the two of them as Maggie scolded the pup.

When she finally sat down with her refilled plate before her, and Rosy safely on the floor, Maggie glanced at Michael. He was already half done with his meal.

"This seems a rather elaborate subterfuge just to come in and talk to the Quilting Bee. Do you really think anyone would notice if you just stopped by the church?"

Michael shrugged. "Probably not. But this whole thing is so convoluted, there's no use taking any chances. All kinds of people are involved, you know. ATF, FBI, Homeland Security, police from Scottsdale, Phoenix and Glendale. Maybe Tempe and Mesa. Even the sheriff's office. It just keeps getting bigger. And people from the church have been involved right from the start."

Maggie stared, stunned at how the whole thing had grown. Exploded, you might say, she thought, groaning inwardly at her own pun.

"And it all started with some young boys setting off firecrackers." She sighed, shaking her head. "Parishioners." Amazing. And now it was valleywide. In some ways the instant communication available these days was not for the best. The copycats were sure to be getting their information from media sources and the Internet.

"It does seem to have begun when the Rivera boys and their friends set off their firecrackers," he admitted. "It's the first explosion anyone reported. Now, of course, any little noise is being called in. The nine-one-one operators are fielding hundreds of calls every night. Because of all the media attention, every little thing gets reported. A lot of it is a waste of time. Dogs or coyotes getting into trash cans, car doors slamming, people just plain dropping things that make noise. Those calls are tying up resources that could be out doing real investigating."

"Are all the new reports false alarms?"

"Unfortunately, no." Michael sighed. He'd finished his eggs and reached for the basket of muffins. He sniffed deeply as he parted the napkin covering them and the scent of

288

the warm muffins hit his nostrils. "Mmm, that smells good." He helped himself to several, throwing a sheepish glance toward his mother. "They're small," he said.

"Yes they are." Maggie dropped her head to hide her smile, taking a forkful of eggs to make the motion appear natural. When she'd finished chewing, she took a closer look at her son. "You seem more like yourself today," Maggie told her son as she offered him more muffins. The ones he'd taken a moment ago were already gone. "I guess you're out and about again."

Michael grinned. "Saw the doctor yesterday, so I'm expecting the all clear from the captain today. I can change into my uniform later. It seemed friendlier to wear ordinary clothes. I don't want to stand out or scare anyone."

Maggie watched Michael pop another of the muffins into his mouth. She really had made them too small. "Seth Moody said something interesting yesterday. He called the police stupid, said of course it was the kid drumming up business for his father who had killed Paul. He figures Paul's death scared Bert, and that's why he turned himself in and confessed to the lesser charges. To avoid a murder charge, he said."

"Paul didn't die as a result of the explosion and the falling tree or the roof. I already told you he was dead when the tree and the roof fell. And it was announced some time ago to both the public and the media that his death was suspicious."

Maggie shrugged. "Seth isn't the brightest bulb in the chandelier. Let's hope he's the only one who feels that way. I do think those young boys are basically good kids, even Bert." She toyed with her fork for a moment. "Do you really have no idea what actually killed Paul? Could it have been a heart attack or a stroke?"

"Nothing so simple. They're waiting on some lab tests; that's why it's so uncertain." Michael ate the last muffin on his plate and followed it up with a long drink of coffee. "That isn't public knowledge," he warned. "So don't go spreading it around the Quilting Bee. I know how you women talk. We don't want whoever killed Paul to get wind that we're on to him."

Maggie nodded before taking a sip of her own coffee, mulling over the ramifications of what Michael told her. "It does put a whole new light on things, doesn't it?"

Michael nodded. "This murder case is really the only part of it that we're working on our own. The feds have co-opted the rest of it, claiming terrorism and various other things."

Maggie sighed. "So Edie was right after all." She stood, picking up the empty plates and setting her coffee mug on top of them. "We may never hear the end of it."

"Domestic terrorism is what they're calling it," he clarified. "I'm sure it was checked, but they don't think there's an Al Qaeda cell here in town. Isn't that what Edie was talking about?"

Small comfort, Maggie thought. Edie would figure terrorism was terrorism and quickly forget that she suspected some ex-pat Middle Easterners.

When they arrived at the church parking lot, Michael hurried around to open the door for his mother. "Don't mention how Paul died, okay? That was just between us."

"You didn't really tell me how he died," Maggie reminded him, though she did nod her agreement to keep the information private. "You only told me *when* he died — more or less."

"Smart aleck," Michael murmured. But he was grinning as he said it.

The others were already at work in the bee room, anxiously awaiting their arrival. Maggie was happy to see Clare smiling and excited — the Clare they all knew and loved. She seemed to be over the melancholia that had afflicted her in those first days after the explosions and Paul's death.

"This is so exciting," Clare said, as soon as everyone had greeted Michael. "We have some *leads* for you." She pronounced the word "leads" carefully, proudly, and with a slight emphasis.

Michael looked over at her, one brow cocked, the side of his mouth twitching. "Have you now?"

Maggie tried hard not to laugh as she seated herself at an open section of the quilt frame.

"Oh, yes," Clare said. "We heard some very interesting things, didn't we?" She glanced around at her friends.

Michael pulled a chair up to the quilt frame so he could converse easily with the women — and so that they wouldn't have to keep craning their necks to look up at him.

"Such as . . ." he said.

"Well," Clare began. "The whole family is rather strange, don't you think?"

"Strange how?"

"We've been wondering if Shannon might be bipolar," Louise said. "The house looked really good, no dust, everything neat. The food table was very nicely done. And she apparently did it all herself. She certainly never asked the church bereavement group to help, and I know someone called and offered. And this is a young woman who doesn't seem to do anything."

Clare picked up the dialogue. "Brad says she works like crazy for days, then she crashes. Not that he used that word, but he said afterward she's tired and she sleeps a lot."

"What about her husband?" Michael glanced down at his notebook. "Seth Moody."

"Shannon and Seth . . ." Edie shook her head as she repeated the names, obviously thinking them too-too cute. "Can you believe those names? It's like twins in a bad novel."

"I think they're cute," Clare offered.

Edie clucked her disgust. "You would. I'm surprised she didn't name her son Shawn or Sheldon to keep the alliteration going."

"Didn't I tell you?" Clare said. "She named him after her favorite actor, Brad Pitt. Paul told me."

Edie snorted.

"She was young," Louise said with a shrug.

Edie shook her head again.

Michael cleared his throat, drawing the attention of all the quilters. "So . . . your impressions?"

"I don't like either of them," Edie intoned. "Especially that young man. Moody. Perfect name for him. Thoroughly disagreeable. Do you know, when I looked into the laundry room, I found him hiding a whiskey bottle in a cupboard. I'm sure he'd added some to his tea." She ended her comment with a click of her tongue. "Not at all respectful, hiding in a back room getting drunk."

"Perhaps he was just upset," Anna suggested, "losing his father-in-law so suddenly and all."

"I doubt it," Clare said. "I don't think he liked his father-in-law much. He doesn't even seem to care for his own son very much," she added. "And he kept calling Max 'that dog'!" she finished, a picture of indignation at Seth's treatment of Brad and Max.

"Maggie and I talked about them on the way home from the reception," Victoria said. "Shannon is making the right moves, but something about her just doesn't seem right. Seth doesn't even pretend. I agree, I don't think he liked his father-in-law at all. I'm not sure Shannon liked him either, poor man. Her demeanor just doesn't speak of a

294

loving daughter who has just lost her father."

"Well, not getting on with his father-in-law might explain why Seth was working out of state," Louise said.

The others all agreed.

"Paul didn't like him either," Clare said. "In fact, according to Paul, Seth walked out on Shannon. Left her high and dry, he used to say, and that's why she moved back in with him." Clare sighed. "I'm afraid that poor little Brad and Max are the only ones really missing Paul."

"And you are," Victoria offered gently. Clare looked at her in silent thanks.

"What about his wife?" Michael asked.

"Well, we don't think they ever divorced, even though she's been gone for years and years," Clare began. "She was there at the church and at the graveyard, and dressed all in black. She looked sad, and I think I even saw a few tears. It looked real too, didn't you think?" She looked around at the other women, several of whom nodded. "But she wasn't at the house afterward. Only Shannon and Seth were there."

"We asked her about that, remember?" Maggie said. "She didn't think she'd be welcome." Maggie turned to Michael. "We heard from the neighbors that there was a scene earlier in the week when she turned up at the house. I'm sure she didn't want to cause a scene after the funeral."

"There was a scene before?" Michael asked.

"Didn't you hear about it?" Theresa asked. "Raquel said the neighbor across the street called the police."

"I'm not up on every event that happens concerning the police in Scottsdale," Michael replied. Maggie was surprised he could do it with a straight face. She smiled for him, pleased at his restraint.

Maggie, with a little help from Clare, quickly brought him up to date on the information they'd received from Raquel.

"He had a gun?" Michael asked.

"That's what she said," Maggie replied. "Though later the neighbor said she couldn't be absolutely sure, but she thought she saw him waving a gun around. You might have to check with Fay."

"Seth does have a gun," Edie said, to everyone's surprise. "Or perhaps Shannon has one, but there is a gun in that house."

"And you know this because . . . ?" Michael asked.

"I asked to use the restroom while I was there. It was when Maggie and Clare had gone outside to see Brad." Edie looked at the two of them. "You can learn a lot about a person from taking a look around the house, and especially the bathroom."

"You looked in the medicine chest, didn't you?" Louise asked.

"Edie!" Anna looked shocked at her boldness.

"Honestly," Edie replied. "Lots of people do it, just out of curiosity. At least I had a good reason for snooping."

"So what did you find?" Clare asked, obviously curious herself.

"It was full of stuff — mostly over-the-counter pain, cold and allergy meds. Even more under the sink. That seems a little suspicious in itself, don't you think? I mean, they only let you buy two or three packages at a time no matter how bad your allergies are."

Michael heard this last with interest. "Meth addicts can make small doses for themselves these days. And your descriptions of Shannon's behavior could indicate meth use."

"You're right," Louise said. "I'm surprised I didn't consider that."

"Like what?" Theresa asked.

"Excited behavior, irritability, anxiety," Michael stated. "Also the same kind of manic behavior you described as bipolar."

"Oh, my," Clare said. "And with a little

boy to care for." She sighed. "It was bad enough thinking she was bipolar. It's even worse if she's a drug addict."

"I'm sure she's a liar too," Edie decided. "There were all kinds of allergy and cold meds, even children's versions. But there were birth control pills in the medicine cabinet, and why would she need those when her husband has been working out of state for the past two years?"

"Perhaps she just got them?" Victoria suggested.

"Oh, no," Edie said. "I checked the date. The prescription was old, almost ready to expire."

"It doesn't mean anything," Maggie said. "Lots of young women take them just in case they meet someone. And many women take them to reduce cramping."

Edie didn't look happy at Maggie's defense of Shannon. "There were also prescription bottles of . . ." Edie took out a piece of paper where she'd jotted down the drug names. "Alprazolam, zolpidem, and hydrocodone. I looked them up online last night. The first is for anxiety and the second a sleep aid. The last is a pain killer, of course. They're all the generic versions."

"Lots of people take the first two," Louise said. "To help them sleep."

"The hydrocodone prescription was in Paul's name," Edie said, triumph in her voice. "So what was it doing in Shannon's bathroom?"

"Good question," Michael murmured.

"Paul didn't take drugs of any kind," Theresa objected. "He was very vocal about it."

"I recognized the name of the doctor," Edie supplied. "It's an endodontist I've used. He must have had a root canal, and gotten the prescription as a matter of course. It doesn't mean he took any of the pills."

"Are you sure it was Shannon's bathroom?" Maggie asked. "Maybe it was Paul's and she's just moved into it."

"That wouldn't surprise me," Edie mumbled.

"Hydrocodone is a very popular drug," Michael said. "If either Shannon or Seth is into drugs, I'm sure they would have grabbed that right away. Maybe even if they aren't into drugs."

"I hear a lot of teens steal it from their parents," Edie added. Michael nodded.

"She might have needed help sleeping after her father was killed," Victoria suggested. "That could explain the first two."

"It had to be traumatic losing him that way," Theresa agreed.

"Especially if she killed him," Edie said. "Or knows who did."

A moment of shocked silence was followed by Michael's calm question.

"What about the gun?"

"Of course. I was distracted," Edie said, glaring at the others. "The gun was hidden in the laundry room cupboard." Edie finished a line of stitches and calmly cut her thread and reached for the spool. "Since I'd seen Seth put a bottle of whiskey behind the detergent box, once I finished in the bathroom I thought I'd check the laundry room. See if he'd hidden anything else in there."

"And you found a gun!" Clare couldn't hide her excitement.

"I don't know why you're so excited," Edie snapped. "It's not as if anyone has been shot."

"It just proves that the neighbor was correct," Theresa said.

"It does show how unstable Seth is," Louise said.

"And I think he was lying about not being in town when Paul died," Clare said.

"Why is that?" Michael asked.

Clare shook her head. "It was an impression, something about the way he talked about it."

Maggie nodded. "I know what she means. I had the same feeling. It was the way he spoke about the explosions, the early ones. It certainly sounded like he'd been around. And the way he looked at me when I asked if he was already here then. Venomous!"

Louise nodded. "When Maggie suggested he was already in town when Paul died his eyes just went all over the place — an obvious tell that he was lying. And it was Shannon that jumped in and said he came when he heard about her dad."

"She calls Paul Daddy," Clare said. "Isn't that sweet?"

Edie snorted again. "Sweet? More like childish. That girl needs to grow up."

Louise nodded. "She does strike me as very immature for a young single mother."

"Tell Michael about the neighbor causing a scene," Theresa said.

"Yes, tell Michael about that," he seconded.

Taking turns, they told him all about the rude neighbor barging in, and recounted Shannon's comments as well.

"Have you seen the backyard at the Tipton's, Michael?" Maggie asked.

"Only from over the back fence," he admitted.

"We noticed that the damaged section of

fence is right near the block wall that the neighbor is complaining about," Clare informed him.

Maggie glanced at the clock, then stood. "I think we should all take a break now. And, Michael, you should come to the break room with us. There's a good chance someone will know about the incident with the neighbor. A lot of the people in that area belong to St. Rose. And lots of them have lived in their homes for years, just like Paul."

"Good idea," Clare said, also rising.

The rest of the quilters followed them out of the room.

CHAPTER 27

Maggie had timed it perfectly. The break room was crowded with members of the Senior Guild. The room was kept stocked with coffee, tea and bottled water. Bakers among the Senior Guild provided fresh baked goods most mornings. Maggie could see Michael perk up at the sight of the fresh apple turnovers and cranberry-orange scones on the snack table. She'd have to remember to tell Michael that the apple turnovers were brought in every week by one of the *men*. Although Michael claimed a lack of time for his inability to cook, she suspected he didn't find it a manly enough hobby. But Stan was a big man, a former Marine and retired Chicago cop, and perhaps he could inspire Michael to try something simpler than his amazing turnovers.

It was ten-thirty, mid-morning for the groups working on craft items for the bazaar. Most of the seniors present knew

Michael and greeted him warmly. There was a lot of shaking of hands, and many back slaps from the men. Hugs from the women. Everyone claimed to be happy to see him looking so well after his recent ordeal.

"We were worried about you, you know," said a tall, reedy woman with an unlikely shade of red hair.

Her companion nodded. "We prayed, and I lit a candle," she said.

"So how are you?" one of the men asked. "Have you caught the guys who got you with that bomb yet?"

"Afraid not," Michael answered, stirring some sugar into his coffee. "But we're working on it."

"So are the ATF and the FBI and even Homeland Security," added Clare.

There were a few laughs, and comments of "That should do it" and "Great."

"It wasn't the kids who turned themselves in?"

"No." Michael sighed. "Their stories check out. They used different types of explosive material, so we know the bomb I found wasn't part of their activity. Neither were the bombs at the substation or the high school."

"How many different groups are involved in this?" A petite woman with frizzy gray hair shuddered after posing the question, which came out as more of a whine than a statement.

"There are likely quite a few, especially now that the explosions have spread across the valley."

"I'm doing my part," claimed a wiry, balding man. "I check the perimeter of my property every night before we go to bed. Make sure there's nothing suspicious out there. In fact, I called nine-one-one the other night. There was a large can upturned against my fence, back in the alley. With all that's been going on I thought I shouldn't touch it."

"Very wise," Michael agreed. "Cliché that it is, it's much better to be safe than sorry."

"What was it?" someone asked. "Was it a bomb?"

The first man shook his head. "Turned out it was nothing. Just an empty can. But they told me I did the right thing to call. There was no way to know what might be under that can, and a bomb might have blown off my fingers or my hand. Turned out it was nothing but an upended can." He frowned. "Gave me a scare, I can tell you. Couldn't help thinking about what happened to Michael here. Not to mention Deacon Adam."

There was a moment of silence as several women crossed themselves in a silent prayer for Deacon Adam. Which gave Maggie the perfect moment to bring up the subject of Paul Tipton's death. "Wasn't Paul's funeral nice? I thought the choir did such a good job."

It was the correct thing to say. Betty, who was in the choir, preened. As others also praised the music, her cheeks turned pink.

"It was a nice service," one of the men said. "Good guy, Paul. Not real sociable, but a great mechanic. Good neighbor too."

"Oh." Maggie couldn't believe how well that had gone — directly to the topic they all wanted to discuss. "Are you one of Paul's neighbors?"

"Yeah. I live one house down."

"Next to the Riveras?" Victoria inquired.

"No, on the other side. The Patricks lived in the house in between us for years, but they had to sell last year. He had a heart attack and she has Alzheimer's. The kids found a care home for her and sold the house." He shook his head. "A lot of the old neighborhood is passing on."

"Or losing their homes in the economic crash," someone added.

There were several solemn nods.

"Were you there when that crazy guy was

yelling at Paul's daughter?" someone asked.

Maggie was delighted with the way the conversation was going. No one would suspect the Quilting Bee of poking their noses into Shannon's affairs with the way the group was directing the discussion. Not that Shannon had any friends at the church who might want to keep her informed, Maggie thought. Rather the opposite, she suspected.

The first speaker sighed. "Yeah. That crazy guy bought the house between us — where the Patricks lived all those years. Such a shame the Patrick boy lives in Las Vegas. Good kid. Moved there when the local construction industry tanked, you know."

"What happened?" Michael asked. "When this guy came into the funeral reception, I mean. How was he crazy?"

"This guy bought the house then had a survey done. I think he was planning some fancy landscaping. Name's Lance Cannon. Ever heard such a name? Sounds like a porn star." As soon as he said it, his cheeks reddened and he looked embarrassed. "Sorry, ladies," he said, as a couple of women laughed along with the men. "Anyway, according to Cannon's surveyor, Paul's fence was a few inches over onto his property. Doesn't seem like a big deal, but Cannon went nuts. Stormed over to Paul's, told him he had to tear it down. A nice block fence that's been there for probably thirty years. And the thing of it is, the guy who owned his property was the one who first put it up."

There were murmurs and comments around the room. Many of those in the break room had been present at the incident the day before.

"Paul took him to court over it, didn't he?" Clare asked.

"No. Cannon took it to small claims court. But Paul read up on it so he was prepared. And he had the information about how he and the neighbor had had it built. In his research he learned that if a situation has been accepted for many years, then it was okay. And he was right. The judge ruled in his favor. Cannon was mad as hell."

Walter nodded. "That would be an eminent domain issue. If the fence has been there for thirty years or so and no one ever questioned it or complained, then those few inches are a part of his property."

"Interesting," Michael said, taking a sip of his coffee. Maggie noticed that his paper plate was empty. And she was pretty sure he'd had one of the turnovers plus two of the smaller scones. And after all of the mini muffins he'd had at her house! One of these days her baby boy was going to have to watch what he ate, and it would be a difficult transition for him.

"Shannon was pretty irritated," Louise said. "She kept saying 'it's only a measly six inches'."

"What's this Cannon guy like?" Michael asked.

Cannon's neighbor shrugged. "Don't really know him. I talked to him a time or two when he first moved in. Small talk, you know. Seemed okay. But then he got into this thing with Paul and he stopped talking to *any* of the neighbors. Ignores us all."

"Except to yell at us," someone added. "I was out getting the trash can one evening and he yelled at me about something or other. I couldn't really hear him and didn't care to go closer to find out what he was ranting about."

"We're all hoping he might be mad enough to sell the place," the first man said.

"Do you think this Cannon could be mad enough to try to get back at Paul?" Michael asked.

"You mean kill him?" The woman who asked the question turned pale.

"The police said Paul's death was suspicious," Clare reminded them. "Remember, they told us at the community meeting last week."

Paul's neighbor shrugged. "Who knows? I guess Cannon is a good name for him — he's definitely a loose cannon." He smiled at his own joke while a few of his friends groaned. "I guess I could see him doing it in a rage — during an argument, you know, one that got out of hand. But killing him that way . . . that would take planning. I don't know." He shook his head. "I don't know him well enough for that."

"He could have," another man said. "I think he has a sly side. I've seen him slinking around in the alley a few times, peeking over fences. So he could have planned something like that and figured he was getting even. Knocking over the fence, you know, even if it was the wrong one. The rest could have just happened."

Michael nodded solemnly. It was good to hear from people who actually knew the man, rather than his mother's friends who had observed him in a temper for a few minutes.

"Anything else?" Michael asked.

He looked around. No one offered anything more.

"Thanks, you've all been a big help. You all know these people better than I do, so your insight is appreciated. I'll pass all this information on to the detectives."

CHAPTER 28

That afternoon, Maggie sat with Rosy on her lap instead of her stitching. And while she missed her usual afternoon pastime, she realized that petting her new housemate was extremely satisfying. She felt quite mellow as she looked down into Rosy's dark eyes. There was nothing like a dog for unconditional adoration.

"They do say that animals like you are good for the blood pressure," she told Rosy, who looked up at her with unreserved love. Her tail thumped against Maggie's thigh. It brought to mind Clare's often gushing stories of her beloved Samson. While Maggie had had many dogs over the years, this was her first lap dog. She could already see that owning a small dog would be a different experience.

Which made her think of little Brad Tipton and the equally little Max. When she'd talked to them after the funeral, Brad had asked her to come walking with them one evening. She'd taken Rosy on some short walks, but mostly the puppy had to make do with her back garden area. Perhaps she'd go this evening.

A mouth-watering scent wafted in from the kitchen, and Maggie resolved to do it. She'd put on a pot of chili when she came in at noon, and it smelled delicious. Michael loved her chili, knowledge, she realized, that was probably there at some unconscious level when she decided to make it. She'd take a pot over to Michael this evening, then head over to Clare's and walk with her and Brad. And of course, if Michael wanted to tell her if he'd heard anything new, well, that would be a bonus, wouldn't it?

Maggie smiled, all the while continuing to pet Rosy.

Michael didn't seem terribly surprised to see his mother on his doorstep. Rosy's leash hung over her arm, and the puppy sat beside her feet.

"You haven't eaten yet, have you?" Maggie asked. "I meant to call, but then Rosy fell asleep in my lap and I hated to disturb her."

Michael shook his head, giving his mother an indulgent smile. At the same time, he reached to take the towel-wrapped pot from her hands. "I haven't eaten, I just got home." He lifted the bundle up closer to his face. "Chili?"

Maggie nodded, and Michael whooped. "Great," he said, taking the bundle straight through to his kitchen.

"I have something else to bring in," Maggie called before returning to her car. When she returned with a plastic carrier, Michael had unwrapped the pot and filled a bowl.

"I'm starved," he said. "Barely had time to grab lunch today.

"Hello, Rosy," he added, too busy ladling to take time to greet her with a pat or an ear scratch.

Then he addressed his mother. "Have you eaten? Want to join me?"

"Yes, I have eaten," Maggie replied. "You realize this just supports my theory that you don't eat properly. I don't know what you have against learning to cook. Lots of men make chili and are proud of the fact."

Beneath his tan, Maggie noticed that his face reddened. Maggie had been trying to get him to eat better for the past year, and apparently it was starting to get through to him if he felt embarrassed. Maggie shook her head. "This chili cooks in the crockpot all day — it's very simple. And that meatloaf recipe I gave you is also easy. You could make it at night while you watch the game and pop it into the oven when you get home from work the following day."

"Ma . . ."

"I know, I know. You're a grown man." She smiled tenderly at him. "But you'll always be my baby."

"I barbecue," Michael protested, already moving toward the table with his filled bowl. Maggie took a glass from the cupboard and poured him a glass of milk, Rosy trailing patiently alongside.

"You barbecue now and then," Maggie corrected him. "If you did it every night, I wouldn't have to get after you."

"So, you came over with this great dinner just to bug me about cooking?"

There was a twinkle in his eyes that let Maggie know he knew exactly why she had come. But two could play that game.

"I'm on my way over to meet Clare. Brad invited Rosy and me to go for a walk with them. I don't suppose you've heard anything new?"

"I have not."

Still eating his chili, Michael glanced eagerly at the plastic carrier Maggie still held. "What else did you bring?"

"I did some baking this afternoon and I

brought you a blueberry pie. I know you like it warm so the ice cream melts, so you should have some as soon as you finish that."

She set the container on the table and stooped to lift Rosy into her arms, then headed for the door.

Michael quickly overtook her, opening the door for her. "Thanks, Ma. You're the best." He placed a kiss on her forehead.

"Don't you forget it." She smiled at him, then stood on tiptoe to place a kiss on his cheek. Rosy took advantage to lick his chin and they both laughed.

"Goodnight, Michael."

Maggie parked at Clare's house and walked over to the Tiptons' with her. Then she waited at the end of the walkway while Clare walked up to the house to get Brad. She noticed that the door opened before Clare got as far as the front stoop. Brad and Max bounded out together, tumbling into a hug with Clare. Maggie saw Shannon close the door behind him, but she didn't even look outside to check on who was meeting her son.

Halfway down the walkway, Brad noticed Maggie and Rosy and trotted quickly to meet them.

"Miz Browne," Brad called out. "You came!" He dropped down to his knees beside Rosy who raised up on her hind legs to lick his face. Brad laughed. "This must be Rosy."

Maggie had to smile. "You have a good memory. I thought I'd join you, since you were nice enough to invite Rosy and me. I've only taken her on very short walks up to now, so we'll have to see how she does. She's still a puppy."

"She's real pretty." Brad rubbed his hand over her back one last time before rising to his feet. "Let's go."

They'd only taken a few steps when Brad questioned her eagerly, "Do you live near Miz Clare? She showed me her house. She said one day, we'll stop in and have lemonade and cookies."

"No," Maggie replied, "I don't live near Mrs. Clare. I live closer to the church, but there isn't such a good area to walk Rosy there. That's why she's only had short walks."

"I think she likes it here," Brad said.

Maggie had to agree. Rosy was having a grand time sniffing along all the lawns and shrubs. In fact, Maggie had to keep pulling her along or they would have fallen far behind the others.

"Your grandma and I used to be pretty good friends a long time ago," Maggie told Brad.

"There was a pretty lady at the church who told me she was my grandma. I never had a grandma before. But mommy doesn't like her. She came to our house to visit and Mommy yelled at her. Mommy yelled 'Leave. You're good at leaving'."

"Is that so?" Clare looked very sad.

Brad nodded. Maggie couldn't help thinking that he was much too solemn for a five-year-old. She exchanged a look with Clare, realizing they shared similar thoughts.

"Doesn't your mommy have friends who come to visit?" Clare asked.

Brad shook his head.

"She must get very lonely," Clare said, then quickly backpedaled. "She has you, of course, but adults usually like to talk to other adults about things *they* like. It would be nice if she had friends with children your age, that you could play with."

"I'd like that," Brad acknowledged.

"Don't you have any friends your age?" The more Clare learned about Brad's life, the worse she felt. He didn't seem to be having much of a childhood. She turned eyes sparkling with tears toward Maggie.

"I have friends at school, but I only see

them at school. I haven't been to school for a while," he continued. "Not since I found Papa. He used to take me. Mommy said she's too busy to take me right now."

"That's too bad," Maggie said.

"Papa and Max are my friends." Brad looked down at the little dog, who looked up and wagged his tail when he heard his name. "And you," Brad added shyly, looking up at Clare.

Clare was so touched, she almost cried.

"And now I have Miz Browne too," he added, looking toward Maggie.

"Does your mom take you to the park, so you can play with the other children on the playground there?" Maggie asked.

Brad broke into a smile, and Maggie and Clare looked happier. Until they heard what he had to say. "Papa used to take me. To the Railroad Park. We'd take Max too, and ride on the carousel and the train. Papa didn't ride on the carousel, because someone had to stay with Max. But we all went on the train."

"But what does your mommy do all day?" Clare asked. "Does she go to work?" She didn't think Shannon had a job, but the woman must do *something* with her time. Raquel had told them no one saw her leave on a regular schedule, so it seemed unlikely she had a job. The house had been spotless on the day of the funeral reception, but no one spent twelve hours a day cleaning, not in the twenty-first century.

But once again, Brad shook his head. "No, she doesn't go to work. Sometimes she spends all day cleaning the house and the yard, but then she gets really tired and she sleeps a lot. Then she gets up and makes coffee and watches TV. But she doesn't watch *Sesame Street* or the other shows Papa would watch with me. I don't like any of the shows she watches. There are always a lot of people yelling at one another. I don't like yelling."

Clare sighed and Maggie shook her head. They could imagine what sort of programs Shannon watched from that brief description. Definitely not suitable for a five-year-old.

"So she must have been happy when your daddy came," Clare said. "Now she has a friend here."

"I guess." Brad's brow furrowed as he thought about something. "She smiled a lot when he came. But he leaves a lot to go to work, and then *they* yell at each other. Mommy doesn't like him being gone all the time."

Maggie had to smile at the cute way he

moved his shoulders when he mentioned his parents fighting, even though the situation was extremely sad.

"Seth likes to yell at me and Max too," he said. "He doesn't like Max."

"It might be that he just doesn't like dogs," Maggie said. "Lots of people are afraid of dogs, even little ones like Max."

"Seth goes off to work?" Clare asked. "I thought he worked somewhere out of state."

"Seth told me he drives a truck," Brad told her. "But he wouldn't take me to see it. I'd like to see a big truck, and maybe go on a ride in it."

They paused for a moment while Samson sniffed at the post of a mailbox. The other two dogs quickly joined him, not wanting to miss out on an interesting scent.

Brad spoke when they began to walk again. "We had to go to a lawyer's office this morning. But not Max," he added quickly. "Just Mommy and I."

"A lawyer's office. How exciting," Clare said. She shot Maggie a quick look that let her know this was something important. Maggie almost laughed. She was interested in seeing how Clare would get any pertinent information about a will from a five-year-old.

"That must have been interesting," Clare

said. "Did they read your Papa's will?"

"I don't know what that means," Brad answered, looking puzzled.

Maggie decided to leave Clare to it. She and Brad had the friendship. Hadn't Brad just named her one of his special friends? She could see Clare thinking, trying hard to come up with an explanation suitable for a five-year-old.

Meanwhile, Brad went on, telling them about his morning. "I had to sit outside and wait while Mommy went into an office with a man wearing a suit. The pretty lady who said she's my grandma went in the office too. She stopped to say hello to me, and she gave me a hug and a kiss on the cheek. There was another lady sitting out there with me, and she was nice. She brought me some crackers and a bottle of water."

Clare thought for a few more paces, still trying to work out how to explain a will to a five-year-old. Of course, children were often smarter than you expected, especially these days. They watched TV and played on the computer — things were very different from when her children were five. Brad certainly seemed much more aware than her own children were at his age. But she didn't get to see enough of her grandchildren to know if this was typical. Seeing them on Skype wasn't the same as seeing them in person every day, or even every week.

"Well," Clare began, "when someone dies — or goes to live with Jesus and the angels, like your Papa did — they leave a paper called a will behind with their lawyer. On that paper, they tell who they want to give their things to. Your Papa might have said that your mommy would get his house and his car. And maybe he left you all those models you used to help him make."

Clare was delighted to see Brad's wide smile. "Oh. I'd like to have the models. Maybe I could have them in my room." But then his smile faded. "I heard Mommy and Seth yelling at each other about a will. I didn't know what it was. But the house isn't Mommy's. That's what they were yelling about. She said the house is Grandma's now, and we'll probably have to live on the street."

Brad looked up at Clare and Maggie, his expression conveying his concern. "Do you think we'll have to live in the street? Will I have to bring my bed outside?" He looked at the street beside them, watching as a car passed slowly by. "Where will the cars go if we're living on the street?"

Clare's heart plummeted. What a dreadful thing to tell a young child.

Maggie hopped in to reassure him. "I'm sure you won't have to live in the street, Brad. She just meant that you couldn't live in your Papa's house anymore. Your mommy and Seth will find another house or an apartment."

"We lived in an apartment before we came to Papa's," Brad said, nodding his head. He seemed relieved to hear they would go to an apartment. "Papa's house is better. I like the yard and having Max. No one in the apartments had a dog." Then he seemed to reconsider. "But there were some other kids at the apartment and I could play with them."

Clare was glad to see he seemed comfortable with that idea. Putting his bed into the street indeed! She frowned over his head at Maggie. But his next statement brought the sparkle back to her eyes.

"Mommy says that I hit the jackpot, but I don't know what that means."

Clare smiled. "Hitting the jackpot means you win something, something big. She must be very happy for you."

Brad gave her a big, happy grin. "Really?"

"That is good news," Maggie told him. "Didn't she tell you what you won?"

Brad shook his head.

"Was she happy about it, when she told

you?" Clare asked.

He shook his head again.

Clare had an idea of what Brad might "win" that would not make his mother happy. Except he'd already said that Fay had inherited the house. But was he right?

"Maybe your Papa gave you his house," she suggested.

But Brad immediately shook his head. "No. Mommy said the house is Grandma's. She told Seth. And she was yelling and crying a lot. She even threw a glass at the wall and it broke. Then she shouted at me to get away from the glass, so I went outside."

Clare's lips thinned.

"Grandma talked to me at the lawyer yesterday. She said she wanted to get to know me. And she said maybe we could go to the mall together." Brad's voice sounded wistful.

"That would be nice. Grandmas can be fun." Clare smiled indulgently.

Brad nodded, once again a too-serious little boy. "I think so too. Mommy said maybe."

"I like to do things with my grand-children," Clare told him. "But they don't live here in Scottsdale."

"Mine do," Maggie said. "And we do fun things all the time."

They spent the rest of their walk talking about activities Clare and Maggie shared with their grandchildren. They both thought it a shame that Brad listened as though hearing a fairy tale. The poor boy had never gone to the county fair, had never baked cookies or had an indoor picnic. Clare decided to invite him over the next time she baked. If Shannon would allow it. She'd have to ask her.

Maggie left determined to talk to Fay about following through on the suggested invitation to the mall. The poor child needed a real adult in his life, now that his Papa was gone.

CHAPTER 29

Clare hurried into the Quilting Bee on Wednesday morning, excitement pouring off her.

"I have such exciting news," she exclaimed, dropping into a chair at the quilt frame and allowing her purse to fall with a soft plop onto the floor beside her. "Wait until you hear."

Theresa entered the room just then, looked around at everyone watching Clare and hurried to join them. "What's going on? Has something happened?"

"Oh, something happened all right," Clare confirmed. She looked toward Maggie. "You haven't told them yet, have you?"

"Just Victoria," Maggie said.

"Oh, good." Clare smiled in satisfaction that the previous day's news was hers to tell.

"Well, come on then. Get on with it," Edie urged.

"Well," Clare began, drawing the word out enough that Edie frowned mightily at her. "Maggie and Rosy joined Brad and me on our walk last night. And I asked him if he'd gotten to meet his grandmother."

She quickly recounted her conversation with Brad about Fay.

"And that's exciting?" Edie asked.

"It will be," Maggie assured her.

"I haven't gotten to the best part yet." Clare looked slightly hurt that Edie should call her story dull when it was only half told.

She was about to continue with it when Raquel burst into the room. Remembering her previous visits, Maggie braced for more disturbing news.

"Morning, Raquel," Maggie said. "How are things going for your family?"

Raquel lost no time pulling up a chair and making herself comfortable. "Bianca's husband insisted the kids leave town," she told them. "Remember, I told you he wanted them all to go stay with relatives in Casa Grande? Well, he and Bianca couldn't get away from work, but he took the kids over on the weekend. Bianca works from home most days, you know, and she called me this morning about another dust-up over at the Tipton house."

"Was it the neighbor again?" Louise

asked, remembering the scene at the funeral reception.

"No. It was Fay again," she replied.

"We were just talking about Fay," Clare stated. And she once again recounted her story about Brad and his hopes of getting together with his grandmother.

"It would be nice if Fay could help raise him," Raquel said. "He's a nice boy, thanks mostly to Paul's influence. But there's no knowing what that Shannon might do."

"I hadn't reached the best part of my story yet," Clare said, more anxious than ever to tell them the rest of her story. But, typically, Edie cut her off.

"So what happened at the Tiptons'?" Edie asked.

Raquel perked right up at Edie's question. "Bianca called me right away. She knows I've been talking to you about all this. She says even though Paul had problems with her boys making noise sometimes, he was still a good neighbor. Always kept up his house and yard, you know. And he would watch their place if they left for a few days so she didn't have to tell the post office or the newspaper that they would be gone. She hopes you'll all be able to figure out how he died." She fingered the fabric of her skirt, folding it over and over around her fingers.

So, she wasn't as calm as she tried to project, Maggie thought, remembering the way she'd pleated and unpleated her skirt during their talk a few days ago. She'd been quite tense that day. Her movement today seemed unconscious, perhaps indicating a somewhat lesser degree of stress.

"So what happened with Fay?" Edie asked. "Was it another shouting match like last time?"

"Did Bianca hear anything they said?" Clare asked. She spoke quickly, something that showed she was excited.

"Oh, yes." Raquel straightened, her hands finally resting calmly in her lap. "She said it was around eight this morning and she could hear yelling, so she stepped outside to see what was going on."

"Oh, darn," Clare said. "A little earlier and I might have been there at the end of our walk."

Raquel shrugged off Clare's comment and continued. "Shannon was standing in her open doorway, and Fay was on the stoop. Bianca couldn't hear much, but one thing came across loud and clear. She heard Shannon say 'It's not enough you deserted me when I was a baby, now you're going to throw me and my baby into the street?' Can you imagine?"

"So Brad was correct about Fay inheriting the house," Maggie said.

"I've been trying to tell everyone," Clare said, completely frustrated. She glared at Edie, who had interrupted her attempt to lead into the story of the will. She took a deep breath as the other women all looked toward her.

"Tell us, Clare," Victoria urged, even though she herself had already heard the story from Maggie. She knew how much Clare wanted to tell it.

"Brad told us last night that they went to a lawyer's office yesterday morning. He said he had to wait in the outer office and I had to explain to him what a will was. But he did say that his parents were yelling at each other about a will."

"Well," Edie conceded. "That is something, but I still don't see why you thought it was such exciting news."

"It's because of what he said *afterward,*" Clare said. She looked over at Maggie, who nodded her encouragement. "He told us that his mother told him that he hit the jackpot, and he asked what a jackpot was. So I told him it means he won a big prize and that maybe his Papa gave him his house. But he said right away that Grandma owned the house. Shannon told that poor little boy that they might have to live on the street! Can you imagine! He asked me where the cars would go if his bed was in the street."

Raquel listened, shaking her head the entire time. "That Shannon never was any good. No respect for her elders. Doesn't seem to be much of a mother either."

"Children often take things literally," Victoria said.

Anna shook her head sadly at the thought of a child thinking he might have to live on the street.

"I'm sure Fay wouldn't throw them out," Maggie said. "She can't have changed that much."

Raquel agreed. "Bianca said Shannon was all worked up and yelling, but Fay was calm and kept her voice down. She thought from Fay's body language that she was trying to be nice to Shannon."

"She is her only child," Anna said.

"True, but even your own child can make you angry at times. And she deserted Shannon and her father, remember," Victoria reminded her. "I suppose that could make Shannon resentful, even after all these years."

"Shannon sounds unstable," Louise said. "If she is an undiagnosed bipolar or a drug addict like we speculated, she probably has dramatic mood swings. Those rages the neighbors have observed, for example. Also, yelling at her husband and telling her child they were going to be thrown out into the street."

"Well . . ." Raquel appeared more eager now, and Maggie was reminded of Clare just moments ago when she couldn't wait to share the news about Brad's jackpot. "Bianca said she had her cell phone out and was just waiting to see if Seth would appear with a gun, the way the other neighbor said he did the last time. But then she said it looked like they just stared at each other for a while, then Shannon stepped out of the way and Fay walked into the house." She turned toward Clare. "Maybe that's when she talked to Brad and invited him to go out with her."

But Maggie shook her head. "He said it was at the lawyer's office."

"Do you think Shannon will allow Brad to have visitations with Fay?" Clare asked.

"She will if she's smart," Edie said. "It's in her interest to keep on Fay's good side, if she wants to stay in the house. Which may be why she allowed her entry this morning."

"She could also be her own worst enemy,"

Louise said. "She seems unstable, raging at her family." She looked at Clare. "And you said Brad described what sounds like manic periods. If she's bipolar, she could be treated. But if these mood swings are because of a meth addiction, she could be real trouble."

"Fay seems settled in where she is," Maggie said. "I can't see her moving back here after all these years. So she might allow Shannon to live there, maybe even rent free. But she'd have to be on good terms with her."

"Brad may be just the one to affect a truce between them," Victoria suggested. "It wouldn't be the first time a mother and daughter put aside differences so they can both enjoy the next generation."

Clare appeared to think this over. "I guess Shannon couldn't really keep her out if she's the new owner."

"That's what I told Bianca," Raquel agreed.

"But if Fay inherited the house, why would Shannon be telling Brad he hit the jackpot?" Theresa's question stirred the others into a fervent debate about what else might be included in Paul's estate.

"There are all those model cars we saw in the house," Clare said. "Brad would love to have them. He even told me he would like to have them on shelves in his room. He used to help his grandfather make them."

"But, really," Edie said. "How much could those be worth? Perhaps another collector would like them, but isn't the fun in it putting them together?"

"I would imagine so," Victoria said. "But we're all crafty types, and we love that kind of activity. A car fanatic might be just as happy to have them already assembled."

But none of them had any real idea of the value of the extensive collection they had seen at Paul's house — or of any other things Paul might have owned. So Raquel soon moved off to join her usual group.

The others continued stitching on the Bright Hopes quilt. They were all enjoying working on a top that was outside their usual traditional style.

"I love these batik fabrics," Theresa said, as she pulled her thread through, then took a moment to run her fingers over the bright cloth. "I've been trying them for some of my Hawaiian patterns and they are just beautiful for the appliqué. The color variations give the patterns movement."

"You have to bring them in for us to see," Anna said. "Do you find the batiks difficult to appliqué?"

Edie had been quiet since Raquel left, thinking. Now she brushed aside Anna's question so she could move on to something new. "Of course she does," she said. "Batiks are very thickly woven, right Theresa?"

But she didn't give Theresa time to answer, just barreled on. "Do you think Paul had made a new will? Because if Fay inherited, it could be a will from back when they were first married. Some people never bother updating them."

"Paul was pretty organized. I'm sure he would have kept his will up to date," Theresa said. "And, Anna, some of the batiks are difficult to sew, but not all of them." She threw Edie a quick, defiant look before returning to her stitching.

Maggie and Victoria exchanged small smiles at the riposte.

"He must have made a new will," Clare insisted. "Otherwise, how could Brad inherit something that Shannon called a jackpot. The thing is, what could there be, other than the house?"

"He lost his son in a tragic accident," Victoria said. "Something like that makes you aware of your own mortality. He seems to have been very devoted to his grandson, so it makes sense that he would want to provide for him. He must have left a recent will."

"He of all people knew what Shannon is like," Clare said.

There were several nods of agreement.

"I wonder how we could find out about the will," Anna mused.

"I believe wills are on file at the courthouse, but it would have to be probated first. I don't know how long that might take," Edie said. "But I can check online. I'll look this evening."

"I have an idea . . ." Clare looked quite pleased with herself. "Let's get our husbands and a few of their friends to offer to redo that damaged ramada. I'll bet Shannon would be glad to have it replaced, and Seth doesn't really look like the handy type."

"Not if he's the one who patched up that fence," Maggie murmured.

"That's not a bad idea," Edie said. "The pieces of the old ramada are still there, aren't they? I didn't go out into the yard at the funeral." Left unsaid was her regret at not doing so. But she had put her time inside to good use.

"Oh, yes, all the pieces were there when I went outside during the reception," Clare said.

"In that case," Edie said, "if the men who work on it are knowledgeable, they might be able to tell if the original one had been tampered with."

"Tampered with?" Theresa repeated. "You mean besides the fireworks that toppled the tree?"

"Wouldn't the police know if it had been?" Anna asked.

"They should," Edie said, hedging a bit. She was a law-and-order advocate, and supported the local police, so she hesitated to speak against their methods. "But they aren't sharing information with us, are they? And how can we proceed to figure out what happened to Paul if we don't have the facts?"

"They can't just walk up to the door and tell Shannon they're there to fix the ramada," Theresa said.

"Clare can suggest it when she goes over this evening," Edie said. "Make it sound like the parish men got together and offered to do it as a gesture toward Paul. Say they know how much he enjoyed using it and they wanted to fix it for his grandson to enjoy."

"But if she doesn't own the house . . ." Anna began.

"She has a point there," Louise said.

But Edie waved away the concern. "Pssht. Why should Fay care if something is done to enhance the property? It will be fine."

"Nonetheless, I think we should try to get Fay's okay," Maggie said.

"Does anyone know where she's staying?" Clare asked. "Would the bereavement committee people know, Louise?"

"It would depend on whether or not she was involved in the funeral arrangements," Louise replied. "And I was under the impression that Shannon handled all of that."

There were a few nods, and Clare frowned.

While they considered, Anna posed a question.

"Who will you get to rebuild it?" Anna asked.

Edie looked expectantly around at the others. "Can Gerald, Vinnie or Carl do that kind of work?" she asked.

"Not Gerald," Clare said. "He has to be careful because of his heart. I wouldn't want him climbing ladders."

"Carl likes to build things," Theresa said. "I'm sure he'd be willing to help."

"Vinnie, too," Louise said.

"Well, then, there's a start. I'm sure they'll know of one or two others who can help out, right?" Edie was smiling smugly at how neatly she'd implemented this new idea of Clare's.

"How will Brad feel about having it fixed?"

Anna asked. "Do you think he'll mind?"

"Oh, no," Clare said. "He'll be happy. He told me he's always sad when he looks at the pile of rubble, because it makes him remember finding Papa."

Clare pulled her thread through the quilt and looked around at the others. "So how do we find Fay?"

"Did Walter know Paul?" Maggie asked. "Perhaps he'll know who his lawyer is."

"Good idea," Clare replied, her face brightening. "I'll go ask him."

With that, she rose from her place at the quilt frame and hurried out the door.

CHAPTER 30

It turned out that Walter himself had drawn up Paul's will years ago. He was kind enough to call the associate who had taken over his practice, to get information on Fay's whereabouts. Maggie called and arranged to meet her that afternoon at the casita where she was staying, part of a resort along Scottsdale Road.

"Maggie!" Fay greeted her warmly, inviting her inside. She was equally genial toward Victoria, whom Maggie introduced as a friend from church.

Fay ushered them inside and toward seats on a long sofa. The casita was comfortably furnished in southwestern style, with saltillo tile on the floor and faux Navajo rugs on the walls. With the high cost of Navajo rugs, Maggie doubted the resort would pay for the real thing, but the room did have a warm, cozy ambiance. There was a small kitchenette, and what appeared to be two bedrooms with a Jack-and-Jill bathroom between.

"This is nice," Maggie commented.

"Yes. I wasn't sure how long I'd have to stay, so I wanted to be comfortable."

"Is your friend staying here as well?" Victoria asked. "I believe you had an escort at the funeral."

"No, Leland had to return to Los Angeles. Business, you know. But he was here for a few days."

"I was happy to see you with someone, Fay," Maggie said. "You've sounded happy in your Christmas notes. Perhaps because of Leland?" she suggested.

Fay smiled, the kind of smile that indicated she might be hiding a secret. "Leland is a doctor, a plastic surgeon. I've worked for him for almost ten years now, and we *have* become close. He lost his wife a few years ago, and this past year we've gone out to dinner a few times."

Maggie found it charming that Fay's cheeks pinkened at her talk of dating. She might have avoided using the word, but that's obviously what it was.

"I'm so happy for you. Now that Paul is gone, there's no reason you shouldn't marry again. What is it they say? Fifty is the new thirty?" Maggie grinned. "You have a lot of good years ahead."

Fay smiled again. "Thank you for that. I've never forgotten that I was still married all these years, however, so I've been careful not to get involved with anyone."

Looking slightly uncomfortable at the conversational direction, she popped up from her chair and gestured toward the kitchenette. "Can I offer you something to drink?" she asked. "I don't have much to offer foodwise, but there are soft drinks and juices."

"Thank you, no." Victoria replied and Maggie nodded agreement.

"We're just coming from lunch," Maggie explained. "We worked on the quilting at the Senior Guild until noon, then we had lunch before coming over. I'm glad to be able to visit a little," Maggie continued. "There wasn't really the opportunity after the funeral."

"No." Fay sat down again but grimaced at mention of the funeral. "I would have liked to attend the reception, just to see some of the people I knew from the church years ago. But I didn't want to create a scene, and that's what would have happened if I showed up."

"Shannon still resents you for leaving then?" Maggie asked.

Fay nodded. "I'm sure it's gotten all around the church by now, how she yelled at me when I tried to visit her and Brad."

"Oh, yes," Victoria told her. "We even heard about this morning's visit."

"I don't know why I'm surprised." She sighed. "I'd really like to get to know my grandson. But at least Shannon relented enough to allow me inside this morning. I thought she would stand guard over us the entire time I was with her son, but she disappeared into the bedroom for over an hour." She frowned. "She seems to have already moved into the master bedroom — at least that's where she went for what I think was a nap."

Maggie and Victoria exchanged a look, remembering Edie's comments about the prescription bottles in the medicine chests.

"One of our Quilting Bee members has been taking Brad and Max along when she walks her dog in the late evening, and she talks about him often," Victoria said. "He seems to be a very sweet child."

"Yes," Fay replied. "He mentioned Clare and their walks when we talked yesterday. He really enjoys those walks." Her fond smile clearly showed how much she loved her grandson. "I believe it's what he looks forward to all day."

She looked down at her hands, then up again. "I was very impressed with young Brad. He *is* a sweet child, and very polite. And he has an excellent vocabulary."

Maggie could see in her face Fay's desire to get to know Brad better. He had captured his grandmother's heart.

"I'm rather surprised, actually," she continued. "There must be more to Shannon than meets the eye for her to raise him so well."

"I think most of that is due to Paul, not Shannon," Maggie told her. "They lived with him for two years, and from what Clare says, he and Paul were practically inseparable."

Fay nodded, though Maggie wasn't sure if she agreed that the two were inseparable, or if the statement confirmed her own ideas about Brad's upbringing.

"So," she said, "does everyone at the church know about the will too?"

"No," Maggie said. "And we're very curious." She shrugged, a small apology for their nosiness. "Clare did hear from Brad that his grandma owns the house. In fact, Shannon apparently told him that they might be sleeping out on the street."

As Maggie expected, Fay was suitably horrified at this.

"What! How could she . . . I would never . . ."

"I know," Maggie told her. "I told Clare that could never happen. Brad too. I walked with them last night. Brad invited me on Monday when he heard I had a new puppy."

Watching their hostess trying to come to terms with her daughter's mean-spiritedness, Victoria jumped in. "You know, I wouldn't mind a soft drink. Do you have any ginger ale?"

Fay looked relieved at having something to do. She stood immediately and moved toward the kitchen area. In a few minutes, she was back with tall glasses of iced ginger ale for all of them, looking composed once again.

"Do you remember Raquel Moreno?" Maggie asked, after taking a sip of her drink and placing it on the glass coffee table. "She stopped in at the Quilting Bee room this morning to tell us about your visit to Shannon's. Her daughter lives next door to your old home." Then she added. "I guess it's your house now."

Fay nodded. "But not my home," she said. "I do remember Raquel. In fact, we talked after the funeral, and she introduced me to her daughter and her family. She even told me about her grandsons and the firecrackers. She told me they wouldn't be going to the house either. She didn't think they would be welcome. We had that in common."

Maggie wasn't surprised. Raquel did love to talk.

"Just what did she say about this morning?" Fay asked.

From her leery look, Maggie thought she expected something bad.

"Her daughter heard Shannon yell something about you throwing them out into the street."

Fay sighed, shaking her head. "Shannon still has a lot of issues, that's readily apparent. And I've noticed that she gets very dramatic."

Victoria nodded. "In many ways, she reminds me of a teenager."

"Victoria taught high school for thirty years," Maggie told Fay.

"At twenty-three, she's still young, and she does not act her age," Fay agreed. "Being a mother should have brought more maturity, don't you think?"

"It depends on the individual's personality," Victoria replied. "Perhaps because she became a mother so young, she may feel she missed out on things other women her age experienced."

"I regret leaving her all those years ago, but I was in such pain." Fay pushed her hair back and sighed. "Paul just didn't understand. He wanted to put it all behind us. Our *son,* and he wanted to just put all his things away somewhere and move on. In fact, he wanted to clear out his entire room — just call in St. Vincent de Paul to empty it out. I couldn't do it."

Maggie heard the pain in her voice, and her heart went out to her.

Fay picked up her glass, then put it down again without taking a drink. "I guess that's all water under the bridge. I doubt she'll ever forgive me. She was a difficult child, and she doesn't seem to have improved much with age or with motherhood." She looked over at Maggie and lowered her eyes with shame. "I guess that's a terrible thing to say about my own daughter. But I did try to see her a few years after I left. Once I was able to come to terms with myself, when the pain had turned into a dull throb instead of a piercing ache."

Maggie wished she was close enough to pat her arm, or give her a hug. It wasn't much, but she wanted her to know she understood what she was trying so hard to share.

"Paul wouldn't let me talk to her. Told me

if I came to town he wouldn't let me see her. Said my leaving once was more than enough. I wondered briefly if he'd told her I was dead." She sighed. "He could be a hard man."

"He must have been in pain, too, after your son died," Victoria suggested.

"I'm sure," Fay replied, but there was doubt in her voice. "I could never tell what he was thinking. A lot of men keep their emotions in check, but I think Paul took it to an extreme."

"Raquel said that she saw you enter the house with Shannon," Maggie said. "I believe her daughter was watching with her cell phone in her hand, just in case it was necessary to call nine-one-one. We heard about that first visit and Seth waving a gun around. Bianca was remembering that too."

"That was frightening." She shuddered. "I wasn't at all sure I should try another visit. But it helped that he wasn't there yesterday. Dumb luck, I guess."

"I wonder what he does with his time," Victoria said.

"Brad told us that he drives a truck and often goes off to work," Maggie said. "Shannon claims that Seth has been working out of state, implying that he's been sending support money back."

"I have no idea," Fay said. "She let me in so I could visit Brad. And I did manage a quick look around the house. I felt entitled to that, since I'm now the owner. The house looked good, all clean and tidy. I was pleasantly surprised." She paused, pursing her lips in thought. "I can't decide if I should sign the deed over to Shannon or not. I don't like the idea that Seth could claim half. There's something about the relationship between those two that bothers me."

Victoria nodded agreement. "I know what you mean. Seth acted very strange that day of the funeral. He didn't seem happy about being there for one thing."

"One of our friends walked into the laundry room on Monday and caught him doctoring his drink with a bottle he hid behind a box of detergent," Maggie added. "And Clare tells us that Brad doesn't like him because he's always yelling at him and at Max."

"He didn't say anything to me about Seth," Fay said. "But then he acted rather shy. He said more when we went outside to visit Max."

"He really loves that dog," Maggie said.

"Max must remind him of Paul," Fay said. Both women agreed.

"Clare has gotten the idea that Shannon and Seth aren't big dog lovers," Maggie said.

"I believe she's right," Fay said. "Brad did tell me he spends a lot of time outside with Max. He said Seth didn't like having Max inside." She sighed again, then laughed lightly. "I don't think I've ever done so much sighing in my life as I have these past few days. But I'm glad that Paul had Brad these last few years. He deserved more than Shannon, and I can tell that Brad brought him a lot of happiness."

"What we're most curious about," Maggie told Fay, "is an odd comment Brad made to Clare last night. He told her that his mother told him he hit the jackpot. He didn't know what it meant and asked Clare about it."

Fay laughed — long and merrily this time. "He did that all right. And I'm sure Shannon resents it mightily."

"But Paul didn't have much of an estate, did he?" Maggie asked. "You got his house, so what was there for him to leave to Brad that might qualify as a jackpot?"

Fay laughed again. "Well, that's the beauty of it. Shannon thought the same thing. She was sure she'd get the house, since she'd been there living with him for two years

351

now. And he loved Brad so much. I suppose she figured if she didn't get it, Brad would, and with him only five years old, it would be the same as if she had inherited. But Paul outsmarted her. I guess he knew how immature she still is."

Maggie didn't understand and she took a sip of her ginger ale while she waited for Fay to continue.

"Paul didn't spend much, and he excelled at saving and investing. We always had money in the bank," she explained. "And he was pretty good with stocks too. I don't know how he managed to survive the bad markets we've had in recent years, but the reading of the will was quite a shock. Though not as much so to me as to Shannon." She laughed again, wiping a tear from her eye. "I must say, after the way she treated me when I stopped at the house that first time, I enjoyed the reading very much."

"Did he have a lot of savings?" Maggie asked.

"You might say that," Fay said, her voice merry. "According to his lawyer, there's over two million dollars in savings and investments."

"Two million?" Maggie couldn't hide her shock. "Wow."

"Yes. Isn't it a kick?" Fay asked, chuckling

as she thought about it once again. "That's one rich little boy. And the best part is that it's all in trust for him. Shannon and her husband — if he really is her husband — can't touch it. They can ask the administrator, who is the lawyer himself, if they need money for Brad — like if he wanted to take riding lessons, for example. But they have to ask the executor, and they have to explain what the money is for. Brad won't get the money free and clear until he's thirty."

"Thirty! My goodness. Paul was being very careful that Shannon didn't get any of it, wasn't he? Didn't he leave her anything in the will?"

"Yes, he did. But nothing of any real value. Some small savings bonds that I think he had given to her as a child, and mementos like photo albums. Even all his models were left to Brad, with specific instructions that they were not to be sold. I don't know if they have any real value, but he loved to make those, and apparently in recent years Brad helped."

"Brad is a lucky boy," Victoria said.

"He deserves it too," Fay said. "He's a lovely child. I hope Shannon and Seth don't spoil him by passing on their own indolence and bitterness."

"Neither of them is very happy," Victoria said.

The three women spent a moment in silence, thinking of the little boy and his parents.

After a moment, Victoria cleared her throat and Maggie nodded to her, acknowledging the gentle reminder.

"Actually, Fay, we had another reason for asking to see you," Maggie said.

Fay raised her eyebrows but did not say anything.

"Clare had an excellent idea — that a few of the men at church could volunteer to rebuild that ramada. Clare says that Brad claims to feel sad whenever he looks at it because it reminds him of finding his grandfather's body."

"Oh, no!" Fay looked stricken. "I didn't know Brad was the one who found the body!"

Victoria and Maggie both nodded.

"I'm so sorry," Maggie hurried to say. "I had no idea you didn't know. Apparently Paul had trouble with insomnia, and also didn't like air conditioning."

Fay laughed, a short laugh that had nothing to do with fun. "No, he didn't. We only had evaporative coolers when I lived there."

"We heard that he put in the AC when

354

Shannon arrived," Victoria told her. "She claimed the baby needed something better than the evap cooler."

Fay shook her head. "The evap was good enough for our kids. But I guess that shows how fond he already was of Brad, that he went along with that."

"It's also good for the resale value of the house," Victoria pointed out.

"I'm sure Paul would have considered that," Fay said.

"Anyway," Maggie said, getting back to where she had left off, "apparently, Paul often went outside to lie on his lounge chair if he couldn't sleep, and then he'd fall asleep out there. When Shannon asked Brad to call his grandfather for breakfast, he went outside and found him."

Fay frowned. "I always hated that the kitchen window doesn't look out onto the back yard. It's very inconvenient when you have small children."

Her eyes clouded over for a moment as Maggie imagined she remembered her late son.

"So it's all right with you if we proceed?" Maggie asked. "We think that three or four of the men could get it fixed up in a couple of hours. Give Brad and Max a shady place to play together."

"Sure," Fay said. "And thank you. Anything like that has to help the value of the property, so how can I object?" She smiled at Maggie. "Shall I come over while the work is being done?"

Maggie and Victoria exchanged a look.

"Why not?" Maggie said. "Maybe we'll all go. We can take picnic food and eat in the ramada after it's finished. I don't see how Shannon could object to that."

"Great idea. There's a very nice barbecue setup back there," Fay said. "We can plan on barbecue for everyone when the work is done. I have an excellent recipe for marinating chicken," she offered.

"And my specialty is beef," Maggie claimed.

They both looked toward Victoria.

"I'll bring the punch," she decided. "I have a good recipe made with different fruit juices. Suitable for little people."

Rising, they shook hands on it, and promised to contact Fay with the day and time of the event after they coordinated with the men.

"Let's hope Shannon and Seth don't cause a ruckus over this," Fay said. Her dark look showed the others that, despite her ownership of the house, she suspected they just might. "She'll probably think I'm getting the ramada repaired so I can sell the house." She sighed.

"Don't worry about it. Just concentrate on helping that little boy. He needs a mature adult in his life, and his parents don't seem to fit the bill."

Maggie stepped toward the door but continued to speak. "Shannon's behavior seems very erratic. Do you think she might be bipolar?"

"I'm embarrassed to say I have no idea," Fay replied. "Paul made it clear he didn't want me involved in raising her. He never replied to any of my Christmas cards. I don't even know if Shannon saw them, or any of the birthday cards I sent. I stopped sending gifts after the first few were marked 'return to sender' and returned. I only learned about Brad last week."

"So she didn't try to contact you when she lived in California?"

"I had no idea she lived there! Do you know where?"

"I don't," Maggie said, "but Clare may. She and Paul would often visit while they walked their dogs. She says they were mere acquaintances, but she has a lot of knowledge about his life."

"Maybe I can talk to her on Saturday," Fay said.

"I'm so sorry," Maggie said, giving her a hug. She knew Fay would understand that she was commiserating about the loss of her daughter during all these years.

Fay's eyes gleamed with unshed tears. "It's my own fault. Not that it makes it easier to bear. I do hope to have a relationship with my grandson."

"This may be just the way to begin," Maggie suggested. She gave her old friend another hug and followed Victoria out the door.

CHAPTER 31

Maggie and Victoria spent much of the afternoon on the telephone, setting up the Saturday workday and barbecue. So when Clare stopped by for Brad that evening, and Shannon came to the door to greet her, Clare assumed it would have something to do with the plans for Saturday. It did not.

"It's so nice of you to come every evening like this," Shannon said.

Clare was so startled by this unexpected, grateful comment, she was momentarily speechless. In the week and a half she'd been walking with Brad and Max, she'd barely seen the woman at all. When she did see Shannon, she'd been distant, ignoring her for the most part.

"Brad will be right out," Shannon continued. "He was just washing his hands before getting Max ready."

"I guess you've heard about the men at the parish offering to repair the ramada,"

Clare ventured.

"Yes. That's so nice." Shannon seemed antsy, moving constantly. She looked back over her shoulder every few seconds — checking on Brad, Clare assumed. She also swayed, as though hearing music, though her movement did not match the rock number Clare could hear coming from the kitchen. "Brad loves being outside in the yard. It's what he and Papa did, you know. Sat outside and put together those cars." She threw her arm out toward the shelves lining the living room wall.

Clare watched her, astonished. Swaying bonelessly, Shannon almost fell over with the wide arm gesture. She was so mellow, Clare decided she might be high. She'd never seen someone who was high — at least that she was aware of. She squinted at the young woman, trying to see if her eyes were dilated.

"Did Paul garden?" Clare asked. It was hard to keep up a sensible conversation when she was distracted by Shannon's odd behavior. But gardening was an outdoor activity, and many retired people loved it. She didn't recall Paul ever mentioning working in his garden, but their conversations had often been brief.

"Not that much. He took care of the yard

— mowing, edging, all that stuff. But he wasn't into flowers, if that's what you mean."

Brad came running down the hall at that point, Max trotting along on his leash, the dog's short legs moving quickly. As soon as Max caught sight of Clare and Samson, he sprinted ahead of Brad and began leaping high into the air before Clare.

Laughing, Clare leaned over to pet him, barely managing to avoid a painful head banging. "Hello, you handsome boy," she crooned, petting him down his long body.

"Hi, Miz Clare. Max is so happy to see you. Me, too."

"Have a good time," Shannon called, as they started down the walk. "You come right back if you don't feel well, Brad," she added.

Brad looked back in surprise. "Thank you, Mommy," he called back. "I feel fine."

Clare was suddenly concerned about more than Shannon's unusual behavior. "Are you okay, Brad? Have you been sick this afternoon?"

"I'm fine," he repeated. "I just didn't feel hungry at dinner."

Clare looked him over carefully. His color was good. His cheeks *might* be a little too pink, but children often had red cheeks. And they were walking on a warm day. Clare refrained from feeling his forehead. It was difficult, but she didn't think he'd appreciate it. And she wanted to remain one of his good friends.

"Your mom is in a good mood tonight," Clare said. "Is she happy that we're going to fix the ramada for you?"

"You are?" Brad said.

Clare explained about the plans for the weekend. "We'll have a good time, once the work is done," she finished.

"I like having the ramada. Papa and I used to sit out there all the time."

"That's what your mom said," Clare replied. "I hope you like barbecue."

"I do!" Brad enthused. "We haven't had any since Papa died. He liked barbecue a lot. And Max likes the bones," he added.

Clare laughed. "Well, we'll be sure that Max has some good bones to chew on."

CHAPTER 32

By the following morning, plans for the construction and barbecue were complete. Maggie alerted Michael to their plan, and he decided to join Carl, Vinnie and Raquel's husband Rodrigo in rebuilding the damaged ramada. With so many men, Maggie estimated the time involved would be a couple of hours at most. Raquel told them that Bianca's husband would have liked to help, but relations between his family and the Moodys were so poor, he was afraid to join in and create a situation.

At the Quilting Bee session, the Saturday plans were the first order of business.

"It's wonderful that Michael is participating," Clare enthused. "He'll know right away if the wood was tampered with, don't you think?"

"I think so," Edie said.

"I don't understand why the police wouldn't have checked that themselves,"

Anna commented.

"I'm sure they did," Victoria said.

"What I want to talk about is Brad's jackpot," Clare said. "What did you find out about that?"

Victoria and Maggie had not revealed the startling news of Brad's "jackpot" in their phone calls the previous day. They decided it was something worth keeping until they were all together in the quilting room. Knowing how excited the others would be at the information they had, Maggie and Victoria exchanged a brief smile before Maggie filled everyone in on their visit with Fay. She kept the information they had gleaned from Fay about the will until the very last.

"And you knew this yesterday, and you didn't tell us!" Clare's indignant comment caused Maggie to bite back a smile.

"I didn't want to have to repeat it five times," Maggie replied. She refused to get flustered.

"Maggie and I decided this was information best kept until we were all together," Victoria informed them. "We knew everyone would want to talk it over."

"Also," Maggie said, "Brad's inheritance doesn't affect anything as far as our debate over how Paul died."

"Don't you think it might?" Clare insisted. "Seth and Shannon might have plotted something together, thinking that she would inherit. Especially if she had an inkling of how much money was involved."

Several of the others agreed with Clare's new theory.

"Millions!" Anna commented. "Imagine!"

"Remember, we talked about the most surprising people leaving behind millions at their deaths," Edie reminded them. "Two million really isn't a whole lot these days."

This brought a wealth of objections.

"It sure sounds like a lot to me," Theresa declared.

"Me too," Anna agreed.

Victoria added her concurrence. "I know inflation has made inroads, but I think two million dollars is an excellent inheritance."

"But how could Shannon have known?" Maggie asked. "Everyone seems to agree that Paul was a very private man. And Fay told us that Shannon was surprised not only to receive so little herself, but at how much was being held in trust for Brad."

"Living in the same house, Shannon could have searched for bank records or such," Louise suggested. "If she's as devious as you're trying to make out."

"That would make her a good actress,

then," Victoria commented. "Fay seemed sure she was shocked at the will's contents."

"She was certainly mad about it afterward," Maggie said. "We know that from what Brad said about his parents' arguments that day."

"You know . . ." Clare began, then paused as she stopped stitching to consider something. "Shannon was awfully nice to me when I picked up Brad and Max last night. Normally, she doesn't even come to the door. But last night, she opened the door for me, and spoke very nicely to me for a few minutes. Even thanked me for taking Brad out, saying he enjoyed it so much."

"She's planning something," Edie predicted.

"Doesn't it make you wonder why she doesn't take him on walks herself?" Theresa asked.

"Maybe she's going through a different phase right now," Louise suggested. "She may even have gotten some medication. How did she seem, Clare?"

Clare stopped stitching to lean over the frame. "I think she was high." She said it in a serious voice, like she was imparting state secrets. "I've never seen someone who was high before, but she acted just the way I'd expect them to. She was restless and agitated even though she was making nice. And she was moving all the time, just little movements, like she might be keeping time to music in her head. But there was music playing in the kitchen and it didn't match her movements at all. At one point, I thought she was going to fall right over. She threw her arm out to gesture and her balance didn't seem quite right, but she did manage to stay upright."

"Could you tell if her eyes were dilated?" Louise asked.

"I tried to, but I couldn't tell. She has brown eyes, you know."

"What you describe could certainly be explained by a meth addict on a high," Louise said. "Though I would expect more aggressive behavior, rather than her being polite like you described."

"You should have seen Brad's face when she told him to have a good time. It's pretty obvious she doesn't usually talk to him that way." Clare inserted her needle into the quilt again. "And then she told him to come back if he didn't feel well."

"Was he sick?" Anna asked.

"I asked him," Clare said. "He told us both that he was fine. He told me he just wasn't hungry at dinner time. I thought his cheeks were a little red, but some children get those red cheeks after a little exercise. I didn't want to fluster him by feeling his forehead. I didn't think he'd like that kind of fussiness."

There was a moment of silence as they all considered this new information.

"What if something happens to Brad?" Edie asked.

Shocked, Anna stopped stitching and turned toward Edie. "Are you thinking that little boy might be in danger?"

"Oh, no." Clare looked ill.

Edie shrugged. "If Paul was murdered, and the police do seem to think so, then what's to stop the murderer from killing Brad to get his hands on the money?" She thought for a moment then added. "Or her hands. Because if that is the case, it would have to be one of them, wouldn't it?"

"His parents?" Anna asked, shocked that Edie could suggest such a thing.

"You don't honestly think that Shannon killed her father?" Theresa asked.

"That Seth isn't a very nice person," Clare commented. "I could believe *he* did it." She emphasized her words with a decisive nod.

"I thought he didn't get to town until after Paul died," Theresa said. "Didn't he arrive afterward, to help Shannon?"

"That's what *they* told us," Edie said.

"We did wonder about that after the funeral," Clare said. "Remember, we even told Michael about it."

"Well," Edie said, "it seems to me that it would be easy enough for him to have arrived earlier. Just because he wasn't staying at the house doesn't mean he wasn't in town."

"And Brad says he's a truck driver, so he could have passed through town even if he wasn't actually living here then," Clare said.

"It's no use worrying about things we have no way of knowing," Maggie decided.

"Maybe we'll know more once we get a close-up view of those ramada boards," Louise suggested.

"Did the police check where Seth was living before he came here?" Edie asked.

"Another thing we have no way of knowing," Maggie told her.

"There must be some way for us to figure this out," Clare insisted.

"We could lay out all our ideas for Michael on Saturday," Theresa suggested. "Then he can take them to the detective in charge, and maybe they can put it together."

"Except that so much of this thing is being handled by federal agencies," Maggie explained. "All the investigations into the explosions have been taken over by the FBI and the ATF."

"Surely they aren't investigating a murder," Victoria said. "If that's what it was."

"True." Maggie thought for a moment. "Michael did say the murder was the only thing they were still investigating. But I can't help thinking there had to be some connection with the explosions and Paul's death. It's too much of a coincidence . . ."

"That's right," Clare agreed. "In the mystery books the detectives always say there's no such thing as coincidence."

CHAPTER 33

Between the Quilting Bee and Fay, all the arrangements to repair the ramada were made. The men arrived at the Tipton house early Saturday morning to take advantage of the cooler part of the day. As Maggie suspected, it didn't take long for them to organize the work and get going. The women planned to come later with whatever they had prepared for the luncheon, but Maggie and Clare were there from the start. The largest part of the job was digging out the old support posts, or what was left of them, and replacing them with strong new ones. While the cement set on that job, they stained the new wood for the roof slats. That was completed around the time the rest of the Quilting Bee arrived.

To no one's surprise, Seth was nowhere to be seen during the backyard activity.

"You'd think he would at least help out," Edie said with a sniff. "He's been living here, after all."

"Shannon is being wonderful," Clare said.

Maggie had to agree. Shannon invited the women into the house, urging them to make use of her refrigerator and/or oven until the work outside was completed.

"No one will want to find wood chips or nails in their food," she said as she helped them store the food in the kitchen. She herself made a large tossed salad as her contribution to the barbecue, and a large fruit salad as well. The men also informed them that she had come out periodically with offers of cold drinks. Maggie wondered if she was turning over a new leaf or trying to distract them with this new friendly Shannon. But what could she be trying to distract them from?

Maggie could see no sign of the vague, mellowed-out Shannon Clare had described seeing on Wednesday evening. Shannon was focused and hard at work on food preparation.

"Where's Brad?" Maggie asked Shannon as they worked together in the kitchen.

"Fay picked him up this morning and took him out. She was going to take him to Fashion Square," Shannon said. "I told her I'd call when the work was almost finished so they could join us for the barbecue." She glanced at the clock. "I called a little while ago, so they should be here soon. Brad's been talking about the barbecue nonstop since Clare mentioned it to him the other day."

"Will Seth be joining us too?" Clare asked.

"I doubt it," Shannon replied.

Her offhand manner did not say much about their relationship, Maggie thought.

"He had a job this morning," Shannon added.

"Oh? On the weekend?" Edie raised one brow. "What is it that he does?"

"He drives."

Maggie thought Shannon's reply rather vague, but she was glad when Edie didn't press the point. Shannon was being friendly and cooperative, and Maggie for one hoped she remained that way. Perhaps Shannon had decided to mend her ways so that she could remain in her father's, now her mother's, house.

Shannon turned toward Maggie, as though communicating her reluctance to continue the conversation with Edie.

"Fay said something about taking Brad to Build-a-Bear. Do you think he's too old for a teddy bear?"

"Oh, no," Clare said, surprised Shannon seemed so clueless about her own child.

"Children love teddy bears, even when they're much older than Brad. And there, he can dress his bear in his favorite team's colors, or as a superhero. It's a wonderful place to go with a child or grandchild."

"They have more than teddy bears too," Louise added. "He might go for a dog or a horse if he doesn't like bears."

As Shannon and the others continued to speak of stuffed animals, Maggie slipped outside to talk to Michael, using the soda she carried out as a ruse to pull him to one side.

"Did anything seem suspicious?" she asked immediately. "Did it really fall because the tree fell on it?"

"You realize the crime scene people already looked at this?" He accepted the can of soda and took a long drink. With the temperatures over one hundred, keeping hydrated was important.

Maggie frowned. "No, I didn't. Why didn't you tell me? Was this whole thing just silly then?"

"You mean you all arranged this only so you could snoop into what happened here?" Michael grinned at his mother.

"No, of course not. We wanted to repair the ramada so that Brad and Max could make use of it. Brad loves to play outside, and it seems that Seth prefers he do it too. Especially at this time of year, he needs shade, and they don't have any large trees." Maggie frowned at her son. "And if the crime scene people already checked it all out, why were you so anxious to help out?"

One side of Michael's mouth quirked upward, and Maggie couldn't help thinking how handsome he was. If only he'd settle down and start a family like her other boys.

"You never know what you might discover," Michael said, still grinning at her. "And I wanted to help. I've heard you talk about Brad, and he seems like a nice kid in a sorry situation."

Maggie couldn't disagree. Then she noticed him glancing toward a shed on the other side of the yard. A smile played at her lips as she regarded the small building.

"Did Shannon invite you all into the shed?"

Michael smiled. "Not quite. But she's been very cooperative. She went in there herself to get Paul's tools out for us to use."

"And am I correct in thinking that no one from any law enforcement agency has been in that shed?"

"You would be."

Maggie eyed her son. "You look like the cat that swallowed the canary. What do you

375

think you know about that shed?"

"Nothing," he replied promptly. He reiterated his position when she frowned at him, and lowered his voice even more. "Honest. I don't *know* anything about what might be in it. But I thought I smelled something. Along with what Edie observed in the bathrooms, I may have enough to get a search warrant and let us find out."

"You smelled something," Maggie repeated, frowning at him. Could you smell explosives? Perhaps the type made of fertilizer smelled, but fertilizer would not be out of place in a garden shed.

Michael nodded. "You know we find a lot of meth labs around here. And they have a very distinctive chemical odor. It's the main way the labs are uncovered." He took another long drink, finishing up the soda and crushing the can. "It could be nothing, but I'm sure there's an odd smell around that shed. I'm hoping that will be enough to get a warrant." He raised the soda can. "But this may help."

Maggie raised questioning eyebrows. "A soda can?"

"I have to dispose of it, right?" He nodded toward the trash cans at the side of the house. "Searching trash cans is allowed, you know, even without a warrant. So when I go to toss out this can, I'll have a look in those cans."

Maggie nodded. She wasn't certain she understood just what he was looking for, but she now knew what he planned to do.

"But what does a meth lab have to do with the bombs that have been going off?"

"Maybe nothing." Michael shrugged. "But if it will get us a search warrant, that's all we need."

"Maybe you could get one of those bomb-sniffing dogs in here," Maggie suggested.

Michael nodded. "Did Brad ever say whether they had fireworks on the Fourth? It's not that long since the Fourth. If they were setting off fireworks out here, I don't know if that would complicate matters, maybe let the dog alert on that."

Maggie shook her head. "I doubt very much Paul would spend money on such things. I've learned a lot about him recently, and I'm sure he would have considered fireworks a waste of money."

"Good. This area was already majorly contaminated. The first responders thought the roof crashing was an accident and didn't bother keeping things intact. They threw aside the boards to get at Paul, for one thing."

Maggie felt her heart squeeze a little

tighter in her chest, thinking again of Brad discovering his beloved grandfather's body. She wondered if the poor child had nightmares.

"In any case," Michael continued, "I've called the captain and filled him in. He's going to check with the various federal agencies and see what they want to do. But if it is a meth lab, that would come under our jurisdiction."

The thought of a meth lab in such a nice family community turned Maggie's stomach. "Actually, exploding meth labs was one of Edie's early suggestions. That or terrorists. If you discover Seth has been cooking meth out here, we'll never hear the end of it."

"Seth, huh?" Michael gave her his cute half smile, the one she always felt would make the girls melt. "Why not Shannon?"

Surprised at the question, Maggie thought for a moment. "I guess it's just natural to assume it's a man doing something like that. Besides, Seth is just a disagreeable character, while Shannon sometimes makes an effort to be nice. Today especially. It wouldn't surprise me at all to find that Seth has been involved with drugs in the past."

"And you would be correct." Michael checked to be sure they were still isolated enough to be speaking privately. "I checked on him and he does have a record. DUIs and drug possession, plus a sealed juvenile record. Could be more of the same, which wouldn't surprise me at all."

Maggie shook her head. "Good luck with your search, then. The sooner we can find out what's going on around here, the sooner poor Brad can get on with his life."

It was a cheerful party that sat down to eat together when the work was done. Fay returned with Brad, a Phoenix Suns teddy bear, and a foldout table for the new ramada.

"Brad told me there was a table under here where he and Paul used to work on the car kits, but it was destroyed when the roof fell."

"Actually, it wasn't," Shannon said. "It was folded up and sitting against the fence. He just didn't see it because of the debris."

However, with the large group, an extra table was welcome. There still wasn't enough space for everyone to sit at the tables, but Shannon pulled out a number of chairs from the garage and the house and they managed well enough.

"Dad liked the outdoors," Shannon said as she looked over the new ramada and the tables under it. "But he brought Brad out here to work on the models because of the fumes from the glue."

"It's nice that your boy likes the outdoors so much," Carl said. "Did your grandpa ever take you over to Chaparral Park to fish?"

Theresa, sitting beside her husband, gave him a tender smile, pretty sure she knew where he was leading with his question.

"Yes!" Brad replied with enthusiasm. "We used to go a lot. It was fun."

"I like to go over, and I have my fishing license and everything," Carl replied. "Why don't I pick you up one day and we can go together?"

"That'd be great," Brad said, grinning from ear to ear.

Shannon thanked Carl too, still in friendly mode. She rattled off their phone number so that Carl could call one day soon. Then she thanked all the men who had worked on the ramada. "It's so nice to have that pile of rubble gone."

"I still don't understand how the whole thing came down," Vinnie, Louise's husband, said. "There was some dry rot, but it didn't look that serious structurally. That tree must have hit it just right to make one of them crack and buckle."

Maggie watched with interest as Shannon popped up from her chair and hurried over to the table, offering Brad more chips when he still had a sizeable portion on his plate. Did she not want to hear about the damage? Was she dreading hearing details of how her father might have been killed?

"I agree, it was a chance in a million that it came down," Carl said. "I don't see any clear reason why the thing caved in. Though the posts on the side near the fence looked like someone was digging around them. Was Paul fooling with something out here?" He glanced toward Shannon. "Was he planting something, or working on the irrigation system?"

Shannon, back in her chair, appeared uncomfortable. In fact, Maggie thought there was an almost frantic look in her eyes. "He might have been. He liked to work in the yard."

"Papa wasn't digging there," Brad said. His decisive tone belied his tender years. "He didn't plant things around here. He said he didn't want to attract bees this close to where we always worked. Or too near the pool. Papa said that even if the plants didn't have flowers, sometimes the bees came around anyway to check them out."

They all stared at the little boy, who

381

continued eating without noticing the reaction his statement had produced. Maggie thought that his appetite seemed to have returned with gusto.

"Was your Papa allergic to bee stings?" Louise asked.

But before Brad could answer, Fay did.

"I'm allergic," she said. "Paul always worried that one of the children might be too. He probably wanted to be safe in case Brad is."

Shannon nodded. "Brad has never been stung, so we don't know if there's a problem."

Maggie observed that her friendly mood seemed to have passed. She now appeared sulky, as though sorry to have to put up with them. She played with a celery stick, pulling off one long string after another, keeping her eyes focused on that instead of the people around her.

"So what made the ramada fall?" Edie asked.

Maggie almost groaned. Not that she didn't want to know the answer to that herself, but she was concerned Shannon would explode if the conversation didn't move on to something less provocative.

"It was the explosion," Shannon declared, dropping the mangled celery stick onto her plate. "It must have been that boy looking for work for his father. He could have loosened the posts beforehand. I don't know why the police believed him when he said he didn't do it. He was trying to damage the fence, and probably even the ramada, so his father could repair them. It would have been a good job for him, much bigger than fixing a mailbox."

"I believe Bert had an alibi for the time Paul died," Maggie said. Raquel continued to give them periodic reports on Bert and his family. She didn't ask Shannon how Bert would have gotten into the fenced-in backyard and done some digging there without anyone noticing. "His mother wasn't feeling well and was up and down all night. He heard her moving around early that morning and got up around three to make her some tea. They were drinking it together when they heard the explosion."

Shannon dropped her fork, and Maggie noted a tremor in her hand as she reached down to retrieve it. Was she now on medication, as Louise suggested? Medications could certainly cause that kind of hand tremor. It was a good possibility, too, seeing that she was suddenly so much friendlier to everyone. Even on the day of the funeral, when she'd planned such a nice luncheon, she had not been overly warm toward any of her father's old friends.

On the other hand, if she had arranged her father's death, hoping for a big inheritance, she might be a psychopath and a good actress. These new observations about what happened to cause the roof to cave in could be making her nervous — another thing that caused hand tremors. There was also the possibility that she'd taken some kind of drug and that it was wearing off.

Maggie exchanged a look with Michael, but he was concentrating on his food. She was sure he was acting unconcerned on purpose, which meant he was *very* interested. Could he possibly be correct, thinking something was going on in that shed? For the sake of all their peace of mind, she hoped so.

And where was Seth? Why didn't he join them for the barbecue? In her experience, all men loved barbecue. Was he really working this morning? Didn't he and Shannon realize he was making himself more conspicuous by not appearing?

CHAPTER 34

As she watched *Masterpiece Mystery* on Sunday evening, Maggie couldn't help wondering what was happening with Michael and the warrant for Shannon Tipton's shed. Or was she Shannon Moody? Maggie realized she had no idea which name Shannon actually used.

Maggie put aside her quilt block — another appliqué rose, one of her favorite blocks. She paused the television and went into the kitchen to get herself a glass of iced tea. Perhaps she should give up on the program and leave it to watch later from the DVR. She couldn't seem to concentrate on the show tonight, finding it impossible to get Michael's comments yesterday out of her mind. Could Seth Moody be manufacturing methamphetamine in his backyard? Right there in that lovely neighborhood of small families, so many of which belonged to the St. Rose Catholic Community. She'd read about the danger involved for an entire area from the fumes given off by the manufacturing of meth. Could that be why Brad wasn't feeling well recently?

Maggie hadn't turned on the kitchen lights, and she stood at the sink looking out her window as she finished sipping her tea. Even with the light bleed from the surrounding units, Maggie could see a few stars in the sky. The moon was a bare sliver of light, and a bright star that had to be one of the closer planets shone so close to it, it looked like a representation from the flag of one of the Arab nations. Years ago, she might have wished upon that star, planet though it was. But she was too old and cynical to do it now.

Oh, what the heck, she thought. She eyed the bright star and wished for a better life for Brad.

There had only been one or two minor explosions in the valley since that big monsoon storm ten days ago. The media presence had lessened, the out-of-town reporters departing slowly as there were no more explosions and no further developments. The local stations continued to mention the story of the Scottsdale "explosions in the night," and especially the exploding flashlight that had injured so many at the church. But there was nothing new for them to report, so the coverage became less frequent. They aired the nine-one-one calls when those were released, and interviewed any parishioners who were present and agreed to speak on camera. Deacon Adam continued to turn down interview requests, saying he just wanted to recover and get on with his life. The Quilting Bee made him a lap quilt of appliquéd hearts — Edie did a quick but beautiful job on machine quilting it for them — and they were impressed with how well he was recovering. His wife, however, was still an emotional wreck.

Maggie heard the soft click of nails on the tile floor and looked down to see a sleepy Rosy making her way over to her side. She'd been curled up in her bed beside Maggie's chair and must have come to see what was keeping her mistress in the kitchen.

Maggie put her tea glass in the sink and reached down for the pup. Scratching her head fondly, she headed back to the living room.

"Let's watch some TV, Rosy. What do you say?"

Maggie sat down again but refrained from picking up her stitching. Instead, she cuddled the young dog in her lap, counting on her warm presence to help distract her mind from its troubled thoughts. Perhaps her boys had known what they were doing after all, gifting her with little Rosy.

Early Monday morning, the media once again descended on their previously quiet neighborhood, dashing Maggie's hopes that it was all over.

Maggie was only half dressed when Michael called — still wearing her nightshirt with a pair of calf-length knit pants she'd donned to take Rosy outside to do her business. The sun hadn't been up long, but habit had Maggie arising early even if she didn't need to. And young Rosy did need to go out first thing.

"Goodness, Michael, it's a little early," she said, knowing from the caller ID that it was her youngest son on the line.

Then, her heart thumping in her chest as her imaginative mind thought of all the reasons he might be calling so early, she rushed on. "Is something wrong? Is everyone all right?"

"No, no," Michael quickly reassured her. "Everyone is fine. I just wanted to tell you that SPD and the DEA served a search warrant on the Tipton property this morning. I think there's a good chance Seth Moody might be arrested."

"So you did find a meth lab in that shed?" Maggie was shocked, though she didn't know why she should be. Heaven knew the Quilting Bee heard of all the drug busts and meth labs found in Scottsdale from Edie, and there were plenty of both.

"Yeah. I was pretty sure we would. There were lots of blister packs from cold medicine in their trash can. There's only one reason you find that quantity of cold meds being used, and it's not for treating summer colds."

Maggie sighed. She hadn't taken to Seth, but she liked young Brad. And she'd had high hopes for Shannon.

"Raquel described Seth as Shannon's 'bad boy' back when she was telling us about Paul's family," Maggie remembered. "It's a shame he never outgrew it."

"I've gotta go," Michael told her. "I just called to tell you to avoid the streets around the Tipton house. There are a lot of vehicles from various law enforcement agencies and from the media. And more media trucks arriving all the time," he added. "I'm doing traffic control and it's a zoo. Take care. Keep away from Appletree Lane. Keep your friends away too."

And he was gone. Maggie disconnected as well, but sat thinking for a moment. Rosy had climbed into her lap when she sat to talk on the phone and was comfortably curled up there. Maggie had been patting her lazily while she talked, but now she had to put Rosy down so she could get up. Rosy whined at her feet while she looked up a number and dialed, then jumped right back onto her lap as soon as it was available.

Fay answered immediately. Quickly, Maggie told her what she'd learned from Michael.

"He said it's a zoo over there," Maggie said, "but I thought you might be able to rescue Brad for the day. I'm not sure it's the proper environment for a young child."

Fay was effusive in her thanks. "I'll go at once. Thank you so much, Maggie. That poor boy."

Maggie heard a door slam before the call abruptly ended. She imagined Fay rushing from the casita to her car, clicking off her cell phone as she went. It wouldn't take her long to reach Appletree Lane.

Before Maggie could get up to finish dressing, the phone rang again. The police raid had apparently happened early enough for everyone to hear the news via the neighborhood grapevine. All of the Quilting Bee members called Maggie, and more than a few neighbors. Between phone calls, she barely had time to feed Rosy and change her nightshirt for a decent top.

Finally, she and Victoria arrived at the church — early, but the parking lot was already almost full. Following the crowd into the break room, they found not only the usual Senior Guild members but many people from the Appletree Lane area. It seemed that the street had been evacuated shortly after her call from Michael. She and Victoria walked in just as the evacuees were explaining their presence to some of the other newly arrived Senior Guild members.

"We were having an early breakfast," a pretty, young Hispanic woman was saying. "The police arrived next door at sunrise, and who could sleep after that? All that excitement. We were just ready to have coffee when the police knocked on our door and told us we had to leave. We barely had time to find the cat, who wasn't happy about being relegated to her carrier." She nodded at the object sitting beside her chair.

"It's real upsetting," an older woman said, hugging a Chihuahua to her chest. "Having the police come knock on your door, telling you you have to leave. That it might be dangerous to stay in our own home!" She ended on a choked sob, and the white-haired man sitting beside her put his arm around her shoulders and murmured into her ear.

"Why?" someone at the back of the crowd asked. "Why'd you have to get out?"

"Oh, I saw it on the TV," another member of the Senior Guild — a tall man with a crew cut — replied. "Said it was about a meth lab and they had to get people out of the way while they cleaned it up."

"A meth lab," Edie said, her voice filled with satisfaction. "I knew that Seth Moody was up to no good." She turned to other members of the Quilting Bee. "Didn't I say it might be a meth lab, back when the explosions started?"

Maggie didn't bother to remind her that her most recent suggestion involved international terrorists.

"Did you smell anything strange?" Clare asked the first woman who had been speaking. "They say those meth labs smell very bad. That's how they usually find them."

"The labs can give off terrible fumes," another man whom Maggie knew as a former firefighter said. "Dangerous fumes."

"But not that one." Edie sent a scathing look toward Clare. "We were all over there just yesterday," she reminded her. "Did you smell anything?"

Maggie decided not to share Michael's

sensory detection skills.

"Let Bianca tell . . ." Raquel urged.

Maggie suddenly realized who the pretty young woman was — Raquel's daughter Bianca, who lived next door to the Tiptons. She glanced around the room, wondering if Ramon and Angel were present before remembering that they had been sent to stay with a cousin in Casa Grande. As her eyes continued their circuit of the room, Maggie realized that someone must have stopped at the store on the way in, as there were more snacks than usual available, some of them fairly decent breakfast fare. Healthy even, Maggie thought, as she noted the granola bars, muffins and cartons of milk and yogurt next to the usual coffee cake and Danish. And everything was going fast as more and more people arrived.

Meanwhile, Bianca continued her tale. "They had the fire department there, and men dressed up in those white hazmat suits."

"The bomb squad is there now." The statement came from a redheaded woman holding onto a walker and standing just inside the doorway. Maggie recognized her from the knitting bag attached to her walker — Barbara, who made lovely baby items for their bazaar. The young woman beside her must be her daughter.

"The bomb squad!"

Maggie heard Clare's voice among the several who exclaimed over this new information.

"Does the bomb squad go along when the police raid meth labs?" Clare asked.

"Not usually," the former firefighter replied. "Maybe they found something tying this in with the bombing incidents. It would make all this upheaval worthwhile if that could be settled," he added.

"So Seth might be involved in the explosions after all," Edie said. She pursed her lips in silent satisfaction, and Maggie wondered if she had a theory that linked him to international terrorists. She and Victoria exchanged a private smile; Maggie was sure her friend was having similar thoughts.

"Do you think Shannon is involved?" Clare asked.

"I don't know how she could not have known what was going on," Bianca said. "At least about the meth lab. He must have been using that shed in the backyard. It's right there next to our fence too, right on the other side of our pool. When I think of how dangerous that was . . ." She shuddered. "Our boys are in the pool all the time."

Raquel pressed her palms together as

though praying. "Bianca said Shannon made quite a scene."

Bianca nodded. "We could hear her yelling, right after we heard a loud bang that must have been the police breaking into the house."

"They broke in?" Clare asked, surprised.

"They do that during raids," Edie replied. "I've seen it on the news when they raid places looking for drugs or fugitives."

Neva, the woman who lived across the street from the Tiptons, nodded. "We heard the noise too, and then later we saw that their front door was broken. We think they arrested Seth," she added.

Bianca nodded again. "When we left, we could see him sitting in the back of a police car. We thought he might be handcuffed too." There were several murmurs of interest at this tidbit. "Shannon was in the back of another police car, but we could tell she wasn't handcuffed. She was fooling with her hair when we drove out of our driveway."

"Where was Brad?" Clare asked.

"That poor child," Raquel said.

"He was okay," Neva replied. "We saw him being led out of the house by a woman officer. She took him over to a car and was sitting there with him. He was in his pajamas and holding onto a teddy bear. I saw her get a small quilt out of the trunk of the car and give it to him."

The Quilting Bee members nodded in silent satisfaction. They had all contributed to the charity that provided small quilts to victims of tragedies. The police kept them in their squad cars for use as necessary. Maggie was delighted to hear that Brad had received one of them.

"We saw him too," Bianca confirmed. "He was wide-eyed and trying to see everything, but he wasn't crying or anything."

"That poor boy," Clare said. "He's already had a lot to deal with, and now this."

"I called Fay right after I heard what was happening," Maggie told them. "She was going to head over there and see if she could take him."

"That was a good idea," Clare said. "I hope they let him go with her."

"Do you think this is related to what happened to Paul?" Raquel asked. "Or do you think Seth might have done some of those other awful things with the explosives?"

"And then tried to blame my sons for it," Bianca said, indignant. "He and Shannon kept insisting that it was the kids in the neighborhood that killed Paul."

"Were there DEA and ATF people there?" Edie asked.

"Yes," Neva said. "FBI, too. And the Scottsdale police. There were people in black vests *everywhere.*"

Another neighbor spoke up. "There was a big bang that woke us up. We thought it was another of those explosions, but when we looked out we saw all those men with Police and DEA on the back of their clothing. I'm glad I had Artie there," he said, gesturing toward a young man who looked enough like him to be his son. "I don't mind admitting that without him, I would have been scared to death. But we could see the big white letters on the backs of their vests, so we knew they were officials and not some kind of gang."

Bianca, Neva and the woman with the Chihuahua all nodded.

"And now the bomb squad and the ATF." Edie nodded. "It does look as though Seth and Shannon may be involved somehow with the recent explosions."

"Do you think they killed Paul?" Raquel asked.

"When the men helped rebuild the ramada, they thought it looked pretty solid," Theresa said. "Carl told me he couldn't understand how it caved in after that tree hit it. He thought it should have been fine."

"Remember, they said something about

the posts being loosened," Clare said. "Someone suggested Paul might have been gardening there, but Brad said definitely not."

Edie frowned. "I still think the explosions at the substation and the high school seemed more like terrorist acts."

"If Seth killed Paul with one of those bigger explosions, he might have gone on to blow up other things," Raquel suggested. "To divert suspicion, you know. Seth was always a bad one, even when he was a boy."

"So he grew up around here?" Maggie asked. She wondered why no one had mentioned this before now.

"He was in the valley when Shannon was a teenager, because that's when she first met him," Raquel said. "I remember Paul complaining about the way she seemed drawn to no-good kids. Troublemakers, he called them." She shook her head. "That poor family. To lose Paul, and now it's looking like it might be due to Seth." She grimaced. "Not that I had any use for him. A very disagreeable sort, that Seth," she added.

"There's something romantic about a bad boy," a white-haired woman said with a sigh. "Romance novels are full of bad boys."

"But in the romance novels, they reform and become mature adults," Louise said.

"It's *taming* the bad boy that appeals to romance readers."

"At least Brad didn't like Seth," Clare remarked, "so it won't be too hard on him, even if Seth is his father. He told me more than once that Seth didn't like him." She frowned. "He also said that Seth yells at his mother and at him, so maybe it's not such a bad thing for Shannon either."

"If she's not arrested too," someone commented.

"Appletree Lane is just a mess," Bianca said. "Police cars and vans everywhere — at least they were when we left. But they were getting ready to move all those vehicles too. The television remote trucks were already down on the next street. The reporters tried to wave us down as we drove off, but we didn't stop."

Neva nodded. "We didn't stop either. I suppose they wanted to ask us about Shannon and Seth, or maybe see what we thought about having to evacuate."

"The ATF and the FBI were there," Raquel said. "And so many police cars!"

No one seemed to mind that she was repeating information that had already been revealed. Of course, people kept coming into the room as they found the work rooms empty, so there was a lot of murmuring as those already in the room tried to bring them up to speed.

Another newcomer brought them up-to-date on the television reporting she'd heard just before leaving her home. "They said the neighborhood was evacuated because they found explosive materials in a meth lab. A bad combination, the reporter said."

There was general murmuring about idiots and stupid fools, and more than a few fearful concerns about how their homes would fare if there was an explosion of some kind.

"The overhead photos from the news copter were amazing," the newcomer continued. "They showed the street before the evacuation, when there were vehicles parked everywhere. Then they showed it again all empty, like a scene from one of those apocalyptic movies. The TV people were all over a block away, behind police lines."

"I wonder what happened to Shannon and Seth," Clare asked, though no one had an answer. "I do hope Fay was able to rescue poor Brad."

"I hope Shannon is not involved," Victoria said in her quiet way. "She might not be the greatest mother in the world, but it would be awfully hard on Brad to lose the only parents he's ever known one after the other like that. And Paul did act as a father figure to him, so it has to be like losing his father. He's only just met Seth, and he doesn't seem to like him, so if he does go to jail it shouldn't affect him too much even if he is his father."

Maggie hoped she was right.

The Quilting Bee did finally make it to their stitching room, and even managed some work on the Bright Hopes quilt. However, they couldn't stop talking about the morning's news. And people stopped in periodically with updates on the situation. At one point, Maggie received a call on her cell phone — an unusual occurrence for her on a weekday morning. But it was Fay, thanking her again for her heads-up that morning.

"Brad and I are at the zoo," she told Maggie. "I gave the officer my number in case they need to get in touch."

The bee women were all glad to hear that Brad was away from the worst of the situation at the house.

"Did Michael tell you anything that we didn't hear in the break room?" Edie asked Maggie.

"Not really. He told me they were serving a search warrant at the Tipton house, and to stay away from Appletree Lane."

"But why would Seth have bombed the substation or the high school?" Anna asked. "I don't understand that part at all."

"As I said," Edie began, "if Seth killed Paul with that explosive charge set under the tree, he might have wanted to create a distraction with the other bombs. A misdirection. It certainly caused a lot of national, and even international, publicity, so if that was his intention, it worked."

"It seems like a lot of trouble," Theresa said. "But now we at least know that Paul's estate was worth killing over."

"And then some," Louise murmured.

"It's a shame it was Seth," Victoria said. "But they do say that most murders are committed by someone close to the victim. I guess that's why the police always look at the family first."

"Well, at least now we don't have to worry about him going after Brad," Clare said.

"Amen," the others murmured. Clare and Theresa made quick signs of the cross.

Theresa pulled her thread through the quilt layers and pressed her needle back in again. "I was very impressed with Brad at the barbecue on Saturday. He's a smart boy, and so polite."

"Do you think he'll stay overnight with

Fay?" Anna inquired.

"I guess it depends on what happens with Shannon," Maggie said. "We don't know if she was arrested or not."

But Maggie frowned as she finished speaking. There was something about the whole situation that bothered her. If only she could nudge the misgiving out of her brain and onto her tongue.

CHAPTER 35

Monday evening Clare and Samson headed toward the Tipton house more out of habit than a belief that Brad and Max would be there and available for a walk. To Clare's immense surprise, Shannon opened the door as she hesitated in front of the house. Samson tugged on the leash, trying to lead the way up the walk to meet his new friends.

Brad peeked around his mother, then ran off into the house. He was back in a second with Max on his leash, trotting down the path to meet Clare. Samson's tail wagged faster as they approached, and Clare had to smile. She realized how sad it would have made her if they had to give up their walks. To her additional surprise, Shannon followed Brad and Max down the walkway, stopping to speak to Clare.

"Thank you for coming. I wasn't sure you would, what with everything going on." Shannon looked back toward her front door, inexpertly repaired for the time being.

"I heard about Seth." Clare refused to say she was sorry. She'd found Seth quite disagreeable.

Shannon nodded vigorously. "I knew you would. News travels fast around here."

Clare was amazed to hear Shannon say this without sounding sarcastic or snarky. And she seemed anxious to talk — a real surprise to Clare. Usually, she barely said a thing, just nodded at her if she bothered to come to the door at all.

"A lot of the evacuees were at St. Rose this morning."

"I had *no idea,*" Shannon went on. "They said Seth was making *meth* in the backyard. And I never *knew!* Bombs, too, they said."

"Bombs?" Clare kept her voice low, sliding her eyes toward Brad in a "don't speak in front of the little one" signal that she hoped Shannon would pick up. "Do they think Seth may be behind the explosions at the substation and the high school?"

Shannon shook her head. "They didn't tell me anything. But I made some deductions from their questions." She nodded gravely, trying to convey to Clare that she knew more than she could say. She lowered her voice to a near whisper, glancing down to be sure Brad was distracted playing with the two dogs. "He probably killed Daddy."

"No! That's a terrible thing." While Clare was not loath to agree with Shannon, she wanted to see what the younger woman would say if she expressed disbelief. "But why would he want to harm Paul? He didn't gain anything by it. Neither did you, so he wasn't planning on benefiting from *your* inheritance. Or didn't you know what was in Paul's will?"

Shannon's open look closed and Clare saw the old Shannon peeking through the new veneer. "We didn't know," she muttered.

Shannon reached out toward Brad, patting him on the head, a move he did not appreciate from the look on his young face. The old calculating look was back in her eyes as she brought her hand back and pushed it through her own unruly hair. Clare was sorry to see the new Shannon retreat; facade or not, her new friendliness was much more to Clare's liking.

"Seth was always a bad one," Shannon finally said. "Daddy never liked him. I guess I should have listened to him all those years ago." Her eyes moved toward the horizon and her voice had a regretful quality Clare had not heard before. "Daddy never wanted me to date him. I used to sneak out to meet him."

She looked down at her son, patting his hair again. Still squatting down beside the dogs, Brad managed a sidestep from his lowered position that amazed the not very agile Clare. But he did get far enough away from his mother to avoid another condescending pat on the head.

"Well, we did produce Brad, and Daddy loved him." Shannon managed a grim smile. "But even with that connection, Seth and Daddy never got along."

"Still," Clare insisted, "if everyone killed the people they didn't like or get along with, there wouldn't be any problem with overpopulation."

But Shannon seemed to have used up her friendliness quotient for the day. She mumbled something incomprehensible, turned abruptly and walked back toward the house.

Clare looked down at Brad, still squatting beside Samson and scratching his ears. Max waited impatiently beside him, pushing his snout at Brad's hand, asking for his share of the attention.

"I think he missed me," Brad told Clare, offering his sweet smile. He gave Samson one last pat on the head and stood, ready for their walk.

As they began along their usual route, the

dogs pushed ahead a little, anxious to sniff at all their favorite places.

"And how are you feeling today, Brad? I heard you went to the zoo."

"Yes." Brad gave Clare a wide smile. "Grandma took me shopping first, because we couldn't go inside the house and I was wearing my pajamas. There were lots of police at my house," he explained. "She got me some new shorts and a Spiderman T-shirt." He smiled at that, pointing to his chest, and Clare realized he was still wearing his new clothes. "Then we went to the zoo."

He babbled on happily about his day with Fay and all the animals they had seen.

When his chatter slowed, Clare asked, "Are you over the headaches and tummy upsets?"

"No."

His simple reply startled Clare and she stopped walking. Brad took several more steps before noticing, then he turned to look at her.

"What's wrong, Miz Clare? Are you sick too?"

"No, I'm fine," Clare assured him. "But, if you're not feeling well, maybe we should go back to your house."

But Brad was determined to go on, even

leading the way — away from his house.

"I'm okay. And I don't want Max to miss his walk. He really likes his walk."

Clare had to smile at that, but it was a sad smile. "I'd hate to miss our walk too, but if you don't feel well . . ."

"I'm okay," he insisted.

Clare and Samson had caught up with Brad and Max now, and Clare tried her best to examine Brad without actually touching him. She realized that his eyes weren't as bright as usual. But was that because of a medical condition, or just the light this evening? How she wished Louise could be here with them! She frowned out of frustration, then quickly turned the frown into a smile. It wouldn't do to have Brad see her looking like that!

Brad, however, had not noticed anything strange about their evening walk. He was watching the dogs, as usual.

"After dinner, Max and me went outside to play in the new ramada," he told Clare.

"That's Max and I, Brad," Clare corrected.

"Oh," he said. "Max and I played in the new ramada. We really like having it fixed."

"I'll be sure to tell all the men who helped rebuild it," Clare told him. "They'll be very happy to hear how much you like having it repaired."

"Now that Seth isn't living in our house, Max can come inside the house more. Like when Papa was here," Brad added. "Seth didn't like Max. Max always growled at him, so I guess Max didn't like him either."

Clare noticed a brief frown wrinkle his brow and wondered if he was bothered by the fact that his father was under arrest and he was so much happier not to have him around. Still, she wasn't going to take him to task for it; Clare believed he was better off without that sorry excuse for a father in his life. Even Max recognized that Seth wasn't a very nice man. Dogs had good instincts.

"Papa is in heaven now, and I'm sure he's looking down and smiling when he sees you two having fun there in the ramada."

"You think so?" Brad appeared so taken with this idea, Clare was glad she'd mentioned it.

"Does Max sleep with you in your room?" she asked.

"Seth made him sleep in the laundry room, but I asked Mama and she said he could sleep in my room tonight. I brought his bed into my room. Mama doesn't want him to sleep in my bed."

"I'm glad to hear he's been sleeping

inside. It can be dangerous to have a little dog like Max outside at night when the coyotes and owls are out hunting."

Brad's eyes widened, and Clare quickly changed the subject. She didn't want to explain what could happen to a small animal in a place like Scottsdale and wished she had not mentioned it. Even Seth must have recognized the danger if he allowed the disliked pet to sleep inside.

As they turned back onto Appletree Lane, Brad suddenly stopped and squinted at Max.

"Miz Clare, do you think Max is okay?" he asked.

He sounded worried, Clare thought. She checked the little dachshund. He appeared as energetic as usual. He'd greeted her with his customary leaps of joy, and with sloppy canine kisses when she leaned over to pet him. He did seem to be looking up at Brad more than usual. Clare was sure the dog usually spent most of his time sniffing at whatever scents he could detect on the sidewalk and among the shrubs and bushes they passed. Could it be that he sensed something wasn't quite right with his human companion? Some dogs were quite sensitive that way. Clare leaned over to pet Max. "He looks fine to me," she told Brad.

"Are you worried he might be sick too? Dogs don't usually catch illnesses from people."

"He just looks kind of funny," Brad said. "Samson does too. Kind of fuzzy."

"Fuzzy?" Clare repeated. That was odd. She took a closer look at Brad, leaning over to look right into his face. His eyes were dilated. She hadn't noticed earlier because the dark pupil blended into the brown of his iris. "Brad, what about me? Do I look fuzzy too?"

Brad looked directly at her and shook his head. But as Clare straightened back up and stepped away from him, he suddenly said, "You look fuzzy now, Miz Clare. Are you okay?"

Relieved, Clare smiled. "Yes, I'm fine. But I think you might need glasses. If I take off my glasses" — she followed her words with action — "now you look fuzzy too. Max and Samson too. And you feel just fine, don't you?" She replaced her glasses in time to get a clear picture of Brad's wide smile.

"Yes," he replied, looking relieved. "Glasses are okay. Papa wore glasses."

They finally made the turn onto Appletree Lane, while Brad questioned Clare about the process of getting glasses. He seemed intrigued by the idea of the optical exam. As Clare explained it all to him, she herself was dying of curiosity about all that had happened at his house that morning. She couldn't, however, interrogate a five-year-old boy. She wondered if Shannon would be around when they returned to the house and if she might be in a friendly mood again.

To her extreme surprise, Shannon opened the door for them when they returned to the house. "I put some cheese and crackers on the table, Brad, and the fruit bowl too. You hardly ate a thing for dinner, so have a snack."

"I wasn't very hungry," he told his mother. "Can Miz Clare and Samson come in and have a snack too?"

Shannon wasn't through surprising Clare this evening. To her immense surprise, she welcomed her in. While Max and Samson curled up under the table to rest, the three of them chatted over melon slices, grapes, cheese and crackers.

Clare told Shannon about Brad's "fuzzy" vision, and they all talked about that for a while. Shannon kept asking Brad if he felt all right, making Clare wonder what was going on. She knew Brad hadn't been feeling well, but she seemed to be dwelling on that fact more than she should. Didn't she know that letting it go was the best way to deal with such things? Brad would let her know if he felt ill, she was sure of that.

Brad ate sparingly, but Clare had always felt that hot weather killed the appetite. She and Gerald often had salads for dinner in the summer time, something he would never agree to in the cooler months. And they had just been out in the heat walking around the neighborhood. While it was no longer 110 degrees out, it was probably around 100.

Brad did eat several crackers and some melon, which seemed to appease his mother. However, when Clare bade Brad and Max goodbye, she noticed that the boy's forehead was beaded with sweat.

"Do you feel all right, Brad?"

"Just tired, Miz Clare. My head hurts again."

"He's going straight to bed," Shannon interrupted. She appeared from the kitchen holding a small tea towel. "I have a cool cloth here. We'll put it over your forehead after you lie down and you'll feel better."

Clare left as they headed for the bedroom, closing the damaged door carefully behind her. She frowned, wondering if Brad might be coming down with something. It couldn't have been good for his health having that meth lab in the backyard. Could something have been released during the search, and maybe be affecting him now?

Clare hurried down the street, anxious to get home and call Louise. She wanted to see what her medical friend would have to say about the possibilities.

CHAPTER 36

Clare had a lot to tell the Quilting Bee the next morning.

"I couldn't believe it," Clare told them as soon as they were settled around the quilt frame, threaded needles in hand. "I just walked by the house out of habit, you know. And there was Shannon, opening the door and calling out to me, all friendly. You could have knocked me over with a feather, as my mama used to say."

"Did Shannon tell you anything of interest?" Louise asked. "The news last night mentioned Seth being arrested, but they didn't say anything about Shannon. If she was already back home, I guess that's why."

"Was she even arrested?" Edie asked. "It seems that she should at least be charged as an accessory. What did you hear from Michael last night, Maggie?"

Clare looked up. "Oh, my, I forgot last night was your evening to make dinner for

Michael."

Maggie nodded. "I wasn't sure he would turn up, what with everything going on. I decided to make a chicken enchilada casserole, because that freezes nicely. I was concerned that I'd have a lot of leftovers."

"And did he come?" Clare asked eagerly.

"Oh, yes. And full of caveats telling us not to get involved. I'm to pass that advice along to all of you." Maggie sighed. "They still don't know if anyone other than Seth is involved in the explosions and meth-making, or even how *much* he's involved. It's a federal case. Seth is a dangerous man — Michael was full of warnings." She turned to Edie. "And, no, Shannon was not arrested. I believe she's just a person of interest at this time."

"Did he say anything about Seth and what they found in that shed?" Clare asked, eager to learn more. "Shannon told me they found both meth- and bomb-making supplies. She claims not to have known about any of it." Edie interrupted with a loud snort, but it didn't stop Clare, who was on a roll. "*And* she told me she thinks Seth killed Paul."

"And do you believe her when she says she didn't know anything about the meth lab and explosives?" Louise asked.

"That Shannon is a sly one," Edie said. "I find it difficult to believe she didn't know what was going on with her husband. Not when he was doing it right there in their backyard."

Clare frowned as she considered. "Well, I did like her new friendly manner. But it didn't last too long. When I asked her why Seth might want to kill Paul, since he didn't gain anything by it, she morphed back into unfriendly Shannon." Clare paused. "Or maybe that happened when I asked if they were familiar with the terms of Paul's will before he died."

"Oh my, Clare," Anna said.

"Those *are* very personal questions," Victoria said.

"Well," Clare said, "I was just trying to find out what kind of motive Seth might have had for killing his father-in-law. She did accuse him. She has to know that everyone will wonder why."

"Do you think you should say things like that to her?" Anna asked. "We don't know if she was involved. What if she's a murderer too?"

"Wouldn't surprise me if she was," Edie declared.

"I don't see how she could be totally innocent," Theresa agreed. "The way Paul died was so elaborately camouflaged, it makes more sense if *two* people were involved."

"I do happen to know that Shannon went into the shed on Saturday morning," Maggie said. "Michael told me she went in there to get Paul's tools for them to use. But she didn't let any of them inside."

"Huh!" Edie smiled in triumph. "So there! She must have known what was going on if she had access to the shed. How could she not? If Seth was doing something illegal in there all on his own, don't you think he would have put on a lock and kept the only key?"

"That would be the sensible thing to do," Theresa agreed.

"I don't see why she wouldn't just open the shed door and invite them to make use of the tools inside," Victoria said. "Going in on her own and not letting any of the men inside seems very suspicious."

"Exactly what I thought." Maggie smiled at her friend.

"And what about Brad?" Louise asked. "Clare called me right after their walk. It seems that Brad still isn't feeling well."

"Uh-oh." Edie said. "Remember when we talked about Brad's inheritance and what would happen to it if he died?"

"But he's so young," Anna protested. Then she realized what Edie was getting at and frowned. "Oh!"

"Could he be suffering ill effects from the meth lab in his backyard?" Victoria asked.

"That *might* be a possibility," Maggie said, "only I think it would have happened prior to the lab being dismantled if that was the problem. Surely they wouldn't have let them back into the house if it was dangerous. And he's been fine all this time."

"Oh, you're right." Clare frowned. "Up until recently, he has been in good health, fairly bouncing down the street. Last night he told me he'd had a stomachache and his head hurt. Then, later, he asked me if Max was okay because he looked all fuzzy."

"Yes, that's what worried me," Louise said. "You know oleander poisoning can cause stomach cramps and blurred vision."

"There are oleanders all along the front of their house," Clare told them, her voice solemn.

There was a moment of silence as they digested the ramifications of this information.

Finally, Victoria posed a question. "Did Shannon seem surprised when you asked her about it? Children with vision problems usually have multiple symptoms. It doesn't come on that suddenly. She must have noticed something if he's that near-sighted."

"No, I don't think so." Clare thought for a bit. "She might have said she'd wondered about it. And she seemed awfully nervous." Clare frowned, then perked back up. "His eyes were dilated. Could that have made his vision blurry? I have trouble seeing, even with my glasses, after a doctor's appointment where my eyes are dilated."

"Yes, that could do it," Louise agreed. "But the question here is, what made them dilate? The sun was still out, and there was plenty of light, correct?"

Clare nodded.

"Then there wasn't an obvious cause."

"Shannon did seem upset when I mentioned it, but I thought she was just concerned for Brad."

Edie clicked her tongue. "I don't know what would happen to his inheritance if he passed away," Edie said, "but Shannon or Seth might think they would be able to claim it — as his parents. Remember, if one of them killed Paul, they were probably under the mistaken impression that Shannon would inherit." Edie paused as she re-threaded her needle. "Trusts are tricky. It all depends on how it's set up. But if Paul went to all that trouble to keep the money

421

out of Shannon's hands, I'm sure he tied it up somehow. Neither Seth nor Shannon seems too smart, in my opinion, so they could be wrong in their assumptions again. But either one of them could slip something into Brad's food. He's much too young to cook for himself."

"Then it's a good thing Seth is in jail," Anna remarked.

Clare looked ill. "Brad said he wasn't feeling well last night, and that makes two nights in a row. Shannon said he was complaining of a headache and that he didn't have much appetite earlier. And he said the same to me too, during our walk. I suggested taking him home when he said he hadn't been feeling well, but he didn't want to. He said Max enjoyed it so much. Wasn't that sweet?"

The others agreed that it was.

"I thought he seemed pale and tired from the start," Clare said.

Maggie knew she was concerned that she figured she did the wrong thing by not insisting they go back. "You couldn't have known," Maggie assured her. "You did what Brad wanted to do."

"Clare called me as soon as she got home," Louise told them. "But I can't make a diagnosis from a third-party description.

You know that, Clare. What you described could be anything from a summer cold or a twenty-four-hour stomach virus to some kind of poison ingestion."

"So someone *could* be hurting that child." Edie frowned.

"Of course," Theresa said. "Didn't you hear Louise mention oleander? But wouldn't that point to Shannon? After all, as Anna just said, Seth is in jail."

"Not necessarily," Louise said. "Some poisons act immediately, but others take much longer to be effective. Either of them could do it, depending on what poison is used. For example, if Seth mixed some oleander into a jar of peanut butter, they could still be using it. Even dumb criminals can be smart when it comes to devious activities."

"What are we going to do?" Clare's question was almost a whine. "We can't let them hurt Brad!"

"But why would Shannon want to harm her own son?" Anna asked. "How could a mother do that?"

"Greed, of course," Edie responded promptly. "He inherited a large fortune that she probably believes should be hers. She might even have killed her father thinking she'd get it. There have been many cases in the news of young children killed by their mothers. As unnatural as it seems, it is not unusual. And there are many examples of patricide as well."

Maggie wasn't sure this was the proper time to tell everyone some other news she'd received from Michael the previous evening. But it could tie in with the poison topic.

"Michael had some other news last night," Maggie told everyone. "And after hearing all this, I wonder if it might be pertinent."

"What is it?" Clare demanded. "Will it help us help Brad?"

"I don't know," Maggie replied, not honestly sure. "But Michael said the toxicology reports finally came back. On Paul," she added, though everyone seemed to understand the reference.

"Well, out with it," Edie said.

"Paul had large quantities of drugs in his system," Maggie began, and was promptly interrupted by Clare.

"Paul didn't use drugs," she said. "He was adamant about not polluting his body unnecessarily. He told me so more than once."

"Oh, yes," Theresa agreed. "He was always telling others at work that they shouldn't take various drugs. Even acetaminophen."

"What about those pills Edie found with his name on the bottle?" Anna asked.

"They give you those automatically when you have a root canal," Edie said. "I had the same. It doesn't mean Paul took any of them. I only used two myself after mine, and I had ten of them."

"Having it in his system doesn't mean he took it voluntarily," Louise suggested.

"Oh, that's right." Clare dropped her needle in her hurry to speak. "Like you were just saying about Brad, Louise. I'll bet Shannon cooked for Paul."

"It wouldn't be difficult to sneak something into his food, especially if it was a heavily spiced dish," Edie said.

"You need to call Michael and tell him about Brad being ill," Louise said. "Or at least call Fay and let her know."

Maggie nodded. It might be a false alarm, but they couldn't take a chance with the child's health. Just in case the wrong murderer was in jail. Or in case the man in jail had a female accomplice, like his wife.

"It has always bothered me," Maggie said, "about exactly when Seth arrived in Scottsdale and how it relates to all that has happened."

"Could it really have been Shannon?" Theresa asked. "Could she have caused those explosions? Would she know how?"

"Maybe you could ask Michael?" Victoria

suggested.

"Good idea," Clare said. "Now that Seth's been in custody for a few days, maybe they know more about his movements." Clare snipped her thread then turned a soulful look toward Maggie. "Do you think you could call him now?"

Good grief, Maggie thought. When had Clare perfected that spaniel-eyed look? With a resigned sigh, she reached for her phone.

The women listened anxiously to her side of the conversation. As soon as she put the phone down, Clare pounced.

"What did he say?"

"We're in luck." Maggie smiled. "He actually knew the answer. Said they checked it out and Seth was working in California the day Paul died."

"So he *didn't* arrive until after Paul died." Clare sounded disappointed. "And Paul died really early that morning, so if he was at work that day, Seth must have arrived here long after it happened."

"Still, if they were smart enough to plan all the explosions, and kill Paul in the middle of it all, I'm sure they would make sure no one knew exactly when Seth arrived. Did people really see him in California, or was he just *supposed* to be there?" Edie's cynical voice had them all wondering again. She had been busily working on her smartphone instead of stitching, looking up to reply to Maggie's new information. Now she turned back to the small screen.

"I've been checking with a friend who is much better on the computer than I am."

"Wow, she must be *really* good," Anna remarked, bringing a small smile to Edie's lips.

"He," Edie corrected.

Clare raised her eyebrows, but didn't comment. "He?" she mouthed to Maggie.

"What did you contact him about?" Victoria asked Edie.

"I asked him if a young woman, who doesn't seem really smart but appears to be in good shape, could get all the information and supplies to cause all the explosions we've had around here online. I mentioned that she might also be involved in a meth manufacturing lab."

"What did he say?" Louise asked when Edie paused. Edie returned the phone to her pocket and picked up a needle. She appeared smugly satisfied.

"He said it's entirely possible. He said people who cook meth are often involved with explosives as well."

The other women exchanged worried looks.

"Didn't you say Seth drives a truck?" Theresa asked. "How can we be sure he wasn't driving to Arizona that last day?"

Maggie pulled out her phone once again.

CHAPTER 37

Michael listened to his mother's long discourse about Brad's health, about Seth's job, and about the chances of Shannon being ignorant of her husband's activities. With interruptions from the others, their conversation took a good half hour. At the end of it all, the others fidgeted impatiently while Maggie listened to whatever her son had to say before ending the call.

Immediately, Clare asked, "What did he say?"

Maggie calmly retrieved her needle and inserted it into the quilt top. "He's going to talk to Detective Warner. He said he — Detective Warner, that is — might want to talk to us. I told him we'd all be here until noon."

Clare was delighted when Michael called back to tell his mother to expect the detective within the half hour. It was less than fifteen minutes. The women exchanged speaking glances. His speed indicated to them all that this was an important case and any and all information mattered.

Detective Warner knew all of the Quilting Bee women from previous encounters when they had provided information on various other cases, so he was willing to listen as Clare told him about Brad not feeling well. Then they all explained why they thought this could be ominous. Louise told him she knew all about the symptoms of oleander poisoning.

"Back when we moved here, I was very concerned with the number of poisonous plants growing in our yard, and in all the other houses on the street. Especially the oleander. Every other house had an oleander hedge," she said with a sigh. "So I did some serious research on the topic of local poisonous plants, and the symptoms of ingestion. Just in case."

"I hope you never had to use that information," Detective Warner told her.

"No, but it came in handy when I started working again. And now," Louise said.

They finished the discussion by recounting church gossip and their own observations, and ended with Theresa's comments about Paul's aversion to drugs of any kind.

"Everyone at work knew how he felt about

that subject," Theresa concluded.

Detective Warner took careful notes and promised to give their concerns due consideration.

The women watched him leave, wishing they could read his thoughts.

"Do you think he will give it 'due consideration'?" Clare asked.

"Yes, I do," Maggie said. "He's always dealt fairly with us."

"I hope he does," Edie said. "But I'm a little more cynical."

"Should I stop by for Brad tonight?" Clare wondered. Concern deepened the creases on her forehead.

"Let Rosy and me come with you," Maggie said.

When they arrived on Appletree Lane that evening, it was once again crowded with police cars and remote media trucks. Maggie couldn't help thinking that the neighbors must be heartily sick of all the disruption. She supposed they would find out soon enough. Raquel was sure to tell them everything she learned from Bianca at Senior Guild tomorrow morning.

For a moment, Clare and Maggie stood at the end of the block watching the circus.

"Déjà vu," Maggie murmured.

"Oh, dear, I wonder what's happened to Brad?" Clare moaned.

Maggie was surprised to catch sight of Michael near the Tipton house. She pulled out her cell phone and called him, wondering why he had not let her know this was going to happen.

"I can't talk now, Ma," Michael said, not even bothering with a "hello."

"I know. Clare and I were coming to get Brad and Max. We're at the end of the block."

"Go home. I'll stop over later." Without a goodbye, he ended the call.

Maggie had to relate the entire conversation to Clare before she was satisfied. Then she wanted to follow Maggie home. As they walked back to Clare's house, Maggie told her why that would not be a good idea.

"There's no telling when he might turn up," she said. "And if it's too late, he might not come at all."

Still, it took all her persuasive powers to allow her to leave on her own, with Rosy and without Clare.

CHAPTER 38

Maggie was glad she'd dissuaded Clare from following her home when Michael had still not turned up as she prepared for bed. Michael rang her doorbell just as Maggie came back inside with Rosy after the pup's final potty trip. Rosy performed her job as watch dog admirably, barking loudly just before the bell went off and for some time afterward.

As usual, Maggie's first response was worry, but Michael quickly reassured her.

"Everything is all right. Every*one* is fine," he began. "But I thought you'd want to hear about this tonight. Sorry it's so late."

"That's okay," she said, looking him up and down. "You look exhausted. Have you eaten?"

"Just a quick hamburger." He glanced at his watch. "Hours ago."

Maggie quickly led him into the kitchen. She pulled out a loaf of banana bread and put it in front of him with a knife and a plate, then began to rummage in the freezer.

"I'll have something in here you can have," she mumbled, deep into mothering mode. Finally, she pulled out a plastic container and closed the freezer door. "Meatloaf," she announced, waving the container. "I'll make you a sandwich."

Surprised by the late activity, Rosy followed closely at her mistress's heels as Maggie busied herself with the microwave and the loaf of bread. Meanwhile, Michael began talking.

"With the information from Clare, we got another warrant for the Tipton house. Shannon was one unhappy lady, let me tell you." He and Maggie both grinned, not at all saddened at the prospect. "And thanks for giving us Fay's number. She met us there and took Brad off for a sleepover. He was very excited. You'll enjoy hearing that he took along a teddy bear and a small quilt that the 'pretty lady policeman' — that's in quotes by the way — gave him last time."

Maggie nodded as she set the meatloaf sandwich and a bag of chips in front of her son. "That quilt program is a wonderful charity. All of us in the Quilting Bee have donated quilts for it."

"I've passed out a few myself, and I can

assure you they are really appreciated. By both those giving them and those receiving them," he added.

While Maggie loved hearing this, she was even more anxious to hear what happened at Shannon's that evening. She retrieved the cup of water she'd heated in the microwave, dunked in a tea bag and sat across from Michael.

"Did you find anything that incriminates Shannon?" Maggie asked. "In anything?"

"Not if you mean something to prove she was poisoning Brad. This is great, by the way," he said, gesturing to the sandwich. He took a big bite, chewed and swallowed before continuing. "Fay took Brad to the pediatric clinic to have blood taken. They'll be checking to see if he has anything in his system that shouldn't be there. There were some new children's cold meds in the bathroom, all open. Shannon said he's been complaining of headaches, which agrees with what Clare told us."

"Do you know how Paul ingested the drugs you found in his system?" Maggie asked. She removed the tea bag and took a tentative sip of her tea. Still too hot. "Both Clare and Theresa said he was against taking drugs. Theresa said he even told the other employees at Gilligan's that they shouldn't use acetaminophen, and most people don't think anything of taking that."

Michael digested this information while he finished off his sandwich. He took another handful of chips from the bag on the table and dropped them onto his plate.

"The medical examiner says it was mixed with food. Whatever his last meal was, some kind of pasta — I don't recall what exactly. Easy enough to hide something in pasta sauce because it usually has a strong flavor. There wasn't enough to kill him right away. He probably felt very drowsy and went outside to lie down."

"And did it kill him eventually?" Her tea finally at the proper temperature, Maggie took a long sip.

"It did. He probably died shortly before the tree and boards fell onto him. Maybe around midnight or one o'clock. It's hard to pin down that kind of thing, you know. It's not like the MEs on television who give precise times. Pure fiction!"

"So Shannon must have been the one to give it to him," Maggie said. "Especially if Seth wasn't in town yet. Also, I can't see someone like Seth cooking. He'd think it wasn't macho enough."

Michael nodded agreement with her conclusion.

"Still, I didn't think she was smart enough to concoct such an elaborate plan," Maggie continued. "How on earth did she calculate that blast to knock the tree over so precisely?"

Michael shrugged. "We may never know. Unless she decides to confess. But she could have managed to knock down the ramada and the tree herself, then set the explosive material to make it appear that was the cause of it all." He popped a chip into his mouth, chewed and swallowed. "She was still screaming that it was all Seth when she went into the back of the squad car. I'm sure you could hear her all over the neighborhood. There were plenty of neighbors standing outside trying to see what was happening."

"Another story that will be circulating all over the church in the morning."

"Seth, on the other hand, claims he did make and sell meth and will plead guilty to that charge. But he says he won't take the blame for anything Shannon did without his help. He says they made meth together, the new small-bottle method. They got high together at night after Brad was asleep. He also sold small amounts to people on his truck route. But he says he had nothing to do with any of the explosions. He says Shannon did all that, found out how to do it on the Internet and was proud of how good she got at it. He also said she set the large ones at the substation and high school because she wanted to try making a bigger bomb. Also, as a distraction — changing the modus operandi — so we wouldn't figure out the whole thing about Paul. His exact words were 'she's nuts, man'."

"She made the flashlight bomb too?" Maggie asked.

"Yeah. Same thing — trying something new and trying to muddy the waters."

"She was proud to be a good bomb-maker?" Maggie shook her head, incredulous. The thought that Shannon might be proud of what she'd done to Deacon Adam turned Maggie's stomach. "So he's blaming her for killing her father. Not very gallant of him, is it? I have to admit I don't much like her, but that is very cold. Did he say why she did it?"

"For her inheritance. She thought he was taking too long to die. Seth says Paul kept a tight rein on his money, and he kept getting after Shannon to get a job. She was frustrated and upset that he wouldn't even let her have money for a night out or an afternoon movie."

"And it never occurred to her to get a job

so she'd have her own spending money?" Maggie sighed. There had to be something wrong with the way her brain functioned. Perhaps Seth was correct and Shannon was "nuts."

"Seth also claimed the bomb supplies we found were for a bomb she had planned to 'get' Fay." He put imaginary quotation marks around the word "get" with his fingers. "Seth said she was trying to figure out how to connect it to Fay's car. I'm sure our computer guys will be able to track her Googling to confirm some of this stuff. If it's true," he added.

"Dear Lord," Maggie murmured. "She could have killed both Fay and Brad that way."

"I'm sure that was part of the appeal," Michael said, his voice dry.

"I know there are terrible people out there," Maggie said. "You know that from listening to the news every night. But I never expected to interact personally with someone so evil. And right here in the parish!"

They sat for a moment while Michael crunched his chips and Maggie sipped her tea.

"So . . ." Michael broke the last chip on his plate and dropped half to an attentive

Rosy, who had been sitting hopefully beside his chair while he ate. He merely smiled at his mother's objection. "Are you going to get on the phone and call all your bee buddies to tell them the news?"

"No." Maggie's decisive reply came quickly. "It's much too late. I'm sure some of them will have heard about it from other people in the neighborhood. In fact, I'm surprised Clare hasn't called me already. She wanted to come home with me, you know, so she could be here when you arrived." Maggie yawned. "I'll tell them in the morning. I'm ready for bed."

Michael helped her clean up the kitchen, then she ushered him to the door. In his hands was a plastic bag filled with Maggie's homemade chocolate chip cookies.

"Thank you for coming to let me know what's happening." Maggie looked over her son, noting the lines on his forehead and his slightly stooped shoulders. "Are you sure you don't want to spend the night? You look exhausted."

"I'm fine," he assured her. "Just tired. It's been a long day."

He stooped to give her a kiss on the forehead. "Love you, Ma."

CHAPTER 39

By the time everyone arrived at the Quilting Bee room on Wednesday morning, the news about the previous evening had made the rounds. Everyone had some version of the story from someone who lived in the neighborhood around the Tipton house. All the bee members had tuned in the morning television programs to catch up on the latest news.

Clare arrived early, hoping Maggie would do the same. Even sitting at the quilt frame to stitch couldn't calm her. She fidgeted in the folding chair until Maggie and Victoria arrived at the usual time.

Clare pounced on Maggie immediately, demanding that she reveal what she'd learned from Michael. She barely gave her time to sit down and pick up a needle. However, most of what Maggie knew had already been reported on the television news that morning. She did make sure to include

Michael's comments about the charity quilts, though.

"There's nothing like a quilt to give comfort," Anna said. No one disagreed.

"I saw Raquel on my way in and she told me Bianca saw them take Shannon off in the back of a police car," Clare said.

"The TV news had footage of them serving the search warrant and showed them carrying off lots of bags of evidence," Theresa said.

"They'll be looking for sources of poison, I assume," Edie said.

Clare nodded, as if she was in on the goings-on of the local police. Maggie knew she'd been thrilled to have Detective Warner listen to their theories. It was all she'd talked about the previous evening as they walked over to Appletree Lane.

"I'm glad Fay collected Brad," Victoria said.

Clare agreed. "I wish we knew if they found any drugs in his system."

Edie's droll voice cut in as soon as Clare's last word was out. "Here's your chance to find out."

Edie sat at the end of the quilt frame, facing the door, while Clare was at the opposite end of the room. But she stood and hurried over as soon as she realized that Fay had entered the room, Brad beside her. Brad held tight to his grandmother's hand, his other hand holding onto Max's leash.

He released Fay's hand to greet Clare and Maggie with smiles and hugs. Then he looked around the room, peeking beneath the quilt frame. "Where are Samson and Rosy? Don't you bring them with you?"

"No, we can't bring them here," Maggie told him. "It wouldn't be appropriate. And they wouldn't like it much either, I'm sure."

"That's too bad," Brad said. Then something seemed to occur to him. "Is it okay that I brought Max?" His forehead creased with concern.

"Of course it is," Maggie quickly assured him. "Max is just visiting."

Brad looked relieved.

"It's nice to see you again, Fay," Louise said.

Everyone was anxious to hear what Fay might know, but no one wanted to ask in front of Brad, which Fay seemed to understand.

"Brad, honey, why don't you take Max outside? He might have to potty after the ride in the car." Fay walked him to the door. "You can look at the fountain too."

Clare grabbed for her purse. "Here you are. I'll give you some coins so you can make a wish." She rummaged through her bag until she found a nickel, a penny and two dimes. "Make one for Max too," she said, handing him the coins.

Brad and Max ran from the room. As soon as he was gone, Fay pulled up a chair and joined the group at the quilt. "I guess you all heard the latest."

"No," Clare said quickly. "We know about last night, but only in general."

"Have they arrested Shannon?" Maggie asked. "Bianca seemed to think so. She hadn't been booked when I talked to Michael last night. They were waiting on evidence."

"More important," Louise said, "how is Brad?"

Fay answered the last question first. "Brad is okay. You were right, and I can't thank you enough for saving my only grandson. They not only found cold meds in his blood, but traces of a substance that probably came from oleander, though we still don't know what she was putting it in."

"So you're sure it was Shannon trying to poison him?" Louise asked.

"I think so, though there isn't enough evidence yet to charge her." Fay emitted a deep sigh. "I think she was giving him cold meds and small amounts of oleander to make it look like he was ill. Then, when she increased the dose later, everyone would assume he was just sicker than anyone knew."

The other women were shocked into silence at such cold-hearted evil.

Fay sighed. "I've come to the conclusion that my daughter is not a nice person. She's self-centered to the point of mania. Even knowing that she's my child, I can't like her."

"No reason you should," Theresa assured her.

Fay rubbed a hand over her eyes. "They told me Seth blames her for all the bombings and for Paul's death too."

"Michael told me," Maggie said.

"Would she have gotten Brad's inheritance if he died?" Edie asked. "We assumed that was the reason behind her actions. But we also thought Paul might have worked to keep it from her."

"And you'd be right," Fay said. "I think Paul was aware of what she is really like. He was never sentimental. That's probably why he took it on himself to spend so much time with Brad. He didn't want her to have the money he'd saved. He knew she'd just spend it all and there would be nothing for Brad's education. He had it all arranged so that if Brad wasn't alive to inherit, the money would go to a scholarship fund at the community college."

Edie nodded. "We thought it would be something like that."

Theresa shook her head. "Shannon did all those terrible things, without knowing that none of it would get her what she wanted. Now she'll be lucky not to get the death penalty."

"What will happen to Brad?" Clare asked. She'd grown to love the young boy over the past weeks. "Both his parents in jail," she said softly, shaking her head.

"I've already inquired into becoming his permanent guardian," Fay told them. "The social worker I spoke to didn't think it would be a problem, seeing that I'm his only other relative."

"Will you be going back to Los Angeles?" Maggie asked.

"Yes. I've already talked to Brad about it."

Brad came back into the room just then and heard what his grandmother said. "Grandma lives near Disneyland," he said happily. "She says we can go one day real soon."

"That sounds like a lot of fun," Clare said.

"Yes," Brad agreed. "I'll get to meet Buzz Lightyear and Aladdin."

"Well, we can't be *sure* of that," Fay

reminded him, not wanting to disappoint him if those particular characters weren't on the scene the day of their visit.

"And you'll be taking Max with you, I guess," Clare said.

"Yes. Max likes it at Grandma's. They have lots of grass there."

"There's lots of grass at my house in California too," Fay told him.

She spoke a little longer about her home before saying goodbye. Brad had hugs for Clare and Maggie, and Maggie observed a tear escape from Clare's eye as she watched him exit the room.

"We've worked so hard on this quilt, we're almost done," Louise observed.

"It was a great idea bringing this in, Victoria," Clare said. "It really has lifted our spirits."

"And it looks like we'll be finishing it up just as the problems are settled," Maggie said.

However, not everything was settled quite yet.

They spent the entire session on Thursday discussing the latest news about Shannon, speculating on her motives and her mental health.

There was more of the same Friday.

Raquel stopped by to tell them that Fay and Brad had moved into the Tipton house.

"Fay stopped by to say hello to Bianca." Raquel smiled, pleased by this news. "Unfortunately, she told her she's cleaning up the house to put it on the market."

"Fay stopped by on Wednesday," Maggie said. "She told us she'll be asking for permanent custody of Brad. She doesn't expect any trouble getting it. Then she'll take him back to Los Angeles with her. Brad seemed very excited at the prospect."

"He told us she lives near Disneyland," Clare said with a smile.

Once Raquel moved on to her own craft group, they continued talking about Shannon and Seth, speculating on who was telling the truth, and who might eventually be charged and convicted.

Shortly before the end of their session, Maggie's phone rang. She checked the number display before answering. "Michael" she mouthed to the others.

"I wanted to let you know before you hear it on the television news," he began. "Shannon is dead."

"What?"

"She was charged with the same drug charges as Seth, until there was more evidence on the other things. She committed suicide in her jail cell this morning."

"But how? Don't they watch for that kind of thing?"

Maggie waved her hands impatiently as Clare asked "what?" over and over again.

"She wasn't on suicide watch," Michael said. "There was no reason to think she might try to kill herself. She was arrogant and defiant in questioning, denying any involvement at all."

"So what happened?"

"Somehow, she managed to get hold of a plastic bag. Late last night, she tied it over her head, then lay down and pulled the sheet up over herself. It's noisy in the jail, so it's not unusual for the guards to see something like that. They thought she was sleeping after all the questioning. By the time someone checked and called the paramedics, it was too late. She wasn't responsive, and she was declared dead on arrival at the hospital."

"So we may never know what really happened," Maggie said, her voice sad.

"The CSI people took a lot of things from the house and shed. They'll keep examining it all, because there's still the case against Seth to prosecute."

"I thought he was pleading guilty."

"Only to the drug charge," Michael replied. "The prosecutor will have to decide whether or not he believes his story about not being involved with all the explosions and bombings."

"Ah . . ."

As soon as Maggie disconnected the call, she was bombarded with questions.

"It seems that Shannon committed suicide," she told them, then went on to explain what else Michael had revealed.

"Well!" Edie said. "There will be some investigating over at the jail after this."

"Do they let them have plastic bags?" Anna asked.

"I don't know," Edie said. "But I'm sure they won't after this."

"That's what you meant when you said we may never know what really happened," Clare said. "You don't believe what Seth is saying?"

"He was on the television news last night," Anna said.

"Yes," Theresa said. "I saw it. He was denying any association with the explosions or bombs. He looked like he enjoyed being on TV."

"How can we believe what he says when we know he lied about so much?" Louise said.

Clare's eyes filled with tears. "I just hope

450

Paul gets some justice. So he can rest in peace," she added.

CHAPTER 40

Two weeks later, the Quilting Bee joined the Browne family for their Sunday brunch.

To the usual family dishes were added Louise's breakfast casserole, Victoria's strawberry/pecan/spinach salad, Anna's homemade honey wheat bread, Theresa's fried tortillas sprinkled with cinnamon and sugar, and Clare's zucchini bread and muffins. Edie provided a quarter sheet cake she'd ordered from the supermarket with a "fireworks" design on the icing, and sparklers to light before cutting. "It's for the irony," she commented. "We're saying goodbye to the explosions once and for all." The nights had been gloriously quiet for the past weeks. All media outlets agreed that the explosions were over, and thank goodness. School was starting and the news programs were busy talking about back-to-school sales. Summer mischief was over and done.

As everyone filled their plates and sat

down to the excellent meal, Hal stood.

"I want to welcome all our guests today, and propose a special orange juice toast to our own St. Rose Quilting Bee for helping solve another murder."

He raised his glass of orange juice high and all the others joined in.

"We should have had mimosas," Frank said.

"Oh, yes, that would have been festive," his wife said, sipping her orange juice.

"A little early," Edie said, arching a brow.

"It's so good to know that the explosions are finally over," Clare said, as she lowered her glass after the toast. "We can go to bed and not worry that we'll be jolted awake at some ungodly hour."

"Amen to that," Theresa said.

"I no longer worry about taking Samson out after dark either, if I want to," Clare added with a smile toward her beloved pet. She'd brought Samson along with her, and after a wild romp with Goldie and Rosy, all three dogs were curled up together in the shade of the acacia tree.

Edie leaned over to catch Michael's attention. "So, are you certain now that Shannon was responsible for all the explosions and bombs not caused by the teens?"

"Yes. All the bits and pieces of supplies

found in that shed connected to the various explosions. And it all traced back to her. She bought everything online with her only credit card."

"Dumb," Edie muttered.

"That's why we catch them," Michael said and everyone laughed.

"But why?" Merrie asked. "I understand that she got the idea when the explosions started, and that she wanted to be rid of her father for his money. But why go beyond that?"

"That's right," Sara picked up on her sister-in-law's thread. "The blasts at the substation and the high school, but especially that flashlight at the church! What was the point of those? They had nothing to do with the earlier explosions, weren't anything like the ones set in the gardens and alleys."

"Seth claims she was having fun and thought bigger explosions would confuse everyone and take attention away from the neighborhood," Michael replied.

"It almost worked too," Maggie said, with a significant look toward Edie. Her crazy theories about terrorists had grabbed everyone for some time.

"I wasn't sure I believed Seth's protestations of innocence," Victoria said. "But I guess that proves he was correct."

"It's so sad," Sara said, then lowered her voice so that the children didn't hear. "How could she do it — kill her father and try to kill her son?" Sara shook her head.

"She was planning to kill her mother too," Michael reminded her.

The newspapers were having a field day with the story, and Maggie had heard that someone was after Seth to help with a made-for-TV movie.

"Shannon figured if she was the only Tipton left, then all the money and property would have to be hers. She completely discounted her mother, and her father's intelligent planning with the trust he set up." Michael shook his head. "You should have seen the stuff she was looking at online. My buddy in the computer division told me. Besides all the pages on bomb-making, she had wish lists of expensive clothes and jewelry. She would have run through Paul's savings in a year. He said she'd been checking out pricey cars and overseas trips, too."

"To nonextradition countries I assume," Edie observed. She was surprised when everyone laughed.

"She was an angry young woman who must have felt that she'd missed out on life," Louise said. "She must have been miserable to do all that she did."

"And mentally deranged," Edie suggested.

"And she blamed her father for everything," Clare said with a sigh. "She called him 'daddy.' How could she kill him?"

"Whatever, it doesn't give her the right to kill her father so she can enjoy her inheritance while she's young," Hal said.

"Well, she thought she'd reap a large financial reward," Michael said. "She must have been madder than ever to learn he'd thwarted her there too. From the grave, so to speak."

His brothers groaned.

"I suppose she did blame her father for everything," Maggie said. "No one takes responsibility anymore. It wasn't Paul who made her have a baby at eighteen. And he certainly did not keep her from looking for a job."

"He told me once that he wanted her to take classes after she moved back here," Clare said. "So she could go off welfare and get a good job. But she wouldn't."

"I wonder what she did all day?" Theresa mused.

"Probably watched television and played around on the computer," Edie suggested. "Making those wish lists and planning ways to kill people. That bomb in the flashlight is the one that really makes me mad. What did she think she was accomplishing with that? She'd already set off the bombs at the high school and substation, the teens had confessed to the early explosions. There was plenty of confusion. That was totally unnecessary, and she must have known it would hurt a lot of people."

Louise nodded her agreement. "It's a miracle Deacon Adam was the only one seriously injured. That was terribly vicious." She looked fondly at Vinnie, still upset at how close he'd been to that dangerous bomb.

"I think Seth is right — that she decided she liked doing it," Kimi proposed. "She'd caused a lot of trouble by then. There wasn't any real point to going off into such a different area except to have some fun."

"Some fun!" Anna repeated with a small shudder.

Maggie was sure they all shared her feelings, the members of the Quilting Bee and her family both.

"I'll sure miss my walks with Brad and Max," Clare lamented. "I love that boy." She sighed, looking down the table to where Gerald sat with Vinnie and Carl. "Gerald thinks we should go back to Missouri to visit the children. He thinks seeing the grandchildren will cheer me up and help me forget Brad. Not that I'll ever forget him," she added.

"Fay asked for your address," Maggie said. "When she called to say goodbye. I'm sure you'll be hearing from her at Christmas time. I suggested she start a Facebook page so we could keep up. I'll let you know if I hear from her there."

"I understand you finished up another quilt this week," Sara said.

"We did," Maggie said. "Back when all of this was going on, Victoria made a Bright Hopes top for us to work on. With all the explosions and sleepless nights, she thought it would be good to have something cheerful to quilt on."

"It's a beautiful top," Clare said. "All batiks in bright colors."

"It was a joy to quilt," Victoria said.

"We should make a quilt for Brad," Clare said. The idea was quickly picked up by the others.

"We could do those little Scottie dogs that were popular in the thirties," Edie suggested. "Don't you think he'd like that?"

Everyone agreed that it was a good pattern for a young boy and would be fun to put together.

"It would make a nice Christmas gift,"

Theresa added.

By the end of the meal, it was all decided. The rest of the Browne family smiled benignly as their mother and the Quilting Bee women talked. Fabric, sashing, quilt styles . . . None of them were into quilting, and Maggie's sons didn't understand most of it. But one thing was certain: They were all relieved that the talk was of quilting and not of murder.

ABOUT THE AUTHOR

Annette Mahon has always wanted to write novels. A voracious reader from her youth, her interest in books and literature fueled her career choice. Mahon has a master's degree in Library Science, has worked in public and university libraries, and even spent a year in a Veteran's Administration Hospital Library. In Fort Wayne, Indiana, she starred in a library cable television show, *The Children's Room.*

When not writing, Mahon works on her quilts. She is addicted to appliqué work, especially Hawaiian quilting.

A native of Hilo, Hawai`i, Annette now lives in Arizona.

The employees of Thorndike Press hope you have enjoyed this Large Print book. All our Thorndike, Wheeler, and Kennebec Large Print titles are designed for easy reading, and all our books are made to last. Other Thorndike Press Large Print books are available at your library, through selected bookstores, or directly from us.

For information about titles, please call:
(800) 223-1244

or visit our Web site at:
http://gale.cengage.com/thorndike

To share your comments, please write:
Publisher
Thorndike Press
10 Water St., Suite 310
Waterville, ME 04901